BLOODLUST CHARITY

by

LISETTE ASHTON

CHIMERA

BloodLust Chronicles – Charity first published in 2004 by
Chimera Publishing Ltd
PO Box 152
Waterlooville
Hants
PO8 9FS

Printed and bound in Great Britain by
Cox & Wyman Ltd, Reading.

BLOODLUST CHRONICLES – CHARITY

Lisette Ashton

He considered her coolly before drawing on his cigar. 'I think you need spanking,' he said, speaking through plumes of smoke.

The words sat between them like the exposure of an ugly secret. The skin on Charity's bare arms once again turned to gooseflesh, but this time she knew the response was generated by revulsion. It was impossible to believe he had genuinely suggested the reprimand and she shook her head with disbelief. 'You think I need…' she said, incredulous.

'Spanking,' he confirmed. 'Don't make me say it again. You need a reminder of who's in charge and who follows orders. Get over my knee, Charity.'

The Story so Far

Todd Chalmers sat alone in the hire car, trying to compose his thoughts into something articulate. 'Charity,' he began, speaking aloud to test the words. 'Your sister, Faith was briefly a vampire…' He shook his head, his voice trailing off as he realised that wasn't the right way to start.

The mansion outside the car loomed large and imposing, a converted manor house now used as a recording studio and the frequent film set for BloodLust's music videos. It was a large gothic building, and Todd considered it reminiscent of the mansions that always appeared in creepy horror films he had enjoyed in his youth. Caught in daylight it was nothing more than an imposing stately home, set in an exclusive Hampstead suburb. But at night it would look like the dinner-party habitat for Dracula himself.

'Charity,' he started again, speaking to the steering wheel. 'Your sister, Hope, helped me effect a cure that brought your other sister, Faith, back from the clutches of the undead…'

Perhaps, he mused, it would have been easier if this were the third book in a trilogy. If that had been the case he could have presented Charity with a copy of the first two novels, waited until she had read both, then told her it was now her turn to face the evil. 'Charity, a coven of sexually sadistic vampires are after your blood. And possibly your other bits. You are the final hope in a virtuous bloodline. It's your destiny to destroy them and… and…' He slammed his fists against the dashboard. 'Fuck it,' he snarled, lighting a cigar. 'I think I'll start by spanking the bitch.'

Prologue

'Have you read your bible recently?'

The gypsy girl seemed resigned to her fate and she spoke with quiet authority. Unmindful that she was naked, defiant in the face of the vampires, she eased herself from the runes on the floor and glared toward the dark one's throne. Orange light from the burning brazier turned her skin into shades of metal that looked as strong and unyielding as her obvious will. Her breasts were magnificent copper domes; her flat stomach was burnished bronze; her legs were sculpted from rose gold. The dark triangle of her pubic bush looked denser at her cleft, as though the curls were matted with the smelted wetness of arousal.

'Have you read it recently?' she repeated. 'Because it will give you better advice than you'll get from me.'

As one Marcia and the mulatto stepped from the shadows. With their slender frames, wan complexions, and crimson smiles they radiated predatory interest. Marcia licked her bloody lips and flicked the fringe of blonde hair away from her brow. The mulatto peeled back her smile to reveal wickedly sharp fangs. Both looked set to advance on the naked gypsy but the dark one stopped them by raising his hand.

He lounged in a throne-like chair, idly admiring his manicure and only seeming to give half his concentration to the surrounding events. His gaunt features and crimson eyes did not make him handsome but there was something about his presence that leant a commanding air. The cruelty of his smile – the corners tipped with fangs and the lower lip glossed by a sheen of blood from his most recent feast – glinted like a silver dagger. 'It might surprise you to learn that I tend not to read the bible too often,' he murmured dryly. 'Books with crosses on the cover somehow discourage my interest. But you must tell me, what's in the good book that you think I should know?'

The gypsy shook her head and scowled at him. 'It's supposed to be ill fortune for the likes of you to feed from my kind, but the runes say you've fed from gypsies before. She glanced down at the marked stones by her bare feet and said coolly, 'The runes say you're going to take me next. Why should I tell you anything?'

His long sigh indicated a shortening temper and he finally glanced up from the study of his fingernails. 'Clearly you are a discerning traveller and are reading very accurate runes,' he growled. 'And as you were reading them for my benefit, I'd really like to know what they say about my future.'

Lilah stepped to her brother's side. 'Let me finish her, sire,' she demanded. 'Let me teach her that impudence is not tolerated.' She had returned to wearing tight leathers; a waistcoat that accentuated her taut, athletic breasts; trousers that hugged her buttocks like a second skin; and high-heeled boots that added unnecessary inches to her commanding height. Trembling with rage, every muscle defined by the exertion of her temper, she flashed her scarlet glance from the dark one to the gypsy and hissed, 'Let me finish the bitch, sire. Please, let me finish her.'

The dark one raised his hand again, bidding Lilah silent. 'You won't ingratiate yourself back into my favour so easily, little sister,' he cooed. 'Even though you've tried to win me over with this truculent fortune teller, and even though you're struggling to look out for my interests now, nothing is going to make up for the way you tried to overthrow my leadership. You're still going to be tonight's sacrifice.'

Lilah glowered but said nothing.

The dark one fixed his glare on the gypsy. 'I asked a question about the virtuous sisters. I wanted to know if they still present a threat to me and my coven. The runes have obviously told you something and I'd like to know exactly what.'

She shook her head and started to argue. 'I'm not telling you any...'

She got no further.

The dark one was out of his throne with chilling speed. Grabbing her in an intimate embrace – one hand clutching her shoulder, the other fixed firmly over her cleft – he carried the gypsy to the wall of the crypt and pressed himself against her.

Her sinewy body moulded to the shape of his masculine frame, but rather than protesting about the chilly fingers that nestled over her sex, she squirmed against him with obvious urgency. The flesh of her pussy lips was tormented by his insidious touch and she pressed herself onto him as though she longed to be penetrated. Her bare breasts were squashed against his chest and she became more intoxicated by his nearness each time she drew breath. The tips of her nipples stood hard and responsive and her areolae became rouged by excitement. When he moved his mouth over her throat, teasing his overlong canines against the pulse of her jugular, she arched her back and looked ready to succumb to whatever he demanded.

He withdrew his hand from her sex, making the egress slow and painfully arousing, and she gasped, the cry torn from her lips like a reluctant kiss.

Placing his arm around her waist and forcing a thigh between her spread legs, the dark one coaxed himself closer. 'What vital secrets do you think the bible could tell me?' he growled. 'What vital information could the good book give me in my search for a way to face my nemesis?'

With her heartbeat hammering recklessly and arousal flooding through her veins, the gypsy sobbed her response. 'Corinthians: thirteen, thirteen. That passage will tell you more than I ever could.'

He frowned, not understanding the relevance and not thinking to hide his ignorance. 'Corinthians: thirteen, thirteen? What does that mean? What does it say?'

Whatever mesmerising skill he employed was broken by the question. The gypsy regarded him with a startled expression, her eyes widening with renewed shock. The arousal that had held her in its thrall evaporated as though never there and she slammed herself against the wall. Blinking repeatedly she noticed something that hadn't been apparent when he resided in the shadows of his throne. But now the revelation was blindingly obvious and she struggled to understand its implications. A night where she was reading runes for vampires was not a singular experience: the undead, besotted with their immortal futures, were regular visitors to those gypsy camps with which she had travelled and she'd previously encountered many vampires. Similarly, because she resided with a band of travellers who were unwanted and hounded from camp to camp, the experience of being stripped naked and faced with mortal peril was nothing new. But this latest discovery was something she had never believed she would encounter.

'Your aura,' she gasped. Pulling herself from his arms, backing away and pointing, she shook her head from side to side. 'My God, your aura! What's happened to it? I've never seen the like.'

Uneasy with her exclamation the dark one frowned. 'What about my aura?' He noticed Marcia and the mulatto had stepped away from him, their consternation obvious. The remainder of the coven were considering him with worried

9

expressions that combined ignorance with uncertainty. 'What's wrong with it?' he asked the gypsy.

Lilah stepped to his side, trying to placate her brother by placing a hand on his arm. 'Let me finish her, sire,' she insisted. 'She hasn't proved to be the fortune-teller you wanted and…'

'It's you!' the gypsy cried. Whatever residue of calm she had managed to maintain was gone as she glared from the dark one to his sister. Her pointed finger wavered between the pair. 'You're the one. You're the missing part of the puzzle.'

Lilah glanced at her, disconcerted by the gypsy's shrill tone and accusatory finger. She didn't understand what the mad bitch was talking about; auras were nothing more than mystical mumbo-jumbo as far as she was concerned, but her frantic tone of voice was beginning to aggravate. Not caring how her brother might respond, only wanting to end the irritation, she started determinedly towards the naked gypsy.

The dark one stopped her. 'You have until midnight before I end your existence, Lilah,' he said quietly. 'Don't make me bring that schedule forward.' Turning to the gypsy, his frown twitching impatiently, he asked, 'What's wrong with my aura?'

The gypsy continued to shake her head, and rather than answering him, seeming to speak only for her own benefit, she said, 'I've never seen the like before.'

'What's wrong with my aura?' he demanded.

'No,' the gypsy told him, 'it's not your aura.' She flicked her disbelieving gaze from the dark one to Lilah. 'That's what's wrong with it. It's shared. You and your sister share the same aura.'

'What the hell does she mean?' Lilah asked. 'What the hell is she talking about?'

The dark one shrugged. 'I'm not properly sure what an aura's meant to be,' he confessed. He had a vague understanding that an aura was some sort of psychic emanation but the mechanics and implications were beyond

10

him. The only thing he felt he could say with any authority was that the gypsy's tone implied the condition was a cause for concern. 'I thought auras were just so much hippy, new-age-traveller bullshit.'

'Is she saying we have similar auras?' Lilah puzzled. 'Or is she saying…'

'I'm saying you have the same aura,' the gypsy cried. Her features were strained with impatience and disbelief. 'You're inextricably linked: your powers, your fortunes, your fates. You must have recently shared a profound, supernatural experience.'

Lilah and the dark one exchanged an uncomfortable glance, both thinking about the magic that had come from Lilah's use of the wish-stone. Rather than granting her the freedom she had craved, or releasing her from the shadow of her brother's memory, it brought the dark one back to life and returned him to a position where he could rule over her. Neither of them bothered to explain the details to the naked gypsy and Lilah racked her brains to work out what this latest development meant.

'What are you talking about?' the dark one asked impatiently. 'What does it mean when you say we have the same aura? How is that possible? And why should we give a damn?'

The gypsy began to laugh, a shrewish sound that combined mockery with self-contempt. 'How could I be so stupid?' she exclaimed. 'If I'd left you to your plan you would have killed yourself tonight when you slew your sister.'

Understanding finally came to Lilah. Her eyes opened wide and her grin was full and bloody, and turning to her brother she said, 'The gypsy's telling us we share a bond.'

'Is that what she's telling us? It doesn't sound like she's talking sense.'

'She's saying our auras are linked.' Glaring at her brother,

11

struggling to contain her triumphant smile, she said, 'If you kill me this evening you'll be killing yourself.'

The dark one glared from his sister to the gypsy, his expression changing from disbelief, to comprehension, to diabolical fury. Roaring with rage he hurled himself at the gypsy and took her in his arms. His leg pushed between her thighs, hard against her sex. He had a hand on her buttock, the manicured nails digging into the plump flesh and squeezing hard. His other hand went to her breast and he kneaded and massaged with avaricious greed. Forcing his mouth over her throat, biting hard into her neck, he drank from her with a thirst that seemed boundless.

Lilah watched in disbelief. She considered warning her brother that it was supposed to be bad luck for a vampire to feed from a gypsy, or possibly reminding him about the consequences that had followed his last impromptu feed from the ranks of the travellers, but commonsense told her this was no time to intervene.

The gypsy bucked and thrashed against the dark one. Her legs tightened around him and, although she was obviously reluctant, she gave herself to him without protest. Her cheeks flushed darkly with the first rush of arousal, then the colour began to fade as the blood was drained from her throat. She cried out, a soft sound that mingled protest and supplication, then fell limp in his arms. Her last movement was a tremor of orgasmic delight that preceded her ungainly descent to the floor.

The dark one stepped away from her fallen figure. He wiped the back of his hand over his bloody lips and glared at Lilah. Although she could see he still despised her for trying to usurp his leadership, she realised a fresh dynamic had been added to their relationship. For the first time since her fears were realised by the wish-stone, Lilah knew her brother could no longer threaten her life. If what the gypsy said was true, it seemed he would now suffer the consequences of any harm that befell her.

'What did she mean?' he glowered. Raising his finger, seeming to realise that Lilah was about to explain the advantage of her unassailable position, he added, 'Corinthians, thirteen, thirteen? What's that all about?'

Lilah rolled her eyes, disgusted with her brother's lack of knowledge. Sensing he was close to losing his temper, and knowing that, despite what the gypsy had said, he would still happily wring her neck, she mumbled an insincere apology. 'Corinthians, thirteen, thirteen,' she muttered. 'The concluding lines to Paul's sermon on the subject of love.'

The dark one's frown remained solemn as he waited for her to explain. In the candlelit darkness of their lair his eyes were lost in the cavernous shadows of his furrowed brow.

'And now these three remain,' Lilah recited. A chill brushed over her forearms as she spoke. The hairs at the back of her neck stood erect and an icy shiver tickled down her spine. 'Faith, Hope and Charity,' she continued. 'But the greatest of these is Charity.'

The dark one shook his head. 'I don't care what it says in the bible. I'm still having her.'

Lilah nodded agreement. It came as no surprise to her that they didn't just share the same aura: they also shared the same desire to vanquish the last of the virtuous sisters.

But this time, she decided, they were going to succeed.

Charity

Act I, Scene I

It was the curse, Charity thought bitterly. It was the Harker family curse and, once again, it had chosen her as its victim. Stumbling alone through the cemetery, lost and scared and struggling not to panic, she clutched her bare shoulders and trembled. She was chilled by the icy fingers of the night but shivering more at the knowledge of how greatly she was exposed and in jeopardy.

Half an hour earlier her world had been perfect. The journalist from the music magazine had insisted on taking a couple of photographs in Piccadilly Circus – Charity on the steps leading up to Eros, then Charity beneath an electronic billboard promoting BloodLust's forthcoming album – and from there they had gone on to dine at an unpretentious Italian restaurant in Leicester Square. The interview was painless and pleasant, a modest gang of autograph hunters assailed her while she dined, and she happily supplied answers and scratched her signature while she enjoyed her agnello brasato. For once the questions were not too intrusive or inane and, rather than concentrating on the salacious rumours that surrounded the offstage antics of her band, Charity was able to talk about her work as a singer and songwriter.

She left the restaurant buoyed with self-confidence. For the first time in too long, certainly the first time since BloodLust had gone platinum, she felt as though she was being recognised as a talented professional in a respectable industry, and not simply considered some lucky schoolgirl who had happened to score a fluke success with a couple of pop songs. She felt so buoyed with confidence that she declined the journalist's offer of a car and took the northern line tube from Leicester Square up to Highgate. But from there, cutting along Swains Lane to try and get back to the Hampstead residence her studio had made available for her and the band, Charity's self-assurance began to falter. When she cut through a gap in the Swains Lane fence, intending to take a shortcut through Waterlow Park, she realised that her buoyancy had all but disappeared and the Harker family curse, once again, held her in its thrall.

'Frick!' she hissed. It was a set rule of the Harker family curse that, as soon as life seemed to be going well everything had to change. And it was a codicil to the curse that everything had to change immediately, and always for the worse.

Charity didn't think the situation could get much worse because she realised her misplaced confidence, ably assisted by her shameful sense of direction, had taken her into the heart of Highgate's west cemetery. An overgrown foliage of sycamores brushed branches against her face and the dense carpet of brambles scratched at her ankles and calves. Eerie monoliths loomed out of the shadows: stone crosses, leering angels and alabaster urns. A row of archways ran to her left and a forest of trees and monuments went on to her right. Brick edgings and rusted wrought iron chains threatened to trip her with every step, and nothing seemed sufficiently familiar to make Charity think she could turn back and resume her journey from a point before she'd taken this ill-fated diversion.

'Frick, frick, frick!' she complained.

She had walked through cemeteries before, but always with someone else and never in such impenetrable darkness. BloodLust had risen to fame and popularity with a ghoulish image that was constantly supported by macabre photos of

15

the all-girl band looking cadaverous and moody whilst surrounded by tombstones. Each of the members bore a deathly pale complexion, overtly heavy eye shadow and blood-red lipstick, and it was a vampiric identity that quickly became their trademark. But just because she had done a handful of photo-ops in some of the country's more picturesque graveyards, Charity wasn't immune to the natural unease that came from walking, alone, through a cemetery so close to midnight.

'Frick, frick, frick!'

She had been forewarned that the magazine interviewer would want to take photographs and subsequently wore a skimpy black skirt that barely covered her bottom, and a sleeveless, strappy top that exposed an almost indecent amount of pale flesh. The outfit was ideal for singing centre stage at the Royal Albert, and had been understated enough to make a monotone contrast against the glamour and colour of Piccadilly Circus, but it felt woefully inadequate for a late night stroll through the overgrown necropolis.

She clutched herself tighter, hoping soon to see some sign of civilisation. Commonsense dictated that if she walked long enough in the same direction she was bound to come to some sort of sanctuary. And while she fretted that such a plan could just leave her following the cemetery's perimeter until morning, she decided it was the closest she had to a rational way out of her predicament. The palms of her hands felt clammy and cold against her bare shoulders and the dewy embrace of a ground fog chilled her. Wading through the mist she was quietly struck by the idea that unseen hands could be clutching at her, their fingers slipping over her ankles and knees, and as much as she tried to shut the image from her mind it refused to release its hold on her and added frigid disgust to every step.

'You're quite a creepy little bitch, aren't you?'

The words came out of nowhere, and Charity stopped walking. She was shocked by the nearness of the man's voice and the insidious lilt in his tone. She tried to glance discreetly around, wondering who had spoken and struggling with the dilemma of whether she should make her presence known or keep herself hidden. The goose bumps that had freckled her bare arms grew more noticeable with nerves and terror tightened its embrace around her bones.

'How the hell can you call her a creepy bitch, Nick?' a woman responded, waspish and shrill with an impatience that was clearly second nature. 'This is the third leg of our grand European tour, and to me it looks like you've brought us to another bloody graveyard. I'd call that a damned sight creepier than anything this little slut could have organised.'

Peering through the shadows, still disconcerted by the vapours of ground mist that clung to the earth like world-weary ghosts, Charity finally caught a glimpse of the trio. He was tall, swarthy and handsome with his formidable physique contained inside the folds of a flowing coat. The striking woman by his side was a full-figured and voluptuous brunette. They had gathered around one of the large marble box tombs, and between them, looking helpless and vulnerable, stood a petite girl. Charity had seen enough of her fans to know how they dressed and she guessed the pallid teenager would be the proud owner of a host of BloodLust merchandise.

Warily, she inched closer.

'I'm calling her a creepy little bitch,' Nick started testily, 'because she's dressed like a necrophile's wet dream, and it was her suggestion that we should gather here.' Defensive and petulant, he added, 'I didn't want to come to this bloody cemetery. I wanted to have a ride on the London Eye. She's the one who wanted to go traipsing around this creepy shit-hole.'

'Just take her,' the brunette decided impatiently, turning

17

away from Nick and the teenager and folding her arms across her ample breasts. Her posture, like her tone, indicated that she had exceeded the limits of her patience.

Hesitant, Nick glanced at her back. 'Don't you want to feed from her?'

The brunette sniffed. 'I didn't think she contained enough blood to carry her here to the cemetery, and I wouldn't want to spoil your feast. Take her and then let's get out of this damned place. These bloody brambles are snagging ladders in my stockings and they're the best ones I got from Paris.'

Intrigued, and going against her better judgement, Charity edged closer. She had her first proper glimpse of the teenager and was momentarily stunned by the ghostly pallor of the girl's complexion. Her skin was so white it seemed to glow with its own luminescence in the snatches of moonlight. Her eyes – large, dark circles – stared reverentially up at Nick as he grinned down.

'You're not really vampires, are you?' the teenager breathed.

He stroked a hand through her long, lank hair. The tips of his fingers grazed her ashen cheek and his bloody smile was tinged with amusement. 'Not really vampires? Why would you say that?'

As he spoke, his soothing voice lulling Charity into a false sense of security, he lowered his hand to the front of the girl's blouse. Skilfully he unhooked the buttons, starting at her throat and working his way swiftly downwards. Her modest breasts were soon revealed to the night and she stood, shamelessly displayed in front of Nick and the brunette. With meticulous care he drew his thumb over the nub of one nipple and the teenager gasped.

Charity swallowed an urge to cry out. Regardless of the rumours that surrounded BloodLust, notwithstanding the exposés that regularly filled the Sunday tabloids, she was not used to seeing this sort of intimacy. Horrified by the indecency

18

a part of her wanted to slip quietly back into the shadows and forget that she had stumbled across this torrid encounter. But curiosity, and a lurid desire to discover what was going on, made her lean closer.

'Why would you think we're not real vampires?' Nick asked softly. 'Don't you want to believe that's what we are? Isn't that what we said we were?'

His thumb worked back and forth over her nipple, teasing it stiff against the coolness of the night and inspiring the teenager to exhale with obvious urgency. Her skin remained deathly pale but her lips were quickly becoming rouged with blatant lust. The circles of her areolae stood dark and her chest rose and fell at a quickening tempo. When she reached out to embrace him, Nick brushed her hands aside and continued to lazily torment the tip of her nipple.

'Stop toying with the little slut,' the brunette complained. 'I don't want to spend the entire night hanging around this poxy graveyard. I've got my own hunger to satisfy.'

If Nick heard her he paid no heed and never allowed his gaze to waver from the adoring smile of the girl in his arms. The teenager pressed closer, squirming against him as he lowered his mouth to her lips and began to kiss.

A fluid heat filled Charity's sex, the arousal coming so suddenly and unexpectedly she almost exclaimed with the shock of the response. Eyes wide with disbelief, heart hammering excitedly, she strained to get nearer without giving herself away. The concept of voyeurism was something she would ordinarily have dismissed as perverted or beneath her, but experiencing the reality – stumbling across this triptych of macabre hedonists in the depths of the cemetery – was more compulsive than she would have believed. Her nipples had become unbearably taut and the slippery warmth between her legs spoke of a dark, inarguable need.

'Don't you want to believe that we're really vampires?'

Nick pressed.

'Yes,' the teenager sighed, her supple body hanging from his and she whispered her reply between kisses. He had consented to let her loop her arms around his shoulders and she pressed herself against him with a need that was prolific and obscene. Her bare breasts rubbed against the starched cotton of his black shirt as she rocked steadily back and forth in his embrace. 'Yes,' she insisted. This time she sounded close to tears of frustration. 'You know I want to believe.'

He pushed her back, effortlessly shrugging her arms away and spreading her over the top of the marble box tomb. Charity couldn't see if he forced the teenager's legs apart or if the girl was simply so eager to succumb to him that she automatically fell into that position. But she guessed the results would have been the same whichever reason was responsible. The hem of the teenager's short skirt slipped up to the top of her thighs, and although the girl was modestly cloaked in shadows, Charity was treated to a brief glimpse that told her the teenager wore no underwear; the sight both sickening and mesmerising. Nick stood between her spread legs, unfastening the front of his trousers, and leering down at her with unconcealed lust.

Mesmerised by the scene, Charity could only watch as he pushed his trousers down and produced the hard length of his erection. The shaft stood long and pale in the moonlight, the glans glistening with silvered smears of his excitement. Gripping himself with one hand, guiding his bulbous tip between the teenager's legs, he chuckled softly as he prepared to enter her.

The teenager moaned as Nick bent over her, his long coat concealing both their bodies. A broad grin surfaced on his lips and his eyes shone crimson with wicked glee. Opening his mouth into a silent roar he tilted his head back and looked ready to lower his kisses to the teenager's bared breasts.

For the first time Charity noticed the peculiarity of his smile. The grin was painfully white in the dark of the cemetery but she could also see the corners were tipped by overlong canines. His bloody leer was more vampiric than anything BloodLust had ever managed with prosthetics and costume make-up and Charity could see he was intent on biting his victim.

'Frick,' she gasped, and then clasped a hand over her mouth, knowing it was too late. Nick paused from trying to take the teenager and the brunette was instantly scouring the graveyard with narrowed eyes. Her body suddenly seemed less voluptuous and was now tense and ready to react.

'There's someone here,' she whispered. 'Someone else.'

'You don't say,' Nick responded dryly. The girl beneath him was briefly forgotten as his glowering red eyes surveyed their surroundings. 'Who the hell is it? Has Lilah sent someone out to follow us?'

The teenager moaned. Disappointment and frustration were clear in her tone. Beneath the folds of Nick's coat her urgent struggles were more than apparent and Charity could picture her trying to squirm her sex on his cock. If she closed her eyes she knew she would see the teenager's pouting pink pussy lips, slippery with wetness and gliding over Nick's swollen glans. It was an image that left her giddy and re-ignited her unexpected arousal.

'Finish her and let's get out of here,' the brunette decided.

'Finish her?' Nick sounded surprised. 'Just like that? Don't tell me you're getting spooked by graveyards, Helen.'

Helen bristled at the suggestion but she remained adamant. 'Believe what you want to believe, Nick. Take it whichever way you like. But if you don't finish the little slut soon I'll do the damned deed myself.'

'I was only saying...' He didn't get to complete the sentence. Whatever he was about to say was brushed aside as Helen pushed him away from the teenager and pressed a deep kiss against the girl's throat. Like Nick's, her eyes were the scarlet of freshly spilt blood and the corners of her smile were made lethal by wickedly sharp canines. She placed one hand against the teenager's bare breast, cupping the unassuming orb and catching the stiffness of her nipple between her knuckles. Her full lips pressed against the teenager's throat, and as she grunted hungrily Charity saw a crimson ribbon creep down the girl's neck.

The teenager gasped, a sound torn from the depths of desire. There were words beneath the cry, intermingled pleas for mercy and more, which were called from the brink of satisfaction. Her body was a liquid wave of writhing flesh that suddenly turned stiff as she crested a pique of elation. For an instant there was colour in her cheeks, a healthy flush that darkened around her lips and the tips of her nipples. Then, as the pleasure receded, the colour faded and she slumped against the marble box tomb as though the life had been drained from her body.

'Frick, frick, frick,' Charity whispered.

Helen raised her head from the fallen teenager and glared in her direction. Her crimson gaze was so intense Charity knew she had been discovered and a shiver of dread made her stomach muscles tighten. The peril of her situation left her cold with foreboding.

'I don't believe our good luck,' Helen growled.

'Who is it?' Nick asked. He peered myopically from her side, his eyes dulled by a lack of comprehension. 'Is it someone from the coven? Can you see who it is?'

'There's a celebrity in our midst.' Helen raised a finger and pointed into the darkness. 'It's the third sister,' she told him, then grinning with obvious delight she stepped away from the fallen teenager and advanced towards Charity. 'The dark one is going to love us. We've gone and found the last of the virtuous Harker sisters.'

Charity's first instincts were to turn and run. She didn't bother thinking where she could go, or how she might now navigate the unknown layout of the cemetery when she had been lost and stumbling blindly along before; now she'd been discovered nothing else took precedence over the idea of putting distance between her and the potentially dangerous couple. But they were on her before she could take her first step.

Nick appeared in front of her, his razor-sharp smile twinkling affably. The brunette, Helen, had her hand around Charity's wrist. Her icy fingers made for a loose bracelet that wasn't uncomfortable, but was clearly going to be inescapable. Insidiously she pressed her body against Charity's and smiled with unconcealed hunger. 'Charity Harker,' she purred. 'I've got both BloodLust albums. I'm coming to get you too, is one of my all-time favourite tracks. '

'That's nice,' Charity replied weakly. She couldn't understand how they got to her so quickly, or why she now seemed unable to resist their unwanted attention. Nick stroked her shoulder, allowing his fingers to linger against the bare flesh of her upper arm. His touch was colder than death, an icy caress that should have made her cringe away from him, but instead she merely shivered and fervently hoped he would continue.

'I don't collect your albums,' he confided, the musical lilt in his tone delicious, making her long to hear more. 'I just collect virtuous sisters.'

His malevolent smile was both hateful and seductive. Charity studied him, sure he was dangerous yet unable to do anything except smile at him and hope he continued to grace her with his nearness. She told herself it was a pathetic way to respond: she was lead singer and songwriter of a gothic rock band that had toured Europe, stormed the charts and gained international acclaim for their hard-hitting image. But the rationale failed to make her move. Even when she remembered what had happened to the teenager, and told herself that this couple would have no qualms about leaving her sprawled and exposed across any of the other cemetery's graves, Charity couldn't bring herself to break away from the brilliance of Nick's charm.

'I've had Faith and Hope,' he told her, 'and having you will complete my set. It's a shame the three of you don't come with a presentation box,' he chuckled.

She didn't understand what he was saying, and she didn't particularly care as long as he continued to smile at her while he spoke. Rather than push either of the couple away, or demand to know what they had done to the teenager, Charity found herself regarding Nick with a guileless adoration she hadn't felt since the days of her last schoolgirl crush.

'The coven's come all the way to London just looking for you,' Helen explained.

Charity glanced politely at the brunette, not surprised to see the woman was stroking her through the flimsy fabric of her strappy-top. Decency and a sense of proportion made her want to slap Helen's hands away, but she couldn't bring herself to make any movement that might detract from the mesmerising glint in Nick's eyes. She was distantly aware of chilly fingers creeping beneath her top, sliding up and over her ribs and reaching the pliant mounds of her breast. Teasing fingertips caught the shape of her nipple, squeezing lightly before releasing then stroking. Caught up in a swelling rush of desire Charity bit back a sigh of unbridled euphoria.

'Why don't you make this easy on all of us?' Nick suggested, and Charity nodded, sure that if he wanted her to make things easy then she would do whatever he demanded. She had never met him before, hadn't known of his existence until she saw him with the teenager, but it didn't seem unreasonable to think that she could devote her life to making him happy. His fingertips were stroking back and forth over the sensitive flesh of her throat and she could feel him teasing the pulse of her jugular. The intimacy of that sensation surprised her and left her wondering why more wasn't written on the sensuous impulses that came from that part of the body.

'What do you want me to do?' she asked softly. Between her legs, Helen had pushed her thigh. She kept one hand under Charity's top, alternating her caresses from the left breast to the right, but she had lowered her other hand to Charity's sex. Her cool caress stroked against the gusset of Charity's thong, sliding softly over the fabric before teasing it to one side. The pressure of her fingers touching warm, moist skin was almost more than Charity could tolerate and she drew a staggered breath as she succumbed to another rush of arousal. She was about to try to find the strength to tell Helen to move her hands away and stop touching, but Nick chose that moment to speak.

'We'd been told you were going to be the strongest of the three,' he said. 'But that's beginning to look increasingly unlikely.' As if trying to prove something he snatched both her hands and pushed them behind her back. Her shoulders were strained by the brusque treatment, her breasts forced more firmly into Helen's eager grasp, and she had to shift her legs further apart in order to maintain her balance. Her gasp was a sound that came without protest, and was simply her body's way of dealing with his unexpected dominance.

He held her wrists in one hand while his other returned to her throat and continued to tease against the sensitive pulse. Attuned to every nuance of the night, Charity could hear his fingertips drawing over her flesh. 'I'm not convinced you really are the strongest. I don't think you'll put up much of a fight.'

Helen snorted. 'No one said she was the strongest, you tit.' Her caustic voice threatened to spoil the mood but Charity was easily able to overlook the brunette's unwanted intrusion. She was happy to have the woman's fingers tease sweet magic from her pussy lips. The tenuous touch squirmed at one moment, and then slyly stroked the next. The friction at her breasts was negligible, little more than an echo of the excitement being fuelled against her pussy, but she could feel herself being drawn by the temptation offered with each forbidden caress.

'The quote says, "the greatest of these is Charity",' Helen scoffed. 'This little slut is supposed to be the greatest. Not the strongest. She's the greatest.'

Charity barely heard the words but the distraction was enough to shake her from her mesmerised reverie. With a combination of shock and revulsion she saw how she had almost surrendered to the pair, and tried not to consider what madness had let her stand still while the bizarre couple fondled her with such intimacy. She tried to pull her wrists free from Nick's hold but the position was awkward and his grip seemed disturbingly powerful.

'I think you should let go of me now,' she said thickly. 'I think you ought to let go of my wrists and move away from me.'

Nick turned his smile back on her and she could feel each of her arguments evaporating like tendrils of graveyard mist. He satisfied himself with a final scowl in Helen's direction, and then seemed to dismiss the brunette as he brought the full weight of his charm on Charity. 'Do you really want me to let you go? Or would you like me to kiss you first?'

This time she came close to moaning with unbidden need. She needed no explanation to understand that he was offering more than a mere kiss, but the prospect of suffering beneath him was so tempting she couldn't contemplate denying herself

26

that pleasure. Raising her mouth to try and meet his, standing on tiptoe in her haste to get closer, she was frustrated when he pushed her head aside to expose her neck. From the corner of her eye she saw his lips curl back, watched the overlong canines glisten in the moonlight, then realised he was going to bite her throat, the idea making her shiver with fresh desire.

'You can't feast on her.'

The man's voice, commanding and surprisingly familiar, echoed across the cemetery. Charity felt Nick stiffen and saw Helen shift posture, as though preparing to attack, and with a flood of sickening guilt she realised how close she had come to succumbing to those dark urges that the pair aroused. Repulsed by what she'd been about to do she pulled herself from Nick's embrace and staggered towards the approaching figure.

Todd Chalmers, illuminated by moonlight and with a frown accentuating his stern features, looked formidable as he bore down on them. 'You can't feast on her because she is truly virtuous,' he declared. 'The lore of the undead forbids you from feasting on nuns and gypsies, but the laws of nature make it impossible for you to feed on the virtuous. Stop wasting her time; stop wasting my time; and be gone.'

Charity stared at him incredulously. She wondered where the band's manager had come from and how he had dared speak so boldly to the couple. Glancing back to see how they would respond she was amazed to discover they had disappeared into the night, and overwhelmed by a thousand questions she turned to Todd with a mixture of relief and gratitude.

But before she got the chance to speak he slapped her hard across the face. Bewildered and hurt she placed a hand against her blazing cheek. 'The Harker family curse,' she muttered, the last words she spoke before her tears began.

Charity

Act I, Scene II

The return journey to the Hampstead residence went past in a blur of embarrassment. Todd kept hold of Charity's wrist, dragging her through the wasteland of the cemetery's overgrowth as though he was a skilled sherpa used to navigating the treacherous route. On Swains Lane, where he had parked his hire car, Todd threw her into the passenger seat and then drove them swiftly through the suburban streets of Hampstead and back to the mansion the band were using. His chiselled features were set in a stern frown and his eyes were narrowed slits of pure fury. Charity only noticed these details in the briefest of glimpses, keeping her gaze lowered as she miserably studied her bare knees and braced herself for the inevitable outburst of his wrath.

The gate's security guards nodded respectfully as he drove past but they seemed to sense the mood of his disappointment, and Charity's chagrin, because none of them made any attempt at their usual exchange of pleasantries.

Without speaking, Todd ushered her through the main front doors. Resuming his hold on her wrist, he hurried her along the corridor that led from the grandiose entrance hall and into the study that he invariably commandeered for an office whenever he spent time in the UK with BloodLust. The furnishings were little more than an ostentatious chesterfield surrounded by wood panel walls and shelves stacked with uniform rows of leather-bound volumes. A mahogany desk took pride of place in front of the draped French windows, and its surface was typically untidy with his usual clutter of paperwork and office minutiae. The air inside the study was still redolent with the memory of the last cigar he'd smoked when in the mansion two months earlier.

Charity blinked against the glare of the harsh lighting while Todd poured himself a scotch. He made no attempt to offer her a drink, and it was only when he lit himself a cigar that she realised she was about to be subjected to the full force of his temper. Frightened, she tried to shrug off the last vestiges of the upset that had come from her encounter in the cemetery and focus on dealing with her manager's outrage. It might have been easier if his anger hadn't been so apparent, and she couldn't decide how best to handle him. She got the impression that he wasn't facing her on the terms of one fellow professional dealing with another, and couldn't shake the idea that she was being treated like an errant child held at the displeasure of an irate principal. Nervously she clutched her bare arms and regarded him with sullen desperation.

Todd downed his scotch in one and then poured himself another. 'I might have expected one of the other band members to behave this stupidly,' he complained, 'but I didn't expect it from you.' His booming voice echoed from the panelled walls and Charity momentarily feared that her reprimand would be overheard. 'Your lead guitar, Angela, is the sort of addled slapper destined to spend her life being fucked or sucking cock.'

Charity gasped, but she wasn't sure if her exclamation was caused by his harsh tone or the vulgarity of his words. She couldn't argue about Angela's morals – the band's lead guitar player was possibly the cause of half the rumours that made BloodLust feature in the tabloids – but Charity had never expected their manager to dismiss her with such coarse contempt, or in such a crude manner.

'And that stoner, Lauren, surprises me each time she turns

up for a set…'

Eyes rounded with disbelief, Charity quietly conceded that Lauren could go a little too heavily on her herbal cigarettes, and that her habit had compromised her professionalism on more than one occasion. But hearing the band's manager dismiss the bass guitar player so callously was not something she'd expected to face. She struggled to find words that would defend her colleagues, and then bit her tongue; fearful she might need all her best arguments to protect her own good name.

'And as for your drummer…' he snapped his fingers as though the name had eluded his memory. 'As for your drummer, the dizzy bitch with the rats-tails hairstyle…'

'Viv,' Charity supplied.

'Viv.' He downed his second scotch and poured a third before taking himself to the chesterfield's club chair. As he sucked on the end of his cigar he regarded her with an expression of barely contained contempt. 'Don't get me started on Viv,' he warned, using his cigar to point, 'because that bitch has caused more headlines than the entire royal family. They say there's no such thing as bad publicity, but she's living proof that that axiom is way off the mark.' Shaking his head, looking as though he was shrugging away the distraction of the band's faults, he went on, 'I might have expected this sort of stupidity from any one of those other worthless cows in the band, but I never expected it from you. I'm disappointed, Charity. I'm severely disappointed.'

The words hit her like a slap and she struggled not to let tears fall. 'I just got lost,' she protested, not thinking to rationalise her argument, hurrying to tell him what had happened so he could calm down and see that she was in need of some sympathy and understanding. 'I'd done the interview – it went really well – and I was making my way back here when—'

'I set rules before I left,' he intoned flatly, the interruption cutting her off more cleanly than a knife. 'I employ security to take you to interviews and bring you back. I keep a garage of cars as well as a round-the-clock staff of drivers who are always available for your use. All I ask is that you keep yourself safe, out of the reach of the public, and out of harm's way.'

'I wasn't looking for trouble,' Charity insisted. She could hear a plaintive note in her voice but she could see Todd wasn't going to respond with pity. 'I just made a bad decision,' she told him. 'Then I got a little lost.'

He considered her coolly before drawing on his cigar. 'I think you need spanking,' he said, speaking through plumes of smoke.

The words sat between them like the exposure of an ugly secret. The skin on Charity's bare arms once again turned to gooseflesh, but this time she knew the response was generated by revulsion. It was impossible to believe he had genuinely suggested the reprimand and she shook her head with disbelief. 'You think I need...' she said, incredulous.

'Spanking,' he confirmed. 'Don't make me say it again. You need a reminder of who's in charge and who follows orders. Get over my knee, Charity.'

She shook her head and fixed him with the indignation she knew his suggestion deserved. 'You're out of your frickin' mind if you think I'm going to let you spank me,' she snapped hotly, and turning her back on him, prepared to march out of the study and end the fatuous discussion, she had her fingers on the door handle before Todd spoke again.

'Fair enough,' he said simply.

She turned to glare at him but he wasn't looking in her direction. He had nestled back in his chair and blew a lazy smoke ring towards the chandelier. 'I can still make a return on my investment from managing the rest of the band,' he pondered, sounding as though he was talking to himself, speaking with the reflective manner of someone in absolute control. 'A replacement lead singer shouldn't be that hard to find. Good luck with your solo career, Charity. And good luck in court when I sue for breach of contract. Don't forget to say goodnight and goodbye to the security staff as you make your way out of here. It's the last time you'll see the inside of this building.'

After the trauma of all that had happened in the cemetery Charity had almost made it past the brink of tears, but their promise came back to her with renewed force. Todd's easy threat to ruin her and cast her out of the band was so shocking she didn't know where it had come from and she wasn't sure how best to handle a response. It crossed her mind that she could simply walk out of the door, and that the repercussions might not be as severe as he was suggesting, but she couldn't bring herself to believe that with sufficient conviction. So tentatively, not sure why she was giving in so easily, only aware that it was necessary, she walked to his chair. He continued to regard her with scorn until she lowered herself to her knees and bent over his lap.

'This is frickin' demeaning,' she told him.

He placed his cigar in a convenient ashtray and nodded agreement. 'You're damned right it's demeaning,' he assured her.

His breath was rank from the scotch, and coupled with the flavour of cigar smoke that tainted the air, Charity could easily have believed she had stumbled into the stuffy realms of an exclusive Victorian gentleman's club. Or back at school and suffering the wrathful displeasure of a severe master. Her chest closed with anxiety and each breath was a vicious struggle for air.

'It's demeaning that I should have to lower myself to punishing you,' he continued. 'And it's demeaning that you should ignore my instructions to such a degree that I have to do it.'

Charity was ready to argue, prepared to push her case and try to wrangle herself away from his knee, but Todd seemed savvy to her attempts at escape. He lowered his legs and urged her to bend fully across his knees, while placing one hand on the swell of her bottom.

She stiffened at his touch, uncomfortable with the salacious intimacy that seemed to be involved in this exchange and still not sure why she was allowing such an indignity. The allegro pace of her heartbeat was swift enough to leave her trembling.

'Count them off,' Todd growled. 'Six slaps, and after each one I want you to apologise for putting yourself in danger.'

She shook her head. 'This is frickin' demeaning.'

His hand squeezed her buttock, and the idea of pulling away, storming out of the study and facing those repercussions he had threatened suddenly seemed like the best solution. But she couldn't bring herself to move.

'We just agreed that this is demeaning to both of us,' he conceded, his fingers remaining clamped to the curve of her bottom, 'now let's not linger on that aspect, and let's see if you can accept your punishment like a big girl.'

Her stomach folded. His condescending tone made her feel like a chastened child and she marvelled at the spectrum she had travelled this evening. During the interview she'd been treated like a respected professional, yet now she was reduced to being chastised in the manner of a naughty schoolgirl, but before she had time to brood on the unfairness Todd delivered the first blow.

The flat of his hand slapped hard against her bottom. The force wasn't particularly strong but the humiliation it inspired was more crushing than she would have believed. The aftershock bristled through her body and she realised she had lowered herself to being spanked by her boorish bully of a manager. The blazing heat burnt against her cheek, and unable to stop herself, she released a small gasp of surprise.

'You're counting,' Todd reminded her.

'One,' she spat from between gritted teeth.

'And you're apologising.'

She drew a faltering breath and struggled to make herself say the words he demanded. The shame of the situation had already gone beyond being intolerable and his insistence that she supplied an apology was almost more than she could accept. But now she'd gone this far to accepting the punishment she could see no benefit in not going along with the final details. 'I'm sorry for putting myself in danger,' she mumbled.

Briskly Todd slapped her rear for a second time, using more force, rekindling the sting of the first blow and branding a fresh handprint of pain against both her cheeks. Charity struggled uncomfortably on his legs, despising the way her breasts were pressed into his thighs and loathing the fact that she was subjecting herself to this ordeal.

'Count,' he demanded.

'Two.'

'Apologise.'

She groaned and glared up at him. 'I've already said I'm frickin' sorry,' she complained. 'Do you really need to hear it another five times?'

His hand returned to her bottom, not slapping this time, simply clutching, helping revisit the burning shame of the spanks he had already administered. The tips of his fingers lingered close to the crotch of her thong and she was appalled by the sense of vulnerability he nurtured. She wasn't sure that he was trying to touch her – although she wouldn't have put anything past the manager now he had revealed this new side to his personality – but she could feel the heat from his hand warming her scantily covered sex. It occurred to her that perhaps the warmth wasn't coming from him, and that it might be her own response that was making her aware of the heat, but she wouldn't let herself accept that explanation.

'Make your apology,' he insisted with forced patience, 'or this will go on a lot longer than is necessary.'

She thought of telling him that it had already gone on too long, but it was obvious that the argument would be counterproductive. 'I'm sorry,' she gasped. 'Is that what you want to hear? I'm frickin' sorry.'

He slapped again, harder than before and leaving a blaze of unwanted fire against her cheek. If she hadn't been struggling to contain her response she knew she would have cried out as the unexpected flare of anguish blossomed: The blistering sting burrowed deep before leaving her aching and breathless.

'You'll apologise without swearing from now on,' Todd decreed.

She thought of telling him that the word frick wasn't swearing, and that she used it to stop herself from falling into the habit of profanity that was predominant with the rest of the band, but she knew this was neither the time nor the place for that discussion. Censured, and anxious to end his belittling sport, she gasped, 'Three,' then added, 'I'm sorry for putting myself in danger. I'm truly, truly sorry.'

His hand returned to her bottom, not striking this time, but resting lazily as he took another draw from his cigar. His fingers stroked idly, chasing nonchalant circles against the bristling flesh and exciting unwanted warmth against her sex. The tips of his fingers absently teased against her pubic curls and her tummy twisted as she realised how responsive she was to his touch.

'I'm not sure I've picked the proper way to discipline you,' he mused, and she warned herself not to be fooled by the hope his sentence offered. The chance that he might suddenly call an end to this degrading chastisement was something she hadn't dared consider but, now he was tempting her with that prospect, she realised she was willing to do anything to bring an end to the torment.

'No,' she agreed, 'this isn't right, is it?'

'Absolutely not,' he concurred, a duplicitous smile in his voice as he added, 'to do this properly I need to be spanking your bare backside.' Charity felt crushed by his words. 'Let's take off these damned panties,' he insisted.

The sick dread that had been nestling in her stomach returned with full force. She contemplated pulling away from him, sure he was trying to take things too far, then stopped herself. If there were only three more slaps to go and he wanted to deliver them while she was without her thong, she supposed she could cope with that humiliation. She tried twice to find the courage to consent, but her throat was locked with unease and she couldn't bring herself to respond.

Not that Todd was bothered in waiting for her approval. He raised the hem of her skirt, his fingers went to the waistband of her underwear, and he slowly began to peel the flimsy fabric over her thighs.

Charity closed her eyes, mortified by the indignity of her predicament and praying for it to come to a swift conclusion. She didn't want to think about the view he would have, or that the secrets of her sex would now be on open display to him. The idea of having Todd Chalmers leer at her private parts was more shaming than any of his blows had already proved. Closing her eyes, fighting back the tears that threatened to spring forth at any moment, she drew a shuddering breath and tried to brace herself for his next blow.

'You'll remember this punishment.'

'Yes,' she murmured, 'I'll remember it.'

'And you'll heed the lesson I'm trying to teach.' His hand returned to one buttock, kneading the plump flesh while the tips of his fingers tickled idly against the slippery flesh of her labia. His fingertips slid easily against her pussy lips and their caress was lubricated by the wetness of her hateful excitement. The intimacy was going beyond anything she could have ever considered decent, and she was on the brink of telling him he had taken things too far when Todd delivered the fourth slap.

Although the thong had offered no protection, she thought this blow seemed far more severe than any of its predecessors. A shock of anguish seared through her cheeks and she stiffened against him as she tried to acclimatise her body to the thrill of the pain. She deliberately avoided acknowledging that her breasts were heavy with arousal, that her nipples were taut and straining against the fabric of her strappy top, and she refused to accept that she could feel the movement of something stirring in Todd's trousers. It was shocking enough to be subjected to her own unwanted arousal without having to suffer the knowledge that he was gleaning excitement from this perverse display of authority.

'Count,' he snapped.

'Four,' she returned, and added a hasty apology before he could demand it from her. Her head thumped with the shame of what she was enduring and her buttocks glowed with the warmth from the punishment. She was aware of her body's other reactions, the wetness of her sex and the pulse that hammered deep between her thighs, but she wouldn't allow herself to admit those symptoms.

'Are you going to follow my instructions in future?'

'Yes.'

His hand slapped down again, the crisp echo whispering from the panelled walls.

Charity had thought she was beyond caring about the indecorous view he might have, but as he landed the fifth smack she noticed his concealed erection twitched against her. The thick muscle, possibly stirred by the same source of arousal that was fuelling her own, seemed infuriatingly appealing and she struggled to push its presence from her thoughts. Concentrating solely on counting and apologising, not allowing her mind to register the fact that her nipples were now a rigid agony in desperate need of attention, she refused to give in to the carnal appetite he inspired.

'You'll do everything I say from now on?'

'Yes.'

'I have your word on that?'

'Yes.'

The sixth slap left her momentarily breathless. He invested all his energy into the final blow and its retort echoed around the room like the shot from a gun. Charity stiffened in a shock of pain and torment, and she was dismayed to discover that her responses were not entirely unpleasant. The warmth he had generated was spreading like a fever, heating the tops of her thighs and nestling like a scalding secret in the core of her sex. The pulse she had noticed earlier now ached with the urgency of a desperate desire and she held herself rigid over his knee, willing the pleasurable sensations to go away.

Todd's hand returned to her bottom, stroking the punished skin and falling disquietingly close to her pussy lips. 'Count,' he prompted.

'Six,' she hissed.

'Apologise.'

The idea of rebellion pushed at the forefront of her mind, but now that the punishment was over, rather than incurring his anger again or drawing attention to the fact that they were both aroused by the episode of discipline, she knew it would be wisest to apologise and move on. 'I'm sorry for putting myself in danger,' she told him humbly. 'It wasn't done deliberately, but I did ignore your rules and you were right to punish me because of that. I'm sorry.'

He patted her graciously on the rear and she struggled not

to moan with her sudden need for him. The urge to surrender was reprehensible yet no less compelling, and she could almost imagine the joyous union that would come from having him take her and sate the longing he had inspired.

Seeming unaware of her response, Todd took another draw from his cigar. 'Then it seems we've reached an understanding.'

She drew a deep breath and contemplated pulling away from him. She didn't like the thought that he had such an unobstructed view of her bottom and sex lips, but the prospect of moving meant she would have to meet his eyes and see the way he regarded her now that she'd suffered his discipline, and the fear of being shamed by that encounter made her remain where she was. Shivering, and urging herself not to notice the increased pressure of his erection as it pressed against her, she studied the timeworn carpet beneath his feet and willed her excitement to abate.

'I'll pour you a drink,' Todd decided, and before she could protest or think of any excuse, he was pushing her from his knee as he returned to the scotch bottle on his desk.

She took the opportunity to stand up, briskly pulled her thong back up, brushed down the hem of her skirt and folded her arms across her chest, before he could properly study her. Then moving swiftly to the door, determined to leave the room now she had the opportunity, she placed her fingers on the door handle and cast a quick glance over her shoulder. 'Don't bother pouring a drink for me,' she said. 'Now you've disciplined me in that belittling fashion, I'm going to go back to my room.'

Todd shook his head and filled two tumblers with scotch, and relighting his cigar, studying her with more compassion than he had shown before, he said, 'We have to talk, Charity. And we have to talk now.'

'Talk about what?' Truculently she returned to the room

and accepted the glass of scotch. She kept one arm folded across her breasts and took the drink without exposing the fact that her nipples remained hard and responsive. 'I won't submit to anything else like that ever again,' she said adamantly. 'I promise you I won't.'

'We have to talk about vampires,' Todd said coolly, and the idea of leaving the room suddenly seemed more appealing than ever. She hadn't wanted to suffer his discipline, and she hadn't wanted to be humiliated in such a shameful way, but a part of her had conceded that it was an inescapable obligation. But now the seriousness of Todd's tone implied a conversation that she felt sure would have more sinister repercussions than a mere spanking. The idea of scurrying to the sanctuary of her bedroom held a greater appeal than ever.

'Those were real vampires you faced tonight,' Todd said calmly. 'And they're not the only ones in town.'

'This is silly talk,' she said without conviction. 'They were just students or fans or something.'

He shook his head. 'We have to talk,' he said firmly. 'We have to talk about your impending confrontation with the dark one and his sister, Lilah. And we have to talk about your role as the last of the virtuous sisters.'

Interlude

Part One

'What is this, Lilah?'

There was no need to glance in his direction because she could hear the contempt in her brother's voice. More than that, and disgustingly invasive, she could sense a part of his loathing as though it was one of her own thoughts or emotions. She supposed that particular feeling was a result of their shared aura. There had been a host of such similarities and they had become more obvious since the gypsy diagnosed the condition. But understanding didn't make the situation bearable and Lilah fought revulsion as she tried to distance herself from the mental weight of his low opinion.

'I asked a question, little sister.' His tone was a thinly veiled threat. 'I asked a question and I expect an answer. What is this?'

Determined that the night wouldn't degenerate into another clash of personalities, depressingly sure of what the outcome would be if that happened, Lilah quelled the urge to deride her brother for his surly attitude. 'This is Regent's Park,' she reminded him. 'We came here when John Nash was laying boundaries back in 1817. Don't you recognise the place?'

He took a breath to the back of his throat and held it like a low growl.

Noise was carrying from the northern end of the park, transporting the sounds of the distant zoo animals as they settled themselves down for the night. Lilah was familiar enough with wild beasts to know that they seldom responded well when they caught the scent of vampires. Their baying and howling was such a commonplace phenomena she wouldn't normally have noticed it, except maybe to think that her brother sounded like he was mimicking some large, menacing rhino.

'I know this is Regent's Park,' he snorted. 'I wanted to know why you've dragged me here, to this damned open air theatre of all places.'

She dared to grace him with her most condescending laugh. 'What a silly question, dear brother,' she murmured. 'Isn't it obvious why I've brought you here? I thought you might like to see a performance.'

There was no time for him to voice his disgust, and only a moment for her to feel the dark shadow of his black mood as it stole obscenely across her thoughts. Lights came on, illuminating the circular stage, and Lilah encouraged her brother to sit back in his seat and enjoy the show she had organised.

Large moths were turned into brilliant motes of gold beneath the halogen glare that lit the stage. The circular podium became a painfully bright arena while the backdrop of trees and grassy slopes leant an ambience that was surreal and almost magical. Lilah settled in her seat and waited anxiously for the first of the performers to take their places.

Marcia and the mulatto walked into the glare of the stage lights, blinking and shielding their eyes. Both peered into the auditorium, seeking out Lilah and waiting for her instruction.

'What is this?' the dark one demanded.

'Don't you want a good champion to go up against the last of the virtuous sisters?'

'I've got a good champion,' the dark one complained. He pointed to the blonde girl in the centre of the stage. 'The mulatto's already shown that she's no match for Marcia. But I can put her up against Charity and, if she fails, I can use

Marcia as a backup.' He sniffed impatiently. 'I've already got that part of my plan established, Lilah. This is a waste of my time.'

Lilah tutted, a soft sound that she hoped covered her frustration with her brother's pigheadedness. 'Don't you want to make sure they're both in top form?' she pressed. 'It's been a while since you've seen either of them face a challenge. Don't you want to go into this confident that you'll be victorious?'

She knew his grudging silence would be the closest he would come to acquiescence and she snapped her fingers as a command for the pair to begin. The mulatto responded first, turning to face Marcia and slapping her hard across the jaw. The blow was crisp and loud, echoing all the way to Lilah's seat on the lower circle of the auditorium.

Not slow to react, and proving herself to be surprisingly capable, Marcia launched herself at the mulatto. She was a blur of extended nails, bared teeth and blonde curls. With no effort she overpowered her opponent and, within moments, the pair were wrestling on the podium. It was a vicious struggle as each scratched and clawed at the other. Sinewy legs interlocked in a parody of a lover's embrace and they squeezed together in a dry simulation of vigorous sex. The shapes of their bodies – lithe, svelte and agile – were clearly defined through the tight fabrics of their clothes.

With her vision attuned to every detail, Lilah could see the rasp of cotton against silk and almost feel the tension of thinly sheathed flesh rubbing against thinly sheathed flesh. Excited by the demonstration of passion and power she subtly rubbed her thighs together. Although she hoped the movement might alleviate the heat between her legs, the maddening itch of her arousal grew more profound.

Marcia snatched the blouse from the mulatto's shoulders and tore it away with one powerful sweep. Struggling to match her ferocity the mulatto flailed her arms, striking and slapping with frenetic speed, her retaliation swiftly quelled when Marcia pulled her bra away, then lowered her lips to the swell of one exposed breast.

'Didn't I tell you that Marcia would win?' the dark one declared. 'Didn't I say the mulatto was no match for her?'

Lilah could sense his smugness as much as she could hear it in his sneering tone. 'They've been battling for less than a minute,' she shrugged. 'Do you really think it's a foregone conclusion so early in the contest?'

On stage the mulatto looked torn between conflicting responses. She struggled to push Marcia away, her dark fist tightening against the blonde's curls as she tried to urge her head aside, but it was clear her torment wasn't a wholly unpleasant experience; along with every insult carried beneath her breath she bristled with the obvious symptoms of pleasure.

Marcia kept her face locked against the mulatto's breast, suckling greedily and biting with blatant force. Her eyes were greedy rounds of satisfaction and dribbles of spilt blood trickled from the union between her lips and the nipple from which she was feeding.

Used to watching her brother's champions go against each other, Lilah could see a host of missed opportunities the mulatto allowed to slip past while she wallowed beneath Marcia, but the sight of her grudging submission was enough to warm the glowing coal of excitement that nestled between Lilah's thighs. She wriggled her buttocks impatiently against her seat and sat forward so as not to miss a moment.

Marcia shifted position; with feline agility she threw herself over the mulatto's face, pushing her sex against her opponent's mouth. The hem of her short skirt concealed the majority of the action but Lilah had watched enough confrontations to know that Marcia was going for a swift victory. All she had to do to win was keep the mulatto against the floor and force her to concede defeat with a supplicating kiss against her sex. Grudgingly, Lilah conceded that this tournament was beginning to look like a foregone conclusion.

'You're wasting my time,' the dark one growled. He started to rise from his seat and Lilah stopped him by placing a hand on his wrist.

The mulatto writhed against the floor with an unexpected burst of enthusiasm, but it was clear that she no longer stood any chance of victory. Above her the blonde's features were twisted with an expression of orgasmic triumph. She squirmed her sex hard against the dark-skinned girl's face and tore the remaining clothes from her body. Milk chocolate flesh was exposed revealing the climactic tension that now held the mulatto. Every muscle and limb was defined beneath the glare of the stage lights as both females wavered on the brink of release.

'You're wasting my time,' the dark one said again. He glared at the hand holding his wrist and waited until Lilah moved her fingers before continuing. 'You're wasting my time, and you're wasting the energies of my best champions. Vampires can be drained too, Lilah. Or had you forgotten that?'

Not allowing her gaze to leave the stage, avidly enjoying the brutal tournament, Lilah kept her tone neutral as she said, 'I hadn't forgotten that vampires can be drained.'

'We rely on blood from fresh victims,' he continued didactically. 'But if you drain the blood from a vampire it will kill them as ably as a crucifix, a stake through the heart or direct sunlight. Drain the blood from a vampire and it will leave them just as dead as the remains of any mortal corpse. If you don't believe me I could happily illustrate my point with a practical example.'

Gritting her teeth, concentrating on the stage and determined not to rise to the bait of her brother's impatience,

Lilah responded, 'There's no need for a practical example. I'm aware of the restraints imposed by our lifestyle. I understand what you're saying.'

'Then is there really a point to all this?'

Frustrated, she snapped her fingers, the crisp echo resounding louder than any other noise in the open-air theatre. On stage a third figure appeared.

'Who the hell is she?' the dark one asked.

Lilah grinned slyly and blew a kiss to the newcomer. 'That's Wendy.'

Wendy was strikingly tall, her imposing height accentuated by a pair of heels and a painfully tight ponytail that sprouted from the top of her head. Her raven black hair was a shocking contrast against her snow-white flesh, and if not for Marcia's pink-flushed cheeks and the mulatto's coffee-coloured nudity, Lilah could have thought she was watching a monotone production.

'Who is she?'

'I found her last night,' Lilah purred, the evidence of that encounter marking Wendy's throat as a wound that looked swollen and tender. 'I knew you'd want to put someone strong up against the virtuous one, and I thought Wendy might have the potential to be a better champion than either of your current favourites.'

Settling back in his chair, the dark one made no comment and only watched.

Lilah had dressed Wendy to appeal to her brother's unsophisticated impulses. She wore black stockings, the seams running directly up from her heels, with matching pants, suspender belt and bra. Her physique was muscular, less athletic than either of the others with whom she shared the stage, and almost manly with her pronounced biceps and broad chest. Her stern features did not make her look pretty and Lilah suspected the kindest compliment the woman had ever received might have been a remark that she was handsome. But Wendy held herself as though she was the epitome of desirability.

'She's a monster,' the dark one mused.

Wendy wielded a multi-thonged whip, the handle fashioned from leather to resemble an oversized pizzle. Lilah didn't doubt she would easily succeed in a confrontation against the other two vampires and thought of asking her brother if he still believed Marcia would be the night's victor.

Wendy towered over the pair as they continued to fight, but her brooding gaze was fixed on Lilah, and waiting until she had received a nod of consent, only acting after she'd been given implicit permission, the freshly made vampire snapped her whip against Marcia's shoulders, the retort ringing around the acoustics of the open-air theatre, Marcia's shriek of pain inspiring the zoo animals to resume their baying.

Lilah writhed on her seat; from the corner of her eye she saw that her brother was not immune to Wendy's charms. The bulge in his trousers was horribly obvious and as unmistakable as his salacious leer, and when Wendy struck the whip down again, striping the mulatto's bared breasts with a stinging flick, the dark one rubbed himself. 'She really is a monster,' he laughed.

'That doesn't sound like you disapprove.'

He made no reply, his concentration fixed on the entertainment she had provided.

Wendy was taking charge of the two vampires with surprising efficiency. Marcia put up the staunchest resistance, struggling to get the better of the newcomer and even making one bold attempt to wrestle the whip from her hand. But Wendy proved to be more than she could handle.

The mulatto, seeming cowed from Marcia's domination, easily supplicated herself before the newcomer. She lowered her head and kissed the toes of Wendy's stilettos with a servility that came close to making her look pathetic.

Marcia made another attempt to snatch triumph from the unexpected turn of events, extending her talon-like nails and aiming a blow at Wendy's face. If her claws had connected Lilah knew the blonde would have flayed skin, yet Wendy brushed the assault aside as though it was no more of a nuisance than a passing fly. She caught Marcia's wrist in one hand, twisted it behind her back, and then pulled the blonde into a reluctant embrace.

'Didn't I tell you she was good?' Lilah said, punching her brother playfully on the arm. 'Didn't I tell you?' With his crimson gaze leering into the night, the dark one said nothing.

Wendy pulled Marcia closer, casually stroking her cheek with the pizzle-shaped end of the whip. Overcoming the blonde's resistance she squeezed closer before extracting a deep, penetrating kiss. The blonde's reluctance was obvious – she struggled in a futile bid to escape – but with one hand trapped behind her back and the full power of the newcomer's formidable force bending her to respond, she had no option except to suffer the unwanted kiss.

The mulatto, clearly trying to avoid Wendy's wrath, raised her kisses up the woman's leg. Her large, dark eyes were turned meekly upward and fixed expectantly on her face. Lilah didn't think the dark-skinned vampire had ever looked more servile and she even noticed the glimmer of a hurt expression on her features when the mulatto was casually kicked aside.

'Both of you bend over,' Wendy demanded, her booming tenor voice brooking no argument.

The mulatto did as she was told, trembling in the throes of either misery, suffering or dark excitement. Marcia was less enthusiastic but ultimately obedient and she eventually lowered herself to the floor. Wendy used the tips of her stilettos to reposition both vampires, directing them to face this way and that and snapping her whip viciously to get the desired result. By the time she had finished Marcia faced stage left, her backside raised in the air, while the mulatto assumed an identical posture and faced stage right. Their shoulders brushed together and both of them shivered each time Wendy's whip cracked down. Allowing her crisp heels to clip like gunshots on the stage, Wendy circled the pair, delivering random blows to backs, buttocks and breasts.

Lilah could have watched the domination for hours. The thrill of the fight had always held a sadistic pleasure for her but the triumph of this swift victory was proving to be absorbing. She didn't normally like to sit back and watch others enjoy themselves, but Wendy was providing compelling entertainment. The woman effortlessly controlled the subordinate vampires, directing one to lick her sex while the other offered herself for feeding.

The sounds of sex carried wetly throughout the auditorium, the rich, guzzling sounds battling against the distant cries from the zoo for their animal intensity, but that didn't stop Lilah from deciding she had made a rare find with the creation of this new vampire. The woman was a natural on stage: confident of where her audience were, and showing the detail of the action to delicious effect.

She pulled the crotch of her panties to one side and bent with the seasoned confidence of a sex performer. Displaying the open split of her sex, taking an exhibitionist's pleasure from revealing the flushed lips of her sodden pussy, she used her whip to control her subordinates and make sure they kissed her without spoiling the view.

Lilah was easily able to see Marcia's pouting lips slip reluctantly against Wendy's silky wetness and she could almost detect the musky fragrance that was left to lather the blonde's mouth. The mulatto was called from her kneeling position, and then instructed to bend her head aside so her throat would be exposed, and all the time, ever mindful of her audience, Wendy made sure that every detail was clearly visible.

She alternated between victims, pushing the mulatto back to the floor as she lifted Marcia and drank from her throat. The dark-skinned vampire was urged to lick Wendy's sex, forced to coax her tongue deep within the pink folds of her cunt, while Wendy greedily bit into the blonde's neck. Acting with the appetite of an indecisive gourmet she pushed Marcia back down, then dragged the other vampire back from the floor.

It was only when the mulatto began to stagger – weakened from blood loss or dizzy with embarrassment Lilah couldn't tell – that Wendy finally relented. However, rather than letting the pair crawl off to recoup their strength she instructed them both to kneel down and insisted they bent over so that their bare bottoms were displayed to the small audience.

'Don't you think she'll make for a formidable champion?' Lilah whispered, but the dark one remained silent. His brow was furrowed and his slumped shoulders suggested he was brooding about something and wasn't enjoying this demonstration as much as Lilah had hoped. She could see his erection still strained at the front of his trousers, and she wrinkled her nose with disgust when she noticed his lust was like an undercurrent to her own thoughts. Not wanting to consider her brother's excitement on such a personal level, she tried to dismiss him from her mind as she concentrated on the stage.

Wendy circled both subordinates, cruelly delivering lashes to one bottom and then the other. Marcia's porcelain cheeks were already the colour of a summer sunset, darkening to scarlet with every blow she suffered. The mulatto clawed the stage with tears of mascara dripping down the perfect bone structure of her cheeks. The vicious force of each lash trembled through her slender body, making the tips of her

breasts jiggle enticingly.

Performing to her audience, Wendy pushed her sex into Marcia's face and demanded to be licked. The blonde obeyed without hesitation, and once again Lilah was treated to the engaging sight of Marcia slurping at Wendy's flushed sex. Remaining calm and composed, showing no emotion or response as Marcia plundered her pussy lips, Wendy took the pizzle-shaped end and stroked it against the mulatto's cleft, making the dark-skinned vampire moan.

Lilah chuckled softly, savouring the visceral pleasure. She glanced at her brother, still anxious to know what he thought about her plans for dealing with the virtuous one, and was rewarded by the sight of his smile. His upper lip had curled back with obvious approval, and trying not to be revolted by the discovery she realised he was massaging his groin as he watched the three on stage.

Blushing, Lilah turned her attention back to Wendy. Marcia continued to squirm her tongue into the vampire's sex, her nose pressed hard against the ring of the woman's anus as she tried to make the penetration deeper. Her breasts heaved with blatant arousal and her nipples stood hard and dark.

Wendy pushed the tip of the handle against the mulatto's sex, and then forced it slowly forward. The thick girth of the length spread her labia and rushed easily into her gaping wetness.

Lilah clutched herself, elated that the new champion was proving to be such a wonderful find. She could almost feel the gruelling entry of the handle as it filled the dark-skinned vampire. She rocked against her seat as she voyeuristically savoured the demands of the penetration. The mulatto's hands became fists and she hammered them repeatedly against the boards of the podium, but there was no sign of her reneging on her obedience to the superior vampire. Lilah even noticed a brief frown of disappointment on the mulatto's face when

the pizzle was finally snatched from her sex.

Wendy moved her domination on to Marcia, and after grabbing a fistful of her curls she pushed the whip's handle into her mouth. The blonde was clearly reluctant to obey, but that didn't stop her from chasing her tongue along its black leather length. She lapped at the dewy remnants of the mulatto's excitement, accepting the head of the pizzle between her lips and greedily swallowing the taste. In absolute control, wielding her domination with effortless ease, Wendy demanded that the mulatto lick her. The dark-skinned vampire responded instantaneously. She flattened her face between the snow-white mounds of Wendy's rear and pushed her tongue deep into the woman's cleft.

Lilah stole a hand between her legs and touched herself. Merely watching others enjoy themselves wasn't usually one of the ways she found her fun, but Wendy was providing such a satisfying show she couldn't tear her attention away. Stroking her fingertips idly against her leather trousers, inadvertently shivering with the prospect of self-pleasure, she released a heavy sigh. Her nipples had turned stiff inside her waistcoat and each subtle movement made her want to groan in a fury of frustrated arousal, but she contained the cry and concentrated on the stage.

Wendy maintained the tableaux, chuckling with scornful amusement. She continued to stroke the handle in and out of Marcia's mouth while writhing her buttocks onto the mulatto's face, her plain features almost made pretty when the trace of a smile finally bristled across her lips. But that glimmer of vulnerability quickly vanished when she snatched the whip away from Marcia, snapped two lashes against the bare backsides, then pushed the thick handle back into the mulatto's pussy. The dark-skinned vampire groaned and Marcia stifled a sob as Wendy's buttocks were pushed back into her face.

'Where did you find her?' the dark one asked.

Lilah laughed. 'It's a funny story.'

He sniffed. 'She was coming out of the Christian Meditation Centre, at Saint Mark's, in Myddleton Square.' His glowering gaze never left the stage.

Frowning thunderously, despising the link they now shared and the way her brother used it to read her thoughts, Lilah folded her arms and tried to throw herself back into enjoying the performance.

Wendy had pulled the pizzle from the mulatto's sex and was now urging it between the blonde's legs. Once again she had positioned herself and her cast so that her audience had an unfettered view of the performance and Lilah caught every detail of the gratuitous penetration. The leather of the handle was greasy with a meld of Marcia's saliva and the mulatto's musk, and it slid easily into the blonde's vagina. Wendy seemed to force it deeper for Marcia and didn't stop until she was shrieking for leniency, but even then, rather than totally bowing to the blonde's cries for mercy, she simply pulled the pizzle free then pushed the tip against her anus.

Lilah pushed two fingers directly against her sex, in little doubt she would easily be able to wring an orgasm from between her legs while she watched Wendy's perverse show, and she idly toyed with the prospect of dominating her once the demonstration was over.

Marcia's cries of protest became a guttural sigh as the handle slipped into her rear passage. Her buttocks were striped with the crimson lines of her earlier punishment and plastered with the lustre of spilt wetness. Arching her back, shivering as the handle slid deeper, her face was contorted with the vicious rage of an unwanted climax.

Slapping a hand against her bottom, Wendy pulled the pizzle from Marcia's anus and thrust the handle under the mulatto's nose. The unspoken instruction was obvious and the dark-skinned vampire didn't hesitate before chasing her tongue against the leather.

Lilah turned to her brother. 'What do you think?' she asked eagerly.

'I think you're an idiot.'

The words hit like a slap. 'Don't you think she's the strongest vampire you've ever seen?' Lilah asked indignantly. 'Don't you think she'll eat the virtuous one and then spit out the bones?'

'She's good,' he conceded, 'but she's going up against the greatest. Corinthians: thirteen, thirteen,' he reminded her. 'Faith, Hope and Charity. But the greatest of these is Charity. This bitch won't stand a chance against the virtuous one. The only thing this performance has shown me is that none of them are good enough. I guess we need to reconsider our plans before we confront the last of the sisters.'

Lilah shook her head, amazed that her brother could hold such a low opinion of her newly discovered champion. She watched him rise and start to climb over the seats as he made his way out of the open-air theatre. 'Where are you going?'

'Wendy isn't good enough,' he called. 'None of them are good enough. You're not organising anything here that will help us deal with Charity. You're wasting my time.' He pointed towards the stage, snapping his fingers and snatching the attention of Marcia and the mulatto, and then with a simple flick of his head he silently commanded them to follow.

'I organised this presentation especially for you,' Lilah complained. 'Where the hell do you think you're going?'

He called something back to her but she couldn't properly understand his words. The acoustics of the open-air theatre were working against her and she thought her brother had said he was going to deal with the problem in his own way.

Charity

Act I, Scene III

The pale face outside her bedroom window glowed more brightly than the full moon. The eyes were wide and avaricious and the lips were twisted in a lustful smirk. And yet, as she tossed and turned restlessly, struggling to find some position that didn't rekindle the discomfort of her sore bottom, Charity remained oblivious to the fact that she was being watched.

Grimly she wished for sleep in the vain hope it would give her a reprieve from the tumult of her thoughts. The humiliation of the spanking stayed at the forefront of her mind, and the shameful memory was awoken each time her buttocks were caressed by the stiff cotton sheets. Her rear felt tender and unduly sensitive to every shift in posture that came as she tried to wind down for the evening.

Charity still couldn't accept that she had allowed Todd to abuse her in such a way and she wanted to deny the excitement his punishment had inspired. The hot need that had broiled between her legs was almost as embarrassing as the way she had so easily submitted to his authority. Remembering the crisp blow of each slap, and the spreading warmth that inveigled its way into her sex, repeatedly made her blush and feel sick with shame.

But it wasn't just the punishment or her vile response that kept Charity awake. Todd's chastisement had to rank as the most humiliating experience of the evening – possibly the most humiliating of her entire life – yet it was the revelation of their conversation afterwards that continued to plague her thoughts.

'Vampires,' she mumbled incredulously. 'Genuine vampires.'

If she had glanced at the face outside the window she would have seen its smile grow wider. She lay flat on her back and the thin sheet that cloaked her body sculpted every curve. The swell of her breasts was obvious and the tips of her rigid nipples were clearly visible. Unaware of her audience she stared blindly into the darkness while she tried to digest all she'd been told - but it was a lot to take in.

After forging her music career with a band that celebrated creatures of the night, and after writing countless lyrics about the fashionable cult of the undead, she was still sceptical when Todd told her that vampires genuinely existed. It was too fantastic to accept, yet his argument was compelling and he coloured his explanation with details about both her sisters and their encounters with the members from a particularly wicked coven. While his stories were too bizarre to be real, she conceded that they were also too outrageous to be lies, so eventually, reluctantly, and going against everything she knew about Todd's dubious character, she decided he was telling the truth.

'Genuine frickin' vampires,' she had mumbled. 'They really do exist.'

'You're the last of the virtuous sisters,' Todd said. 'You're the world's final hope of vanquishing this coven forever.' He had said a lot more, regaling her with anecdotes about Faith ripping the heart from a vampire's chest, and Hope dabbling in dark magics to pull her sister back from the clutches of the undead, but by that point she had found herself suffering from information overload.

There had been a gift from Hope, a silver crucifix that matched the one Faith always wore, and Todd took the liberty of securing it around Charity's neck. There was also the news that Faith was in a relationship with another girl and the disquieting revelation that Todd seemed to regard Hope with genuine affection. But on this occasion she knew the details of her family's well-being would have to remain a secondary consideration. More important was Todd's assessment of the threat with which she was faced.

He had mentioned individual members of the coven; the dark one, Lilah, Marcia, the mulatto and the couple she had encountered in Highgate. He even suggested that there could be new vampires within the group, freshly made from innocents snatched off the streets of London. But after their lengthy discussion all Charity really remembered was his parting phrase, 'It's your turn now.'

Those words remained with her like the echoing knell of an iron cemetery bell. She was expected to face the vampires and the battle would be her bloodline's final confrontation against the forces of evil. Still trying to accept that concept, and appalled by the duties Todd said she would have to perform, she kicked the sheets aside, leaving her body exposed to the room, the face at her window leering with raw approval.

Her breasts were silvered by moonlight and her naked figure was transformed into a monochrome image of feminine perfection. Painfully restless, and anxious to find some position that leant itself to comfort, she twisted and turned, then smoothed her hand against the swell of her sex. Her pussy lips were warm and oily with viscous excitement, and reacting as though she'd been burnt, shocked by the sudden rush of lust her own touch awoke, Charity snatched her hand away.

The face at the window smirked with greedy excitement and something in the movement of that smile finally caught her attention. She saw she was being watched, and unable to contain the response she shrieked in horror.

Danny flicked the catch on the windows and stepped into the room. Grinning with his usual insouciant charm, he caught the light switch and graced her with a cheeky wink. The bedroom was instantly illuminated. 'I thought this was your window,' he chuckled, 'but I couldn't be sure without the lights. I wondered where you were hiding yourself.'

Her heart pounded at a manic tempo. Shock, terror and relief wrestled inside her like a cauldron of bubbling emotions. 'What the frick were you doing out there?' she demanded, snatching the sheet back over her body, covering herself and clutching the cotton protectively against her breasts. Her fear quickly mutated to anger, and keeping one arm across her chest, holding the sheet tightly in place as she leapt from the bed, she used her other hand to beat Danny's shoulder. 'Have you been taking stalker lessons? Or is this just a little freelance perving?'

Danny laughed uncertainly, but clearly puzzled by her reaction he tolerated her ineffectual pummelling without complaint.

'You frickin' scared me,' Charity told him. 'You scared me senseless.'

His ever-present grin continued to grace her. 'This isn't the apology I was expecting from you,' he said, and it was all he needed to say to make her realise that she had forgotten their regular supper engagement. Appalled by her own lack of sensitivity, and quickly deciding that her anger was as misplaced as her terror had been, she stopped hitting him and threw herself into his arms. On the verge of tears, and at the mercy of her seesawing emotions, she leant against him and struggled not to cry.

Hesitant, and possibly a little wary, she guessed, Danny embraced her. 'I didn't really expect an apology,' he murmured. 'I was only kidding when I said that.'

She sniffed back her first response and took a couple of breaths before trying to speak. Danny was Angela's brother and an unofficial member of the BloodLust entourage. While they'd been touring and recording he had become Charity's best friend and she suspected, if not for the pressures of media scrutiny and her crippling workload, their relationship might have already grown into something more physical. He had boyish good looks, and the sort of athletic build she always found attractive, and she often wondered why neither of them had tried to take things any further. Admittedly, Danny had enthused wildly about the schoolgirl uniform she wore for one of their more popular videos, but she dismissed that moment of lechery as nothing more than a polite flirtation. Most evenings they met up – when they were in the Hampstead mansion they usually congregated in the kitchen for a midnight snack – and chatted easily and without affectation for hours. His sense of humour and gentle cynicism often proved to be a breath of fresh air after the hype and pomposity of the music industry. But she had never indicated that she might want more from him, and aside from an occasional reference to how she looked in a schoolgirl uniform, Danny had never behaved in any way that was likely to jeopardise their friendship.

'I was…' she began, faltering, not sure how much she dared say or where she could begin. There was no way she would tell him that Todd had spanked her, and she couldn't see Danny accepting the assertion that vampires actually existed, but without either of those details she was left with no honest explanation for her absence from their engagement. 'I… I just forgot,' she said, swallowing down the truth. 'Can you forgive me?'

He laughed the matter away as though their regular supper date was of no importance. 'I really wasn't expecting an apology,' he chuckled. 'I just came to your window to make sure you're okay.' Taking hold of her shoulders, studying her eyes with quizzical concern, he asked, 'What's troubling you? You look upset, and you screamed when you saw me. Is something wrong?' Genuine worry creased his brow. 'I don't have spinach stuck between my teeth, do I? That isn't what scared you, is it?'

His typical vanity made her giggle, and she managed to shrug off some of her unrest, but not so much that her worries fully abated. 'There's no spinach between your teeth,' she said, shaking her head, adamant that she wouldn't draw him into anything that had happened in Todd's study. 'You look as handsome as ever. Almost too handsome.' Glancing coyly up at him, trying not to think that there was only a thin sheet concealing her nudity, she added, 'I guess it's just been one of those days.'

'I guess,' he agreed. 'Do you want to talk about it?'

Lowering her gaze, pushing herself back into his embrace, she shook her head again. His broad chest felt somehow right against her near naked body and the strength of the muscular arms around her made her feel secure and protected. It was the first time she had felt safe since her tube ride led her to that horrible encounter with Nick and Helen, and she quietly cursed the fact that it was Todd Chalmers who rescued her and not someone deserving of her gratitude, like Danny.

'Should I just go?' he suggested, and Charity could feel the words trembling through his chest as he spoke, the movement vibrating against her nipples in a way that was exciting without the dark and sinister overtones that Todd had inspired. 'I can leave now if you want me to,' he said, turning back towards the window. 'I shouldn't have called around to see you like this. That was wrong of me. You look like you want to be alone. I'll go.'

'No.' She pulled him tighter into their embrace. It had been awful trying to come to terms with the night's revelations on her own, and even if she couldn't share any of her fears or experiences with him, she still couldn't bear the idea of being left by herself. 'Please don't go,' she implored him. 'Not yet.'

'Something's troubling you,' he stated. 'Was it the magazine interview? Did they give you a hard time? They weren't asking those same tired questions about Lauren and Viv, were they?'

'No, the interview went fine,' she assured him.

'Angela hasn't landed herself with another celebrity kiss-and-tell romance, has she?'

'I don't want to talk about what's troubling me,' she said firmly.

'But if…'

Charity stepped out of his embrace and allowed the sheet to fall to the floor. Presenting herself to him naked, allowing him a moment to savour the sight of her unclothed body, she said, 'I don't want to talk about anything, Danny. Now you're here, perhaps we can do something more than just talk.'

His smile wavered as he admired her, the appreciation in his eyes growing steadily more obvious. 'You're not wearing any clothes,' he observed, then speaking hurriedly, holding out his hands in a gesture of appeasement, he added, 'not that I'm complaining, of course.'

Not hesitating – not daring to hesitate now that she'd made this decision – Charity stepped back into his arms. 'I'm not wearing any clothes,' she agreed, her voice a husky timbre, suiting the thickening atmosphere of the room. 'I'm not wearing any clothes, and I'm in no mood to talk,' she added. 'So care to suggest how we could spend the remainder of the evening?'

'We could…'

She silenced him with a kiss, cupping his face in her hands, standing on tiptoe and pressing hard against him, pushing her tongue between his lips. Whatever resistance he'd been trying to assume was banished in an instant. The hands that had been holding her at a distance pulled her into a crushing hug and the thickness of his erection twitched against her thigh. One hand went to the small of her back and the pressure of his palm against her skin was delicious and invigorating.

The air had felt like syrup before; now it was almost too dense to accept into her lungs and she struggled to find breath. Inhaling deep as she kissed him, savouring the scent of his sweat and the wicked undercurrent of his arousal, she writhed against the bulge of his excitement and felt it grow. Danny kept his hand on the small of her back and moved the other to her breast. His touch was light at first, inquisitive and softly caressing before he made his grip more demanding. A thumb brushed her nipple and she gasped as a thrill of pure pleasure erupted from the tip. The sensation was nothing like the shameful excitement Todd had awoken, and this time the urgent need between her legs felt pure and wholesome and right.

'Are you sure we should be doing this?' Danny asked.

She held his gaze, smiling coyly and savouring the taste of his kiss. Chasing her tongue across her lower lip, seriously contemplating his question before responding, she said, 'We don't have to do anything if you don't want. The next move is up to you.'

He didn't waste any time vacillating. Picking her up in his arms, carrying her the short distance back to the bed, he laid her down and towered over her. The desire in his eyes was the exact expression she had needed to see and made her realise that she had been right to believe there was an attraction between them that extended beyond their platonic friendship. Eagerly helping him remove his T-shirt, delighted by the sight of his gym-toned abdomen and sun bed tan, she told herself she was doing the right thing.

There was only one reservation that niggled at the back of her mind.

Todd had called her the last of the virtuous sisters, and said she needed to retain her purity and chastity in order to win her battle against the forces of evil. Charity wasn't sure how much credence she ought to give to that suggestion but she treated the notion with a lot more scepticism than the concept of vampires. It didn't seem feasible that Todd could spank her bare backside, cruelly humiliate and excite her, then say she was meant to carry herself like the contemporary version of a vestal virgin. Yet, when Danny moved his head over her breast and took her nipple into his mouth, she wondered if she wasn't damning herself to defeat before she'd taken the first move against the coven.

Not that she felt able to push him away. He held the tip of her breast between his lips and trilled his tongue against the end. A flurry of warm bliss spread from the nub and brought her to the brink of tears rich with frustrated joy. Gasping happily, she stroked his scalp and basked in his nearness.

Danny shifted his head from one breast to the other. He had yet to remove his jeans, and the coarse weave of the denim was maddening against her inner thighs, but Charity knew she could cope with that torment, and gently bucking her hips, savouring the pressure of his bulge as it pressed through the fabric she moaned with burgeoning need.

'You're sure we should be doing this?' he mumbled.

The words were spoken against her flat tummy as he lowered his kisses. The scratch of his five o'clock shadow rasped against her flesh, contrasting with the soft pressure of his lips. She knew where his mouth was going and felt dizzy with the promise of pleasure that lay ahead. Snatching air to reply, almost shaking with her arousal, Charity couldn't respond too quickly. 'I'm sure,' she said earnestly. 'I want this.'

His mouth reached the thatch of curls that covered her sex. 'Then we both want the same thing,' he said, nuzzling through the triangle of hairs, inhaling deeply as though drinking the scent of a fine bouquet. 'I guess I've wanted this for a long time.'

She trembled and raised her sex to meet his mouth. He

placed a light kiss at first, a gentle caress of his lips grazing softly against the dewy folds of her sex. There was barely any contact, a whisper of his nearness gliding against the most sensitive part of her body, but it was enough to have her in the throes of accelerating need. Charity wanted to writhe from side to side, desperate to release some of the incredible tension he was fuelling, but she held herself still for fear he might think she was having doubts. Holding her breath, anxiously anticipating the thrill of his next kiss, she closed her eyes and savoured the tickle of his breath against her thighs, and then he pushed the tip of his tongue against her clitoris.

The explosion of bliss was euphoric and she bit her lower lip to contain a scream. Sparkling eddies of arousal blossomed from her pussy and she squirmed beneath the rush of an encroaching release.

When he lapped at her, tasting her wetness, she came close to choking with delight. His head bobbed lazily up and down as he licked her sex and she hurtled quickly toward the moment of climax. Shivering with the growing warmth, amazed by the intensity of her response, she could feel the unpleasantness of the day being banished as Danny transported her to undiscovered realms of joy.

But there was one brief moment of panic that threatened to spoil her pleasure; as he adjusted his position, settling between her thighs and tasting her wetness again, he squeezed his hands beneath her buttocks and the memory of Todd's spanking was fully reborn as his fingertips grazed her aching rear. Then he returned the tip of his tongue to her clitoris and all doubts were pushed from her mind. She melted into the bed as he licked and continued to clutch her rear, holding tight and pressing the constant, nagging ache, but that flurry of discomfort only augmented her need for him.

When he raised his head again, his chin glistening with her

spilt arousal, she knew she had to have him. Acting without hesitation, not giving herself the time to think about any regrets she might have, or any implications that Todd's warning could still hold, she sat up and reached for the waistband of Danny's jeans. Her fingers glossed against the smooth muscles of his abdomen. The cool metal clasp of the belt was frigid to her touch and she had difficulty trying to coax the buckle open, but with clear determination she began to tug it free.

'Wasn't I doing that right?' Danny grinned, and she gave him a sour smile.

'Fishing for compliments?'

He shrugged as she pulled the belt free and then began to work on the button at the waistband of his jeans. The swell of his erection pushed at the front of the denim, making her painfully aware of his nearness. The heat of his arousal radiated through the fabric.

'Maybe I was fishing for compliments,' he conceded. 'Or maybe I was just wondering why you'd stopped me.'

Her fingers held the tag of his zipper and she knew it would only take one smooth flick of her wrist to expose him, and the idea made her inner muscles clench with fresh hunger. 'You were doing everything just perfectly,' she told him. 'And I think you know you were.'

He managed to look simultaneously confident and slightly bashful. 'If I was doing it right, then why have you stopped me?'

Charity pulled the zipper slowly down. He wore no pants beneath his jeans and the length of his solid shaft pushed easily through the opening split of fabric. The swollen dome of his glans was wet with a polish of pre-come and his shaft pulsed as it spilled into view. 'I stopped you from kissing me so you could show me your other talents.'

He chuckled and pushed her back to the bed as he kicked

the jeans from his legs. 'So this is a talent show, is it?' he teased. 'Are you auditioning me?'

She wanted to laugh, entertained by his playful banter, but her mood wouldn't lend itself to amusement. The tip of his length was brushing her inner thigh, sliding upwards and nearing the lips of her pussy. She drew a heavy breath, anxious to feel him inside her – and only slightly worried about the consequences. 'Yeah,' she confirmed, assuming the attitude of an unscrupulous impresario. 'I'm auditioning you. Show me something good and I might find a regular spot for you to fill.'

He stopped her from saying anything else by placing his mouth over hers. She could taste the sweet musk of her own excitement and the flavour was made unbearably arousing when his tongue plundered between her lips. She closed her eyes, wallowing beneath him as his length swayed against her thighs and his lean body rested lightly on her. 'I'd always hoped you'd want me this way,' he murmured.

She wanted to open her eyes, anxious to see him and enjoy the honesty of his expression as he said those words, but momentary panic suddenly held her in its grip. She fretted that if she did open her eyes his smile would be the same scarlet leer she had seen on the vampires in Highgate, and the idea left her frigid with fear and she could feel that mounting horror threatening to kill her arousal.

He kissed her again, and then lowered his lips to her chin. Nuzzling her crucifix aside, gently kissing the hollow of her throat, he began to move downwards again. But it was only when his mouth brushed against her breast, teasing the tip again, that Charity dared look at him again. His eyes were the same tranquil blue they'd always been. His smile, whilst full and rouged with arousal, wasn't glistening with too many teeth or bloody from a recent feed. Relieved, and perplexed by her own overactive imagination, she willed herself to relax so they could properly enjoy their time together.

Danny held his shaft in one hand and rubbed the bloated tip against her pussy lips. The folds of flesh melted for him and her inner muscles convulsed with a rush of hunger. She held her breath and prepared herself for the exquisite sensation of having him push inside. Aware of her own fretful need for him she knew it would take little more than the act of penetration to push her beyond the brink of orgasm. Steeling herself for that pleasure she remained stiff and ready for him.

'No,' Danny decided, and Charity stared at him, bewildered and wondering where the refusal had come from. 'If we're going to do this, we'll do it right,' he said firmly, and moved from between her legs and snatched her discarded sheet from the floor. Wrapping the cotton over one shoulder, looking like a last-minute attendee at a toga party, he tested a sheepish grin and said again, 'If we're going to do it, we'll do it right.'

She frowned; whatever they'd been doing felt perfectly right to her. 'What do you mean, we'll do it right? Where are you going? I thought we were going to…'

'I didn't come up here to perv at you through the window, then talk you into a quickie.'

She opened her mouth, more than willing to argue that it had been nothing like that, but Danny didn't give her the chance to interrupt.

'If we're going to take our relationship to the next stage I'd like to seduce you properly. I'd like us to be civilised and adult and maybe celebrate the night over a bottle of something special. Angela always keeps a bottle or two of Dom Perignon in the fridge. I'll go and get one.'

'We don't need champagne,' Charity insisted. 'We only need each other.' Frustrated, she realised he hadn't heard and watched him leave her bedroom. She didn't know whether to be impressed by his style and gallantry, or disappointed because he'd interrupted their moment of passion, but before

she got a chance to settle on either emotion she realised there
was another face at the bedroom window.

'Frick!' she gasped.

Charity

Act I, Scene IV

'Who the frick are you?' Charity demanded; a redundant question because she already knew the answer. Todd had told her about the coven and described its members with enough detail that she instantly recognised the visitor. Tall, commanding and wearing leathers that hugged her statuesque figure, Lilah cut an unmistakable figure.

The vampire lunged through the open window, accompanied by two others, and Charity remembered Nick and Helen from their encounter in the cemetery. She tried to shy away from the pair as they bore down on her but they were swift and strangely compelling. Clearly working to their mistress's instructions they stood close to Charity, intimidating her with their nearness. Both had scarlet eyes and smiles that glistened with vicious potential.

Nick licked his lips as he leered at her bare flesh, and Helen stroked chilly fingers over Charity's arm. 'Didn't I say this one was as big a slut as the others?' she said to Lilah. 'You saw what she was about to do with that lad, but it wouldn't have surprised me if she'd turned out to be another lezzer. Being a lezzer is something of a tradition in the Harker family.'

Lilah ignored Helen and snatched a discarded bathrobe from the floor. She tossed it against Charity and her imperious expression and air of confidence left no doubt that she was in absolute command of the situation. 'Put this on,' she snapped. 'You're coming with us.'

There was no opportunity to argue, and the chance to cover

herself from the inquisitive attention of Nick and Helen was too welcome for Charity to refuse. She wrapped herself in the towelling robe, punched her arms through the sleeves and tied the belt around her waist. Trying not to let her nerves show, determined that they wouldn't see she was petrified, she held herself defiant and asked, 'Who the frick are you, and what do you think you're doing bursting into my bedroom like this?'

Lilah didn't deign to acknowledge her question. 'You know where I want her; let's go downstairs,' she said, glaring at her subordinates, and acting without hesitation Nick and Helen grabbed Charity and began to drag her out of the room. She considered struggling and toyed with the idea of shouting for help, but prudence kept her silent. The trio looked determined and Charity felt certain they would respond violently against anyone who came to her rescue. She believed the house's staff would be able to deal with most security threats but she didn't think they would know how to cope with an attack from a gang of determined vampires. And, knowing that Danny would be headed back to her bedroom in moments, she didn't want him suffering because he was unfortunate enough to be in the wrong place at the wrong time.

Not that Charity believed she would have slowed them even if she had dared to show some resistance. Nick and Helen each held an arm and virtually carried her out of the room, along the galleried landing and down the mansion's majestic, sweeping stairs. Lilah led the way with a confidence that said she knew her way around, and it was her familiarity that raised a niggling doubt at the back of her mind. There was no hesitation as the woman guided them past Todd's study, and when she was faced with a choice of two doors hidden beneath the stairs, she ignored the route that led to the recording studio and confidently selected the one that lead to the darkened gloom of the wine cellar. Aside from her reservation about what they wanted from her, Charity wondered how the vampires had come to know the house's layout so well.

A bare bulb, dim and ineffectual, smudged the shadows back to the corners. Cobweb bunting looped from the low ceiling to the racks, giving the air an atmosphere of decay and neglect. Charity hadn't forgotten that the house came with a well-stocked wine cellar, but it was still something of a nasty surprise to rediscover this unpleasant chamber beneath the comfort and luxury of the band's abode.

Lilah and her cohorts had made obvious preparations. A pall-cloaked altar stood waiting for them with a solitary black candle burning on its centre. To the left of the flame was a crystal goblet, filled with a liquid that looked thick and dark red. To the right there was a long silver dagger and its blade glimmered like a maniac's grin.

Charity's stomach clenched with trepidation.

Nick and Helen took her to the foot of the altar and made her stand so she had her back to the candle, goblet and blade. Lilah stepped slowly in front of her with a playful smile lilting on her lips. For the first time she met Charity's gaze and her expression melted into one of approval. Reaching for her face, stroking an errant lock of hair from Charity's brow, she purred, 'You're not going to disappoint me, are you? I've been told you're the greatest.'

'I've been told you're a frickin' bitch,' Charity returned, Nick caught his breath, and Helen raised a hand and looked ready to strike Charity for her rudeness.

Lilah waved the insult aside and glared at Helen until she lowered her hand, then turning her attention back to Charity, she said, 'A gypsy told me that you're a threat to my coven.'

Charity shook her head. 'No,' she corrected, 'I'm not a threat to your coven – just you and your brother. Your followers will

71

fall by the wayside without leadership. My mission is only to destroy you and the dark one.'

Nick and Helen stiffened, glancing at Lilah for her response. Charity got the impression that the pair weren't used to anyone defying their mistress and thought they were waiting for an instruction to administer punishment. She warned herself not to continue antagonising the vampire but she was loath to let the woman believe herself to be in control.

'Your mission is to destroy me and my brother?' Lilah repeated. Her tone could have been more condescending, but not much, and she released the most patronising giggle Charity had ever heard. 'You're a little girl with a mission, are you? That must be very exciting. Did a grown up tell you about this exciting adventure?'

Charity set her jaw determinedly and fixed Lilah with the stoniest glare she could manage. 'I've been set the task of finishing the battle my sisters began. I'm going to destroy you and your brother.'

'You're showing more bravado than either of your sisters,' Lilah mused, 'but the mask doesn't fool me. I can hear your heartbeat and it's beating so fast it's like listening to a rattlesnake's tail. Terror's coming off you in waves.'

'My heart's not beating fast because I'm scared of you,' Charity said evenly. 'I must have an allergy to your bullshit.'

Lilah was on her in a second. Before Charity realised the woman had moved, before she even knew Lilah was going to advance, the towelling robe had been torn open and the vampire was pressing a dark kiss against her breast. She gasped and tried to step back, but Nick and Helen held her firm. There was no choice except to endure the vampire's mouth while she suckled against the stiffening nipple.

'No,' Charity begged, but Lilah's cruel chuckle promised no measure of lenience. The vampire's icy fingers stroked Charity's bare flesh, smoothing over her naked hips and waist.

Her long fringe chased tantalising caresses as she moved her head from side to side and sucked with mounting ferocity. 'Please,' Charity sobbed. 'Please, no.' But her begging only urged the vampire to press her kiss with greater force. Charity's nipple was pinched between the woman's teeth and the agonising pressure was exquisite. She held her breath, not wanting to be swayed by the barrage of delight that battered her breast, but the pleasure was too enormous to be denied. Gasping with frustration, hating the insidious heat that Lilah effortlessly inspired, Charity trembled with mounting arousal. Weakened from need and drawing as much breath as she could manage, she whispered again, 'Please, no.'

Lilah stepped away from her, smiling as though she had won a small victory. She left the folds of the towelling robe hanging open, and because Nick and Helen still held her wrists, Charity had no opportunity to conceal herself from the trio. Refusing to let them see the effect they were having on her she almost choked on the sob that wanted to rip from her throat.

'Are you going to continue being argumentative?' Lilah asked, and not daring to incur the vampire's wrath again, more fearful of her own responses rather than the punishment itself, Charity sullenly shook her head.

'There are rules that we vampires are meant to obey,' Lilah went on, nodding, satisfied. 'We shouldn't feed from nuns. Gypsies are out of bounds. And we can't drink from the virtuous.'

Charity's eyes glazed over as she realised the vampire was repeating the same lesson that Todd Chalmers had earnestly instructed earlier in the evening. Vampires avoided nuns because of the risk of encountering crucifixes. They avoided travellers because, for some reason that was dictated by ancient lore, gypsies could only be taken; they could never be made. It was a peculiarity that had clearly fascinated Todd, and he had guessed it was probably due to an archaic protection spell, but its implications were lost on Charity. As the memory of that information recurred to her, she wondered why her mind had thought the fact important enough to retain when she had more pressing things to remember.

Oblivious to Charity's meandering thoughts, Lilah's smile tightened hungrily. 'Nuns, gypsies and the virtuous,' she reiterated. 'And you fall into that latter category. Which is why I haven't simply drained you and left you in a puddle of ebbing mortality.'

Charity didn't understand what the woman was saying, or how it applied to her, but she guessed Lilah was coming to her point. It was difficult to concentrate past the thought that her body was on open display, or the knowledge that both Nick and Helen were gracing her with lurid glances. Trying to ignore them, not wanting to miss anything that could be used to her advantage, she willed herself to think beyond the embarrassment of her exposure.

'I fed from your sister, Faith,' Lilah announced, 'but only after her virtue had been spoilt by my brother's blood. Nick defiled your other sister, Hope, although I think Toad Chalmers had a larger hand in her fall from grace.'

Charity looked away, not wanting to hear these details about her sisters, or listen to the gloating tone of Lilah's smug voice. She drew a breath, intending to ask the vampire to get to the point, but Lilah was moving before she could speak.

The vampire snatched hold of her face and held her jaw so eye contact was unavoidable. 'I'm taking no chances this time,' Lilah growled. 'My brother and I will win our battle against you and we'll manage that a lot easier if I get rid of your virtue before we go any further.'

'What do you think you're going to do to me?'

Lilah snatched her gaze away and fixed her colleagues with an impatient glare. Nick and Helen turned Charity so that she was facing the makeshift alter, and in the same fluid movement one of them pressed a knee against the back of her leg and she was forced down to her knees. The stone floor of the cellar was cold and uncomfortable but she quickly decided that was an insignificant matter, and when Lilah began to mutter ominous Latin phrases she realised there were far greater causes for concern.

The flame of the black candle burnt long and tall, guttering with the casual movement of air that breathed through the cellar. The goblet and the silver dagger loomed large in her vision with their unspoken promise of menace. Swallowing twice, waiting until she was sure her voice wouldn't falter with nerves, Charity asked, 'What do you think you're going to do with me?'

Lilah paused from her Latin recitation and frowned. 'I'm removing your virtue,' she said simply, then picked up the dagger. 'I'll remove it surgically if I have to, but one way or another we're getting rid of it tonight.'

Charity made a final effort to break free but it was futile. Nick and Helen were unrelenting and maintained a hold on her that she knew she couldn't escape. Their fingers were buried beneath her arms and the nails bit with malicious fury.

Lilah continued to recite Latin, drawing the silver dagger through the air as she described the shape of an inverted cross. After dipping two fingers into the goblet, wetting the tips with a viscous smear of its contents, she daubed blood across Charity's forehead and cheeks.

'You must be really frickin' scared of me,' Charity observed, managing to sound braver than she felt.

Lilah frowned, pausing from her Latin as she licked the blood from the tips of her fingers. Her tongue chased the thick redness away with the quick movement of a snake anticipating its prey. 'I'm not exactly quaking in my boots,' the vampire decided lazily. 'But I won't be taking any chances.'

Casually she slapped Charity's face, effortlessly delivering a blow that made the girl see bright stars. 'Now stop interrupting and let me concentrate on this damned spell.'

Shocked to the verge of tears, Charity remained mute as Lilah resumed her chant, dipped her fingers back into the goblet and flicked them absently through the air, dousing Charity's breasts with a splash of crimson liquid.

But it was the silver dagger that held her attention. Fearful of what the woman might be planning, aware that she had no means of defending herself if she decided to use the blade, Charity kept her gaze fixed on the weapon as the vampire paraded back and forth in front of her. Lilah continued to chant, mumbling her way through parts of the language that were clearly awkward, but Charity could sense the change in the air.

The candle sputtered with a fresh surge of life. The light bulb grew momentarily brighter than shattered with a nerve-racking pop, and as the crackle of broken glass hissed against the floor Charity realised she now had to believe in the power of dark magics, alongside her newly found acceptance of vampires.

'Taint the virtuous one…' Lilah proclaimed.

Charity didn't know if she'd given up on the Latin, or if this part of the spell called for the words to be spoken in English, but she wished she didn't understand what was being said.

'Let her taste the forbidden tastes… let her fall from grace…' The vampire stroked her fingertips across Charity's mouth and her lips were smeared with a thick film of blood. The coppery flavour was nauseating. 'Recant your virtue,' Lilah demanded.

Charity glanced up and saw the vampire was towering over her. The dagger was raised high above her head and her posture showed off every inch of her superb figure. Her breasts were swollen against the tight leather of her waistcoat.

The jeans clung to her slender hips and thighs, glistening like well-oiled skin. Mesmerised by her beauty, suddenly infatuated with need for the goddess above her, Charity made no objection when Nick and Helen pulled her to her feet.

'Do you want to recant your virtue?' Lilah asked softly. 'Or do you want me to taint you?'

Charity stopped herself from licking her lips, unwilling to taste the flavour painted there. She met Lilah's scarlet gaze and tried to remember why she had considered the woman to be an adversary. Surrender seemed like such a desirable option that it took all her efforts of restraint not to beg the woman to take her.

'Make a decision,' Lilah urged sweetly. She lowered the dagger and drew the tip lightly against Charity's breast. There was no pressure in the way she held the blade, the razor-sharp edge didn't even graze the flesh it stroked, but the threat of danger honed her arousal to a brighter degree. Charity caught her breath and sobbed with frustration.

'Recant your virtue. Or let me taint you.' The vampire's hand slipped against her side. The icy fingers stole downward, over her hip, her thigh, and across to the curls that covered her sex. Charity held her breath, not daring to let herself enjoy the woman's touch but unable to resist the sultry heat she ignited. When Lilah's fingers combed through her pubic bush, deftly seeking out her sex, she simply held herself rigid and silently surrendered to the moment.

Goosebumps freckled her arms and, from a distance, she realised Nick and Helen had finally released her from their grip. The opportunity to pull away had now become a reality but Charity could only stand motionless as Lilah's fingers began to push into her wetness. She sighed with the first penetration, her inner muscles grasping greedily around their unexpected prize. Lilah's thumb brushed the pulsing nub of her clitoris and Charity's eyes opened wide with the shock of pleasure. The kiss against her breast had been a magnificent revelation in the joys she'd been denying herself, but this teasing took her delight to a new plateau. She regarded the vampire with genuine reverence and struggled to remember why she'd been trying to resist the woman.

'Which is it going to be?' Lilah murmured.

Charity could barely hear her. She was aware of the fingers slipping wetly in and out of her sex and wanted nothing more than to revel in that escalating pleasure. Lilah's touch was maddeningly cold but the warmth from Charity's pussy was more than compensating for that minor inconvenience. The only heat that seemed stronger was the burning weight of Faith's silver crucifix resting against her throat.

'Are you going to recant your virtue?' Lilah asked, plunging her fingers deeper.

The slender digits slid easily into her wetness. If she had closed her eyes and concentrated she knew she would have heard the wet slurp of her sex suckling against the vampire's hand. The idea left her sick with a combination of shame and arousal but that embarrassment got her no closer to pulling away. A swell of mounting pleasure rose between her legs and she knew Lilah would be able to satisfy the need that festered there.

'Are you going to recant your virtue?' Lilah repeated. 'Or are you going to let me taint you?'

'What do you want from me?'

'Just an answer.'

Drawing a heavy breath, shivering with the effort, Charity teetered on the brink of orgasm and shook her head. She didn't know how so much pleasure had come on her so quickly. Nor could she understand how she was able to wallow in an excess of delight in the macabre surroundings of a candlelit cellar with attendant vampires watching while she and Lilah become intimate. All she could understand was that

Lilah was promising to satisfy her needs.

Nothing beyond that mattered.

'Make a choice,' Lilah urged. 'Recant your virtue, or beg me to taint you. Do both if you like, or simply stand there, letting me finger your slippery little pussy. We can both wait here for as long as it takes until the last of your virtue has ebbed away.'

Even though she could detect the disparaging tone of the woman's voice, Charity would have been happy to listen to her until dawn. The fingers between her legs were sliding in and out with a brisk tempo, pushing her steadfastly toward the release she craved. Every muscle in her body trembled and she chugged breath as the moment of climax was almost wrung from her hole.

With a vicious sweep of her arm, Lilah snatched her hand away.

The fingers that had been filling Charity's sex disappeared and she was left to feel so hollow it was almost as though she had been eviscerated. The gaping hole between her legs felt so empty she had to blink back tears as she studied Lilah with bitter disbelief.

'Recant your virtue,' Lilah insisted.

She snatched the goblet from the altar and pushed it under Charity's nose. The cloying scent of the blood was an undertone to the aroma of musk that lingered on the vampire's fingers. Charity watched the contents splash lightly within the glass and felt the tepid wetness speckle her lips. The suggestion that she should drink was repulsive and vile but no less tempting because of that.

'Drink this and recant your virtue.'

Miserably Charity shook her head, and frowning, hurling the glass to the corner of the cellar, Lilah raised the dagger high in the air. 'If you won't recant,' she hissed, 'then you'll beg me to taint you.' She pressed the tip of the blade against

Charity's nipple and pushed.

Anguish and ecstasy tore her responses in conflicting directions and it was all Charity could do to stop herself from shrieking. She didn't know if the sound would have been borne from pleasure or pain but she felt sure it would herald the scream of her orgasm.

'Give up your virtue now,' Lilah insisted. 'Tell me that I may do what I want with you and then we can satisfy those needs you're harbouring.'

No longer sure why she was refusing, despising herself for not giving in to the pleasure Lilah promised, Charity shook her head. She wanted the woman more passionately than she had ever wanted anything but she couldn't bring herself to say the words demanded. Despising herself for her own desires, and hating the weakness that wouldn't allow her to surrender, she shook her head. 'I can't,' she gasped. 'I really can't.'

With a roar of frustration the vampire pushed her to the floor. 'There's a big confrontation coming,' Lilah hissed. 'And you're going to lose.'

Charity was beyond caring. She yearned to submit to the powerful woman and only wished she could make the vampire understand how she felt.

'Let me take her,' Nick suggested.

'No,' Helen said quickly, sinking to the floor by Charity's side and stroking her throat. The clumsy touch of her fingers was nothing like Lilah's exquisite caress but Charity was still ready to submit to the woman. She stared up at the three pallid faces above her, not caring which of them took her, just wishing one of them would end the torment of her frustration and stop waiting for her permission. Her body ached with the desperate need for an end to the torment of this teasing and she silently wished one of them would simply bite her.

'Don't let Nick have her,' Helen insisted. 'It's my turn to

feed from one of these Harker sisters. Let me have her.'

Lilah rolled her eyes and kicked Helen out of the way, then tossing a contemptuous glare in Nick's direction she sneered with disgust. 'You're a pair of clueless bastards. Neither of you could take her unless she was begging for it. Until we've removed her virtue none of us can touch her. Don't you listen?'

'I could take her,' Helen declared confidently, and almost as though watching events from within a dream, Charity realised she was pushing her head to one side and baring her teeth. She held her breath, and the ferocious looking bite loomed closer as Helen tore the neckline of Charity's robe to one side. Attuned to every nuance she could feel the deep pulse of her jugular beating steadfast beneath Helen's hungry leer. She braced herself for the shock of the attack and trembled with anticipation when Helen placed a hand against her breast. It crossed her mind that the vampire was only holding her steady, so that she didn't struggle when she was bitten, but she was still excited by the knowledge that the woman's fingers rested where they did. Needing to feel that dark, painful kiss, she knew she wouldn't struggle.

But Helen pulled away with a squeal of disgust, and momentarily Charity was shocked from her reverie. The vampire was clutching her hand, cursing vehemently as tendrils of smoke curled up from her open palm. Charity remembered the silver crucifix around her neck and wondered if that was what had hurt Helen. She put her hand against the burning silver and wondered if she should offer some sort of apology.

'Cretin,' Lilah cursed, kicking Helen aside. She still held the dagger and used it to describe another inverted cross in the air. Then mumbling more Latin, spitting the words with impatient urgency, she used the blade to slice a wound across the palm of her own hand.

81

Charity gasped as she watched the line of blood quickly well in the vampire's palm. With mounting panic she tried to scramble backwards when she realised what would now be expected from her.

Lilah pushed her bloody palm towards Charity's face, smothering her mouth. 'Drink,' she coaxed gently. 'Taste me, and let me end your suffering.'

Arguing was beyond her. As she inhaled the fragrance of the vampire's blood, and realised it was intermingled with her own musk, she knew she could no longer fight. The wetness against her lips inspired a thirst she hadn't known and the opportunity to surrender now seemed inevitable.

'Drink and be tainted,' Lilah urged.

Charity drew a long breath, savouring the scent of the woman's flesh and trying to remember all those arguments why she'd been trying to resist. Refusal now seemed like a pointless exercise and she couldn't recall one of the reasons that had been so important earlier. Hungry to taste, she extended her tongue and tried to lick the blood from Lilah's palm, which was snatched away before she could. Lilah tossed the dagger aside and pulled Charity up from the floor, and with a cruel smile curling her upper lip she wiped her bloody palm over Charity's breast.

The lubrication was like nothing she had felt before: too thick to properly allow their flesh to glide together but all the more exciting because of the unusual sensation. Both her nipples stood hard with longing and she realised the woman holding her was victim to the same symptoms. Remembering how Lilah had suckled her, and recalling every sweet moment of that unsolicited pleasure, Charity basked in the pleasure when Lilah's palm rubbed fluidly over the aching tips of her breasts.

'Do you want me to take you?' Lilah asked.

Nodding anxiously, eager to be accepted by the goddess

that embraced her, Charity finally found the strength to say the words she had been struggling to manage. 'Yes,' she sobbed gratefully. 'Yes, please, take me.'

Lilah's smile was spiteful. She tossed her head back and gestured for Nick and Helen to leave the cellar. Charity noticed Nick's scowl and heard Helen grumble with disappointment, but neither of them defied their mistress and they dutifully retreated.

As soon as they were alone, Charity regarded Lilah with desperate hope. 'Take me, please, take me,' she begged, wishing the woman would hurry up and do whatever was needed, not sure how much longer she could silence the inner voice that said she was insane for surrendering.

Lilah snapped her fingers and pushed Charity to the floor, and whatever spell she'd conjured was banished before the crisp click had finished echoing from the cellar's stone walls.

Appalled by the position she found herself in, shocked when she realised what she'd been doing and how close she had come to surrendering, Charity glared up at the woman with bewildered disgust.

'It's going to be so easy to take you when the final confrontation does come,' Lilah cooed. 'I may not have taken your virtue, but this evening will tear a hole in your self-confidence. This evening is going to fester in your mind and you're going to spend every waking moment letting your doubts beat you down.'

Charity tried to deny that there was any chance of that happening but she could understand exactly what Lilah was saying. The thought of facing the vampires had been daunting before. Now, shocked by the discovery of her own weaknesses and easy supplication, she dreaded the prospect of encountering the undead again.

'My brother wants you for tomorrow night,' Lilah confided. She bent and placed a chaste kiss against Charity's forehead.

'I guess I'll be seeing you then.'

Shivering against the grimy floor, Charity didn't dare to raise her head as the vampire left her alone. She realised the Harker family curse had struck again and her worst fear had come true: the battle was lost before it had even begun.

Interlude

Part Two

'...You placed your fingers against my breast; You made me think our love was blessed; Then you tore the heart from outta my chest...'

'This is one of your songs, isn't it?'

Angela glanced up from her cocktail, surprised by the question. It was her eighth or twelfth drink of the evening and the world around her had started to become comfortably confused. While she was no longer sure which nightclub she was in, the plush decor and smart attire of the clientele assured her that she was in a celebrity bar at one of the more exclusive venues in Mayfair. Charity's lyrics were being screamed at a deafening volume through the speakers and the backing track was loud enough to throb inside Angela's head like a harbinger of the hangover she expected the following morning. Quite how the man had made himself heard over the music was a mystery, but she found it more remarkable that he associated her as a member of BloodLust. The heavy make-up and stylised costumes of the band meant that recognition only usually happened to Angela when she was either on stage or posing for a photo opportunity.

'I'm right, aren't I?' he pressed.

He was handsome, in a sinister fashion, and Angela thought he seemed more attractive because of the two gorgeous young women that fawned by his side. They both looked young, sexy and exciting, wearing ultra-short skirts that exposed the full length of their long legs, and low-cut tops that revealed enticing valleys of cleavage. The blonde appeared cool, pale and aloof: self-assured and painfully arrogant. The dark-skinned girl simply sneered with obvious disdain.

Angela tried to shake off a haze of drunkenness, wondering if the stranger might be one of those record industry moguls whom she ought to recognise, or at least accord some respect. His face didn't seem familiar but she conceded that, after all she'd drunk so far this evening, her judgement probably wasn't the safest indicator. 'Do I know you?' she asked. 'Have we met before?'

'That's your lead guitar, isn't it?' He cocked his head to one side and held up a silencing finger so she wouldn't interrupt him as he listened to a tricky little chord change in the middle eight. A broad smile broke his face, as though he found the melody truly satisfying. 'I'll bet the instrumental version of this track is well worth hearing.'

She couldn't stop herself from grinning. Angela had heard flattery before; she had been told she was the raunchiest thing in the charts; the only reason why guys ever bought her band's CDs; and that she had the music industry's best backside. Men raved about her and more than a handful had said she was the one who put the lust in BloodLust. Countless times she'd been told that she stood out as the most desirable when the band had performed a video dressed as schoolgirls, but this stranger's approach was something new and she liked him because he dared to be different.

She sipped her cocktail. 'You have me at a disadvantage,' she said, considering him carefully, idly wondering if he might be as dangerous as he appeared.

'That's how I like my women.'

Instead of sounding corny or trite, the line made her laugh. They chuckled together as he shrugged the blonde from his shoulder and extended a hand.

'...*You had me day and night without any rest; You said*

86

our loving was the world's fucking best; Then you tore the heart from outta my chest...'

Whatever name he used to introduce himself was lost beneath Charity's final reprise of the chorus, but Angela was no longer worried about such minor details. She still had no idea which nightclub they were in but reasoned she was in the sanctuary of a bar and felt sure assistance would be available should she need any help. She accepted his hand and watched him brush the dark-skinned girl away as he stepped closer.

'You play the vampire image very well,' he told her. 'I can understand why the act is so popular.'

Once again she was amazed by the easy way he made himself heard over the roar of the music. His dulcet tones were almost mesmerising and she couldn't stop herself from warming to him as he appraised her with an approving smile. 'You sound like you're quite the BloodLust fan.'

His expression was noncommittal. 'My one complaint is that you could play your role as a vampire with more conviction. Aside from that minor quibble the whole act is very enjoyable. I'm definitely a fan.'

He continued to hold her hand while he spoke and Angela was struck by the coolness of his touch. The lack of warmth was not particularly pleasant but she felt no overwhelming urge to pull away. Contrarily, she thought it would be quite exciting to have the stranger's icy hands smooth their way over every inch of her bare body. The idea made her shiver and she hid the response behind another sip of her cocktail.

'More conviction?' she repeated, trying desperately to follow the conversation and not appear like an empty-headed drunk. 'I don't understand. How do you think we're failing?'

He shook his head and moved his lips close to her ear. 'I didn't say you were failing,' he whispered slowly. 'I'm just saying that you don't perform as though you've ever surrendered to a vampire,' he explained. 'You don't act as though anyone's ever drunk from you.'

Surprised by the excitement his words generated, she caught her breath. The music continued to throb around her, fading from the BloodLust track to a rap hit that was tipped to be next week's number one. Angela didn't notice the change in melody as she studied the stranger with renewed interest. 'I still don't get what you're saying,' she admitted. 'How could I perform as though someone had drunk from me? What would be the difference in the way I played the guitar?'

He plucked the cocktail glass from her hand and passed it to the blonde, and then placing a hand on Angela's hip he guided her to the railing that overlooked the central dance floor. 'Perhaps what I'm saying would be better illustrated if I showed you,' he suggested. 'You'll indulge me for a moment, won't you?'

Like most of the celebrity bars that Angela had ever patronised, this one was set above the main dance floor and had its own bar staff and security to cater to a select few of the beautiful people rather than the masses who gathered below. Leaning over the railing, peering down on gyrating bodies beneath a pulse of lights, Angela allowed the stranger to position himself behind her.

The blonde appeared at her right, no longer holding the cocktail glass, and with her interest focused on the crowd below. The dark-skinned girl stood by Angela's left, her gaze flitting blindly from one figure to another in the throng beneath them. Behind Angela, the imposing stranger placed a hand on each shoulder and pressed himself against her backside.

She caught a startled breath; the stiffness of his erection was obvious against her buttocks and she briefly wondered why she was letting this unknown man take advantage of her so easily. Her short skirt was cut to an immodest length – designed to catch the interest of the paparazzi – but short enough to leave her exposed to the languid caress of the stranger. It crossed her mind that her thin cotton panties only protected her sex, and she wondered if she was being unwise for allowing him to continue. His chilly fingers had moved from one shoulder and were already smoothing against her buttocks. She knew her clothes would offer no protection if he wanted to push the underwear aside and explore the secrets of her, but that fear engendered a flush of warm, fluid desire.

She swallowed and considered easing away from him while there was still a chance, but before she could act on that impulse the blonde stroked affectionately against her arm. Angela regarded the woman with doubt, taking no reassurance from her placatory smile. The nightclub's lighting gave her eyes a crimson hue that was almost disconcerting. The same effect transformed the dark-skinned girl so that she looked like something from a lurid horror film.

Angela had a reputation for being the band's wild child, and her promiscuity was well documented through the tabloids, but she had not anticipated spending the evening being seduced by a stranger and his female companions. Yet, although she told herself that such a liaison wasn't what she wanted, the concept of resisting seemed painfully out of reach.

'I can give you the lesson you need,' the stranger told her. 'But I'll want something in return.' He was whispering the words into her ear again, stroking the hair away from her cheek so he could kiss her lobe while he spoke.

She trembled within his embrace. The music was too loud for her reply to be heard but she felt sure he understood when she nodded assent.

'I don't give lessons like this for free,' he murmured, gyrating his hips as he spoke, rubbing against her in a way that was overtly sexual. The nape of her neck prickled with mounting excitement and this time she didn't try to conceal her shivers;

there didn't seem to be any point in concealing her responses. 'I want you to know that I expect to be paid back in full.'

She was no longer concentrating on his words. The blonde was caressing her inner arm, exciting the flesh more fully than Angela could have expected. The light caress of her fingertips was a punishing tease that made her skin acutely sensitive.

More daring than her companion, the dark-skinned girl stroked her fingers over the swell of Angela's breast. Her attention was less subtle and, although Angela's top protected her from the brunt of her touch, she couldn't remain immune as one pliant orb was kneaded and caressed. Her chest swelled as she revelled in the torment and her breath was reduced to short, strangled gasps.

Behind her the stranger's hands were everywhere. He held her shoulders, stroked her face, and then touched her bottom. The thrust of his erection remained continuously hard against her and she rubbed against him to show her mounting impatience.

'Are you going to agree to my terms?' he enquired softly, and she dragged herself back from a dreamy haze and tried to work out what he'd been saying.

'What is it you want?' she asked, not bothering to hide her lack of comprehension, just anxious for him to continue. In her voice she could hear the subtext to her own cry that said: whatever he was asking it was a price she would gladly pay. 'Just tell me what you want and we can negotiate.'

'I'm going to teach you what it's really like to be a vampire,' he assured her. 'Don't worry; I'm a skilled instructor. And all I'll ask in return is that I can teach the rest of your band the same lesson. Do you think we might be able to reach an agreement?'

She held her breath and shook her head. He had excited her to a plateau of unarguable need but she was determined not to be such an easy conquest. The blonde was chasing invisible circles along her bare arm, while the dark-skinned girl had inspired her nipples to stand hard and erect. The alcohol she'd already consumed had mellowed her mood so that her inhibitions had all but disappeared. Yet she'd played this game enough times to know she shouldn't give in without some small show of defiance. 'I doubt there's anything you could teach me, or the rest of the band,' she said, ignoring her body's needs, trying hard to distance herself from the escalating excitement. 'We've had stylists, designers and all manner of experts work on our image. I'd be surprised if Count Dracula wasn't listed on the payroll somewhere. I don't think there's anything we don't know about the whole vampire experience.'

The stranger stroked another loose strand of hair away from her cheek and the icy brush of his fingertips banished the last of her resistance. 'That sounds like you're laying down a challenge,' he murmured, his lips just grazing her neck. 'Not that I'm complaining; I so enjoy rising to a challenge.'

She heard the words, but even if she could come up with some clever retort there was no time to respond before he bit her neck, and the brief sting of pain was easily forgotten in the rush of pleasure that came when he began to drink. Angela arched her back, pressing onto him as she heard the greedy wet sounds of his thirst being sated. The flood of warm liquid against her throat was scorching after the frigid caress of his kisses, and she basked in the heady experience of having her lifeblood drained away.

The blonde held her right hand, raising the wrist to her lips and kissing softly. Angela felt the cruel tease of teeth being drawn against the delicate area, and when the woman sank her fangs into the flesh she gasped with genuine gratitude. The dark-skinned girl at her left raised her other wrist and bit with the same seductive torment.

Helpless, and revelling in the bliss of their attention, Angela squirmed more forcefully against the stranger behind her. It had long been a fantasy of hers to be taken in a crowded place and she realised this was as close to that scenario as she could have ever hoped. The dancers beneath her remained oblivious to what she was doing and none of the guests that lounged in the celebrity bar made any comment or complaint about her behaviour. Even when the stranger unzipped himself – and Angela felt the cold, clammy flesh of his penis touch her bottom – she knew that no one had noticed this latest act of indiscretion.

The blonde moved her lips from Angela's wrist and kissed her mouth. The rusty taste of fresh blood flavoured the exchange and made the moment all the more intimate. A tongue pushed between her lips, and before she realised what she was doing she began to return the kiss with the same frenzied urgency.

At her left the dark-skinned girl lowered the hand she held and returned her fingers to Angela's breast. No longer content to simply tease the orb through the fabric of her top, she unfastened two buttons and placed her hand inside. The tip of Angela's nipple was caught between a finger and thumb and the bead was gently teased to its full stiffness.

But it was the stranger behind her who continued to hold her attention. 'Isn't this going to help your performance?' he asked, his words slightly slurred, a tone she had often heard in those who'd drunk too much too quickly, and she giggled at the thought that she might be responsible for his mild inebriation. But her mirth didn't last long because the humour was snatched from her when his chilly fingers moved to her buttocks and began to ease the gusset of her panties aside. They drew lovingly against the peach-like flesh of her rear as he deftly exposed her sex, and when he traced a finger against the dewy folds she almost collapsed with her need to climax.

'Isn't this going to give you a better understanding of what being a vampire is really about?'

She would have agreed with anything he said, even though she could no longer make sense of his words or their meaning. He had fired an appetite between her legs and the desire for satisfaction crested high above every other need. She didn't have the strength or the inclination to consider the scandal she might be causing, or fret about the consequences of giving herself to a trio of strangers. Todd Chalmers had recently berated her and the other girls for their unladylike behaviour, but he hadn't argued when Lauren sagely pointed out that no publicity was bad publicity.

The blonde continued to kiss her while the dark-skinned girl moved her hand to Angela's right breast and teased the nipple to aching hardness. Her entire body felt alive with need and she groaned quietly as she urged one of them to take her to the brink of orgasm.

'Don't you think the rest of your band would benefit from this sort of tuition?' he asked again.

The blonde tore her kiss away from Angela's lips, as though giving her the opportunity to reply. Angela was amazed by the way the three of them were able to work on her with such choreographed precision and overawed by the easy way the two women deferred to the stranger. Her enjoyment was too great for her to overanalyse the phenomena but she quietly congratulated herself on having the good fortune to fall in with a team of such skilled lovers.

'Well?' he pressed. 'Do you think the rest of your band could benefit from my tuition?'

With each pulse she could feel herself growing weaker, and falling under the shadow of his spell. 'Why would you want to teach the others?' she asked, the effort of speaking a greater strain than she had anticipated, and the question left her breathless. 'Why don't you forget about the rest of the band? Why don't you just make me your protégée?'

He laughed, and in the same moment pushed his erection against her sex. The rounded end of his glans smoothed between her labia, and the split of her sodden lips melted for him. As he thrust forward she ground her hips back and allowed his length to slide easily inside her pussy.

Her eyes opened wide with the discovery of fresh pleasure. The blonde resumed her kiss and pressed her athletic body closer, the swell of her breasts against Angela's bare arm.

The dark-skinned girl unfastened two more buttons, indecorously exposing Angela's breasts. Cupping one, and catching the nipple between the knuckles of her second and third finger, she squeezed hard.

Tightening her inner muscles around the shaft that penetrated her sex, wallowing in the joy of the stranger's thickness as it ploughed in and out, Angela knew she was hurtling towards a climax that would eclipse every pleasure she had ever enjoyed before.

'It would be tempting to take you on as my sole protégée,' the stranger told her. 'I doubt any of the others could prove themselves to be better pupils.' His tongue lapped at her throat, each tentative touch timed to coincide with a forward thrust of his penetration. 'But I think it's only fair that you let me try to elevate them to the standard you've now reached.'

Angela pushed the blonde aside and waved her hand at the dark-skinned girl until she stepped away. Gripping the railing tight, aching from the exertion and desperate to sate the pulsing urge that pounded between her legs, she squeezed him and tried to match the rhythmic tempo of his entry. The music around her was too loud to be heard; the exhibitionism of what she was doing continued to act as an aphrodisiac but it had long since ceased to be important. Her need for an orgasm was now an overwhelming demand and she rode him with fevered urgency.

His shaft was thick and long and their position allowed him to buffet raw bolts of pleasure through her sex. The swollen dome rubbed vigorously against the sensitive spot deep within her pussy and bludgeoned the neck of her womb before retreating to the verge of her labia. Each time he pushed inside it felt like the first penetration and she choked back the need to scream as her pleasure reached a powerful crescendo.

'You'll let me teach them, won't you?'

She closed her eyes and lost herself in the intermingled music and the tempo of his rhythmic pounding.

'You'll arrange for them to submit to me, the way you've just surrendered yourself?'

He paused as he waited for her reply, and she knew he wasn't going to give her that final rush of pleasure until she made a promise. 'Yes, I'll do whatever you ask,' she panted, frustrated by his manipulation but powerless to fight her needs.

He thrust into her and again bit her throat, and this time the pain was muffled by the surging joy of her orgasm. His erection pulsed within her and his viscous spray filled her cunt. Even though he had been riding back and forth within her warmth, his shaft remained cold but his release was a molten flow. He pulsed repeatedly, biting harder as he buried himself deep inside her.

Angela was momentarily lost in a world of unbridled delight. Every muscle trembled as she was torn between the crushing joy of her climax and the delicious agony that came from his mouth sucking her neck. She could hear the fading pulse within her temples and marvelled that she had never enjoyed such an extreme of passion. The hot douche of his seed left her paralysed with elation and she held herself rigid for fear of collapsing in a satisfied heap. Even as she was mentally climbing down from the pique of her release, weakened and dizzied from the whole experience, she knew she had never encountered any force as strong or divine and wanted a repeat performance.

The blonde grabbed her arm before she fell to the floor. Innocently, and with a speed that left Angela blinking, she fastened the buttons on her blouse and brushed her skirt down. The dark-skinned girl subtly placed herself in front of the stranger while he tucked his erection back into his trousers.

If she had thought about it, Angela might have suspected the pair were used to assisting the stranger with this post-coital aftercare, but her mind was still reeling and her thoughts were a chaotic jumble. She accepted the stabilising presence of the blonde's arm and gave the stranger a faltering smile, which he returned: red and bloody.

The crimson tint she'd noticed in his companions' eyes now tainted him. Not sure where the thought came from, only certain that it was absolutely right, Angela suspected her own smile would have that same dark red lustre and she no longer believed it was a trick of the nightclub's lighting. Suddenly hungry, she regarded him with a wicked grin and licked her lips, and her smile grew broader when the sharp tips of her canines scratched her tongue.

'You want more, don't you?' he observed. Again he was making himself effortlessly heard over the pound of the music, but this time the trick didn't impress her because she felt sure she would now be able to manage the same subtle feat.

'Yes, I want much more,' she replied with no hesitation, then pushing the blonde away, sure she would be able to support herself now that she seemed to have regained some strength, she stumbled against the stranger and stared up into the depths of his scarlet eyes. 'I want so much more, and you're going to give it to me.'

'Tomorrow night, I'll meet you at your house. You'll make sure your fellow band members are there too.'

'Are you going to show them the same pleasure you've just shown me?'

'Do you think they'd like that?'

Angela considered this. Lauren and Viv would die of gratitude if she introduced them to this powerhouse of pleasure but she guessed, like everyone else who followed BloodLust, the stranger would want their lead singer in attendance. The realisation cast a pall of unease across her thoughts as she saw that she wouldn't be able to honour her promise and pay the price he demanded.

Charity was renowned for being the most boring member of the band; the songwriter who spent her evenings scribbling lyrics and scoring new melodies; the virgin who spent her late nights chastely chatting with Angela's baby brother, Danny. For all the sultry pouts and daring poses she assumed for their videos, for all the revealing costumes she wore when on stage, Charity didn't play the sort of adult games for which Angela lived, and she had made it clear that she never would.

Angela could feel her good mood slipping, like the wet trickle of semen that began to seep slowly down her inner thighs. 'Charity won't be interested,' she said dejectedly. 'But I can get the others to come. If they had any notion about what you're offering I'd have to fight Lauren and Viv back with a shitty stick.'

'You paint such pretty pictures with your words,' the stranger mused. 'I can't believe you're not the lyricist with that precious gift.'

Angela missed his sardonic tone. 'Lauren and Viv would both jump at the chance to meet you,' she assured him. 'But there's no way I would be able to interest Charity in a party like the one you're suggesting.' She dared to meet his gaze, expecting to be faced by his thunderous anger, but his confident laughter surprised her.

'Don't you worry about Charity,' he whispered. 'I'll see to it that she puts in an appearance. I just want to get you and the rest of your band prepared before you show her what I've taught you. Do as I tell you, and Charity won't spoil the night for any of us.'

Charity

Act II, Scene I

Charity walked boldly into the kitchen and found Danny slumped on one of the breakfast stools. He was dressed again and his entire demeanour looked as beaten as she'd felt after encountering Lilah. In one hand he held a fork and stabbed unenthusiastically at a plate of apple pie. Even though it was lathered with fresh cream and looked exceptionally tempting, he stared at it blindly and with no apparent appetite.

She supposed it might be too early for him to enjoy such an unorthodox breakfast, or that something else could have caused his obvious bad mood, but in her heart she knew he was angry that she had fuelled his arousal and then disappeared without an apology or an excuse. Determined to raise his spirits, and adamant that her own enjoyment of life wouldn't be spoilt by anyone whether they were living or undead, Charity marched purposefully to him. She glided effortlessly through the sterile environment of stainless steel fixtures and fittings, resolute that nothing would stop her now she had decided on this course of action.

'Charity?' The crisp click of her heels on the linoleum made him look up before she was halfway across the room. His initial reaction was to smile when he saw her, but that response was tempered by a narrowing of his brow. Even the sight of the clothes she wore – the schoolgirl uniform he'd raved about with such lecherous approval – failed to soften his frown. 'Where the hell did you disappear to?' he asked. 'I thought you and I were getting closer. I felt bloody stupid when I got back to your bedroom and found you gone.'

She didn't answer until she was on top of him, and then she knew mere words would be insufficient. Straddling him as he sat on the stool, draping her arms over his shoulders and making her intentions obvious with the blatancy of her body language, she pushed her lips against his and kissed. It wasn't the teasing exploration they had shared before. It wasn't even the hesitant surrender she'd been preparing to make when he left her room to find a bottle of champagne. It was the passionate kiss of a woman with needs that demanded satisfaction. She pushed her tongue between his lips and held his head steady so she could devour him with the hunger of her desire. Deliberately she pressed her groin against his leg and rode slowly along his thigh.

He tore his face away and regarded her with a wary expression. Briefly, she noticed, her uniform drew his attention; the tailored blouse moulding tight to her breasts and the thin fabric not concealing the dark circles of her areolae. The classic combination of a pleated skirt and knee-high socks revealed an enticing expanse of bare thigh. She wondered if he might suspect that everything beneath the skirt was also bare.

Danny wilfully shook his head and snatched his gaze back up to her face. Fighting to remain unmoved, stabbing his fork viciously into the apple pie, he grumbled, 'I thought we were getting closer.'

'We were getting closer,' she confirmed, stumbling over the words as she tasted his mouth again. 'We are getting closer,' she assured him. 'And nothing's going to get in the way of that now. Nothing.'

For an instant she thought he was about to relent. A hand went to her blouse, stroked the starched white cotton and tested the swell of her breast. His touch was electric and she could feel the positive crackle of energy passing between them, and she could feel the lips of her pussy grow dewy with a liquid rush of excitement.

Using more willpower than she would have thought him capable, Danny pulled his fingers away, and she could tell he was employing a magnificent effort when he wrenched his mouth from her kiss and struggled to find breath before speaking. 'Where did you go, Charity? Why weren't you waiting for me when I got back to your bedroom? If you had second thoughts you could have said and I would have understood. You didn't have to piss off like that.'

She paused for a moment, trying to read behind the hurt that lingered in his eyes. 'I'll tell you everything that happened,' she promised. 'But now isn't the right time.'

He inched back on the stool and stopped her from resuming the kiss. 'What do you mean when you say "now isn't the right time"? Why not now? Why can't you tell me?'

'I can't tell you now because you wouldn't frickin' believe me,' she gasped. 'And by the time you did believe me, by the time I'd explained everything so you did understand and accept what had happened, you wouldn't be in the mood to do this.'

She could see he was going to ask what she was talking about, and silenced him by placing her hand on his groin. The kiss had excited her, filling her with a fuller version of the delicious longing she'd experienced when he surprised her in her bedroom, but now she discovered it had also aroused him. Through the denim of his jeans she could feel the twitching muscle of his hardness and doubted he would be able to make any further resistance. That simple understanding took her carnal hunger to a new level and she was determined they'd finish what they'd started earlier. Considering the unsatisfied ache that throbbed within her loins, she believed it was imperative that they finish things this time.

Danny finally reciprocated, and when she kissed him again he touched his tongue against hers and mumbled, 'I thought you'd changed your mind. I thought you didn't want me.'

Still riding her hips back and forth, continuing to glide her sopping sex lips against his thigh, she replied without breaking away from him. 'I didn't change my mind. And I never stopped wanting you.' Casting her thoughts back over the events, she added bitterly, 'Someone tried to sway my opinion. But they didn't make a lasting impression.'

His hand returned to her breast and this time he squeezed, and Charity almost collapsed onto him as a surge of pleasure was wrung from her. 'If I knew what you were talking about, I guess your explanation might make sense,' Danny smirked.

Pushing her breasts against him, rubbing her sex more forcefully against his leg, she giggled. 'You're frickin' right it would.'

After Lilah had left her alone in the cellar, Charity felt utterly vanquished. Humbled, and certain that all was lost, she dragged herself back to her bedroom and sought solace from a phone call to her sisters. Considering all that Todd Chalmers had told her about her destiny, she had expected to be met by their upset, outrage or disappointment, but they were anticipating that she would defeat the dark one and remain immune to the insidious temptations of the vampires. And yet in one night, barely two hours after discovering that vampires truly existed, she believed she had lost the battle and failed her sisters.

But instead of being maligned for almost succumbing, and rather than suffering reproach for her lewd behaviour, Hope had told her she was doing well, and Faith opined that Lilah could be irresistible. Neither remark was the reprimand Charity thought she would receive, and the encouragement of her sisters gave her a chance to see the encounter in its proper perspective: Lilah had merely been trying to scare her and dent her confidence. The fact that she hadn't driven home her advantage implied that she didn't have one. Yet, Charity realised, it took Hope's clearheaded assessment of the situation to make her see that point.

When the conversation slipped into the minutiae of gossip, family updates and shared interests, Charity realised that Lilah hadn't properly frightened her, or even come close to damaging her confidence.

It had been a long telephone call, stretching over the best part of two hours, but it was a cathartic experience. Hope spoke enough commonsense to make Charity understand that Lilah was no real threat, and Faith offered sufficient practical advice to make her understand that, while one battle might have been surrendered, the war wasn't yet over.

She had come away from the conversation sure of three things: she was going to defeat the dark one; she could trust Todd Chalmers on most matters except those involving money; and she shouldn't let the fight against vampires interfere with her love life.

It was this final certainty that prompted her to find Danny and make proper amends for not being in her bedroom when he returned. She had showered, selected the clothes she knew would appeal to him, and gone to complete their unfinished business.

'What's come over you, Charity?' Danny asked. His obvious doubts didn't interfere with his arousal and she could hear his need for her in the breathlessness of his words. 'You're not usually like this. What's gotten into you?'

She pulled the erection from his jeans. He was long and hard, the lean shaft fitting snugly in her fist. She squeezed him, relishing his warmth and enjoying the deliberate pulse that beat through his length. 'I was wanting this to get into me,' she murmured salaciously. 'I haven't spoilt my chances, have I?'

The remainder of his hesitation was fleeting. Wrapping an arm around her waist and returning her kiss, he lifted and sat her on the breakfast bar. Her buttocks rested lightly on the polished counter, and with urgent force he pushed between her thighs.

Anxious to feel him closer, needing to have the warmth of his body pressed against hers, Charity crossed her ankles behind his back. His erection was crushed between them, and she knew they would have to change positions if she wanted him to properly satisfy her needs, but for the moment it was enough to have his manly presence held tight against her. Yielding to his kisses, allowing him to unfasten her buttons and release the zipper on her skirt, she pulled the T-shirt over his head and struggled to push his jeans down over his hips without interrupting their intimacy.

His embrace banished all the worries and doubts that had lingered at the back of her mind. She had fretted about Todd's insistence that she must retain her purity, she worried about Lilah's assured dismissal of her in the cellar, and even though her sisters had given her nothing but encouragement, she still fretted that she was making the wrong decision by giving herself to Danny. But as he stroked the smooth flesh of her freshly exposed breast, she realised those doubts were misplaced. Nothing that felt so good or wholesome could possibly be wrong and she didn't believe it could precipitate her downfall.

Danny pulled the skirt away from her and gasped when he saw she was naked beneath. His eyes shone with lecherous approval and Charity almost melted beneath the genuine appreciation that broadened his smile. Unembarrassed by her nudity, excited that his need for her mirrored her own desire for him, she again curled her fist around his hardness and tried to pull him to her aching sex.

Gently he removed her hand and continued to admire her. 'If you can't tell me where you went…' he said, stroking the soft skin of her inner thigh.

'Which I can't,' she broke in testily.

'At least you can tell me why you're wearing the schoolgirl outfit.'

She drew a deep breath before responding, surprised that he had excited her to the point where she found words such a chore. 'I could be wearing it for any of three reasons,' she began. 'It might have been the only thing I could find in my wardrobe. Or I could be wearing it because I've noticed the way you squirm whenever you see me in this uniform on video.'

He blushed and graced her with the full impact of his bashful charm. It was a difficult trick to manage while he was half-naked and stroking so close to the heat of her pussy lips, but somehow he maintained his boyish innocence without looking like a charlatan. His shaft twitched and a glistening pearl of pre-come swelled over the eye of his glans.

Danny's fingers moved from the top of her thigh and chased light circles around her belly button. The teasing was delicious but infuriating. It aroused and excited her need, but ultimately it took her no closer to the release her body craved. She wanted to tell him that she needed to feel something more intimate, but she quickly silenced her internal voice of impatience. Whatever happened between them was going to occur at its own pace and she was determined that it wouldn't be hurried.

'You said you could have been wearing the uniform for one of three reasons,' he reminded her, his voice as soft and light as his fingertips. 'What's the third reason?'

'Perhaps I'm trying to send you a subliminal message,' she suggested. 'Perhaps I've come to you dressed like a schoolgirl so you'll know I want to be educated.'

His eyes widened and this time he instigated their kiss. Charity was thrilled that the exchange was so different from the intimacy Lilah had shown her. Whereas the vampire's

105

mouth was cold and demanding, Danny's lips were sensitive and practically smouldered with the heat of his desire. When his tongue slipped into her mouth and his hands moved to her neck she wasn't chilled by his touch, or fearful of what would happen next. He aroused her sexually but he also filled her with a sense of trust that she knew wasn't misplaced. The sultry need between her legs ached for satisfaction and she tried to press against him with renewed urgency.

Danny eased out of her embrace and regarded her with a shy smile. 'I can't believe you wore that just for me,' he marvelled.

She reached out and tried to encourage him to come back to her but he only stepped away until she was forced to slip from the work surface. He told her to stand where she was and circled her pensively. In a way she could understand why he found the attire arousing; the polished surfaces of the stainless steel cabinets threw back a hazy reflection and she conceded that the schoolgirl uniform did have a definite sex appeal. With the skirt removed and wearing only the knee high socks and an unfastened blouse, she looked painfully young and wickedly corruptible. The modest swell of her breasts peeped from beneath the open blouse and the neatly trimmed tuft of her pubic mound appeared like a freshly exposed secret.

'You can't believe I wore this for you?' she repeated. 'Who else would I wear it for?'

Danny shrugged. 'You were the one who disappeared from the bedroom.'

Charity shook her head. 'I've told you I'll explain all about that at the right time. I thought we'd already agreed that now isn't the right time?'

He stepped closer, brushing the hem of her blouse aside and placing his hands against her hips, and the firmness of his fingers was enough to make her forget the nuisance of his question. When he curled a hand round to her bottom, cupping one buttock, she pushed against him with all the hunger of her renewed longing, and before she could reach down to the swaying length of his erection he lowered his mouth to her breast and licked the tip of her nipple.

She shivered and made no further attempts to lead events. Bristling beneath the sensation of his lips around her stiff nub she arched her back and almost moaned as the pleasure welled within her. Danny raised his head, kissed her throat, chest and stomach, and then lowered himself to his knees as his mouth paid homage to the remainder of her exposed body.

She drew a faltering breath, delighted to be the subject of his affection and uncaring that they were exploring each other in a place as public as the house's kitchen. Charity had never seen Angela or Viv in there and she knew Lauren only bothered with the room when it was late on an evening and she was feeling adventurous enough to try baking grass-laced brownies. This early in the morning, when her fellow band members were still sleeping off the effects of their celebrity lifestyles, Charity felt confident they wouldn't be disturbed.

Danny combed his nose through her pubic curls and Charity stifled a sob. She knew he had excited her earlier, and she wanted to progress things further then, but he hadn't filled her with the rich, fluid desire that now held her in its thrall. Shivers racked her frame and she knew the trembling wouldn't stop until he finally satisfied the urgent need that broiled within her vagina.

His tongue slipped against the wet folds of her pussy lips, the sensation of having his mouth brush against her so intimately almost more than she could bear. She could feel the caress of his breath each time he exhaled, and she realised that Lilah's attention had been bereft of that particular pleasure.

Daintily, Danny drew his tongue against her labia again. Charity's eyes widened, every muscle in her body turned rigid and she pushed her fingers into his hair so she could secure her hold on his head. She didn't know if she was trying to move him away or hold him in position so he could continue to treat her to the miracle of pleasure his mouth was bestowing. When he stroked his tongue against her for a third time, using the tip to tease the folds of flesh apart, she released a shuddering breath and realised she had been right to decide to take their relationship to this level.

'Danny,' she gasped, and he shook his head, nuzzling against her as he made the movement, the tip of his nose lightly brushing her clitoris, a wealth of pure pleasure erupting from her sex, leaving her weak and dizzy. She tugged his hair, still unsure if she wanted to move him away or make him stay where he was and do more. 'Danny,' she repeated, this time with more urgency. 'Stop doing that and frickin' listen to me for a minute.'

He glanced up, his lips and jaw glistening with her musk, but she could see concern in his expression. 'You're not having second thoughts, are you?' he asked.

She shook her head, pulling him up from the floor, aware that her hands were shaking as she took him into her embrace. 'No, I'm not having second thoughts,' she insisted. 'I just wanted to tell you that I'm going to collapse if you keep me stood in the middle of this room.'

He nodded, and scooping her up in his arms, carried her effortlessly back to the breakfast bar and encouraged her to lie back. She remained still as he kissed her breasts again. His lips encircled her nipples, teasing the taut buds to full hardness before he flicked the tip of his tongue against her sensitive flesh. Elated by the excitement he inspired, she writhed against the worktop and surrendered to the pleasure he evoked, the tip of his glans teasing against her pussy lips. While his mouth worked on her breasts his fingers gracefully roved over the rest of her body. His touch continued to be perpetually light, exploring her. The promise of release inched frustratingly closer and Charity could almost taste the bittersweet flavour of the climax she craved, and when his lips returned to her sex she wanted to curse him for teasing her so wickedly. She heard him swallow and knew he was savouring the flavour of her excitement, then he straightened up between her legs and stroked the back of his hand against her face.

She regarded him warily, wondering why he had once again chosen to interrupt their play. 'What's wrong?' she whispered. 'Why have you stopped?'

'Are you sure you want to do this here?'

She held her breath and wondered what had possessed him to ask such a question. Sprawled over the kitchen work surface, exhibiting her glistening pussy lips, she marvelled that he could think she had any reservations. Reaching for his erection, grasping it and rubbing the swollen dome against her labia, she bristled beneath the contact and bit back the urge to shriek with her need. 'Why wouldn't I want to do this? What makes you think I'm having doubts?'

'Last night we were going to consummate our relationship properly, in your bedroom, after sharing a bottle of champagne,' he said. 'Now, this morning, you want me to simply fuck you over the breakfast bar. Are you sure this is what you want?'

She retained her hold on him and slid his glans against her lips again. The flesh of her pussy melted open for him, and when she rested his pulsing tip against the nub of her clitoris she could barely stand the thrill of her encroaching orgasm. Her entire body sparkled with glorious need and she knew that, regardless of where they were or the lack of a contrived seduction, she had to have him between her legs.

'This is what I want,' she insisted, then shaking her head, deciding those words weren't nearly enough to convey the depth of her desire, she added, 'No, Danny, this is more than what I want. This is what I need.'

He nodded and placed his hands on her hips, balanced perfectly between her legs. 'Okay,' he said.

Attuned to his body as much as she was her own responses, Charity felt him stiffen as he prepared to thrust forward. Anxious to feel that penetration, desperate to have him sink inside her, she braced herself for the magnificent rush of pleasure that would come when he finally impaled her on his shaft...

'For fuck's sake, Charity!' Todd Chalmers exploded, the manager's voice echoing through the kitchen.

Charity turned her head, shocked by his tone and appalled that he had caught her in such a compromising position. She saw him thundering towards them, and there was no mistaking the fury on his face. His hands were balled into fists and his cheeks were purple with barely contained rage. 'Is this your idea of retaining your virtue?' he demanded.

Charity

Act II, Scene II

They were in Todd's office before Charity understood what was happening. He had pushed a startled Danny aside in the kitchen and issued some warning that was too stern to brook argument. Then she was being dragged naked through the house, her protests loud enough to draw the most embarrassing attention. But the enormity of her predicament only really came home to her when Todd hurled her into his office, threw her onto the chesterfield and locked the door.

'What the frick do you think you're doing?' Charity demanded.

'I could ask you the same question,' he returned, his cheeks flushed and his eyes positively blazing with fury. When he mimicked her outraged tone she understood that his temper had reached breaking point, and prudently she hesitated rather than confronting him with a display of her own anger.

'Last night I told you it was imperative you retained your virtue,' he thundered. 'And this morning I find you've spread yourself across the kitchen table like you're an alternative to the continental breakfast.'

Charity flushed and looked away from him.

'What are you doing for lunch,' Todd asked nastily, 'the groundkeepers? Or the estate's security staff?'

The insult struck her like a slap across the face. What she and Danny had been sharing was special but Todd dismissed their relationship as though she gave herself to every man that entered the house. Infuriated that he could damn her

111

with such a galling slur, and no longer able to contain her resentment, she rushed at him with her fingers clawed into talons.

It didn't matter that she was naked and embarrassed. It didn't matter that her sex was uncovered, or her pert breasts with nipples stiff. It didn't even matter that he was her manager and a physical confrontation could irreparably damage their working relationship. All that mattered was teaching Todd Chalmers that she wouldn't be insulted or humiliated.

But he easily caught her wrists and pulled her onto the club chair. His strength and speed were so unexpected she could feel the will to fight evaporating as if it had never been there. Frustrated and defeated, she almost moaned when she realised he now held her in the same position from which he had dominated her the previous evening.

Her stomach was pressed over his lap, her bare breasts were pushed onto his thigh, and he held an uncompromising hand against her exposed backside. The similarities were so striking she briefly considered that she might have imagined the past eight hours and was still suffering the indignity of his first disciplining.

'No,' she wailed, 'you can't do this to me again.'

'Can't I?'

'You can't,' she insisted, trying to pull herself away. 'I won't let you.' The sensation of vulnerability made her feel weak and threatened and she urged herself not to let him know that she was daunted by the unspoken threat of his authority. 'You can't do this to me,' she pleaded. 'You can't.'

He sighed reflectively and nodded. She was staring at the floor, unable to turn because of the way he held her, but she felt the gesture nonetheless.

'Perhaps I shouldn't,' he conceded. 'I don't believe it will do any good, anyway.'

One hand rested between her shoulder blades, making sure

she couldn't raise her head and escape. The other squeezed a buttock and his fingers buried deep into her pliant flesh. Charity stifled a sob and tried to find the leverage to pull away. If she thought it would do any good she would have beat her fists against his leg until he released her, but she suspected Todd's willpower was formidable and she knew he was enjoying the superior position.

'It's not like you paid any heed to what I said last night,' he snorted. 'And I didn't think your discipline could have been much more exacting then.'

She wondered if he might be offering some chance of a reprieve. His words suggested a slim hope that he would relent and spare her the indignity of being spanked, but the prospect of being released without suffering was banished as soon as he slapped her bare bottom. 'I guess I'll have to try harder this time,' he pondered. 'I guess I'll have to try a lot harder.'

She stiffened, stung by the sudden discomfort and mortified by the fact that he was punishing her again. After all the careful teasing she and Danny had enjoyed, her rear was inordinately sensitive. Todd's brutal blow jarred through her frame and turned her buttocks into a searing blaze of agony. She bit back a cry, not sure if it would have sounded like a cry of discomfort or an encouraging sigh of delight.

'Stay still, damn you,' he grumbled, landing another brisk slap.

She flinched from the wicked bite of his palm and tried not to dwell on the pain. Through his trousers, pressing hard against her abdomen, she was aware of the unpleasant pressure of his erection. The thickening length twitched lethargically as he raised his hand and aimed another blow.

'Don't you think this is difficult enough without you wriggling your arse all over the place?' he demanded.

She didn't care if it was difficult for him, and would have

said as much if she could find the breath for words. He repeatedly smacked her rear, reddening the flesh and inadvertently exciting her cheeks with his cruel attention. The first few blows warmed her buttocks until she imagined they were glowing a dull cherry-red, and each subsequent smack crackled with a painful bolt of delicious discomfort. Again and again he slapped her bottom and the crisp echo resounded flatly back from the walls.

'Why are you doing this?' she wailed.

'I'm doing it for three reasons.'

She held herself still, recalling that she had heard something similar in the kitchen. It crossed her mind that Todd might have been watching as she and Danny became closer and she wondered if he'd been spying on her, and timed his interruption at a critical moment. Shaking her head, assuring herself she was being paranoid, Charity grudgingly awaited his explanation.

Todd's hand returned to her bottom, not smacking this time, only caressing her as he spoke. His touch was slightly more bearable than the punishment, but while he wasn't hurting her the contact was still infuriatingly invasive. His palm slipped over one aching cheek and irritated her blazing buttock, perversely sparking wanton responses from her tender flesh.

'I'm doing this for three reasons,' Todd began loftily, 'and the first is to make you understand that you need to keep your virtue.'

She shook her head and tried to pull away, but he was skilled in the art of retaining control. The hand between her shoulder blades slipped to the back of her neck and caught a fistful of hair. Moving her head became a painful exercise and clambering upright was now impossible. The hand on her bottom squeezed with quiet authority and Charity knew she wouldn't be able to extricate herself from his lap until she had

114

his permission.

'You have no right to dictate to me about my virtue,' she gasped, glaring at the floor, wishing she could fix him with the same ferocious expression she was wasting on the carpet. 'You're in no frickin' position to—'

He slapped her bottom lightly, cutting off her protests with the simple gesture. 'I think you'll find I'm in the ideal position to dictate about whatever I like,' he countered. 'And you'll do exactly as I say unless you want this spanking to continue for the rest of the day. My arm will eventually grow tired, and we both know I have several appointments that I can't cancel, but I employ enough staff who would trade their pensions for a chance to spank your bare arse.'

She said nothing, not daring to challenge him in case he decided to make good on his threat. It was bad enough suffering beneath him, but the prospect of enduring this humiliation under the hand of any of the house staff filled her with a debilitating dread. Breathing deeply, wishing she could distance herself from the heat he had generated, she remained motionless over his legs. 'What's your second reason?' she asked meekly, despising the discipline and wanting to move the conversation away from the contentious subject of her virtue.

He snorted and squeezed her rear. The tips of his fingers brushed against her sex lips and she choked back the urge to shriek. Her labia were oily with arousal and her stomach churned as he touched her pussy, the small bristle of pleasure he inspired a treacherous blow that hurt worse than any of his vicious slaps, and she tried to convince herself that her response had nothing to do with sexual excitement.

'The second reason why I'm disciplining you is because of my disappointment,' he said, seeming oblivious to her reaction, speaking in a bored monotone.

He released her hair and she was able to peer awkwardly up

at him and study his face. She could see his fury had lessened but there was no mistaking the genuine reproof in his frown. He studied her coolly. 'I know what occurred between you and Lilah last night,' he told her. She swallowed and started to shake her head, but his fingers returned to the nape of her neck and before she could mutter a word of complaint he was holding her tight and she could only face the floor. 'I know what occurred and you need to understand that it is not acceptable for you to keep information like that from me.'

She blushed, appalled that he had learnt of her near surrender in the cellar. Her cheeks burnt as ferociously as her buttocks and she tried not to dwell on how much Todd now knew about her private life. Until he'd arrived back at the house yesterday he'd been nothing more than a manager – a business acquaintance who was familiar with some members of her family – but his involvement with her personal life went no further. Now he seemed to have settled into the role of her protector and authority figure and she was disquieted to believe that he had omnipotent knowledge about every salacious act she committed. 'Who told you about what happened in the cellar?' she asked thickly.

He shook his head. 'It doesn't matter where the information came from. It's enough that I know you were almost tainted. And it's a sorry state of affairs that you didn't tell me about it yourself. Your silence on this matter implies a lack of trust and that needs to be dealt with now.' Sighing heavily, he added, 'And I think that oversight needs to be addressed by something stiffer than a mere spanking.'

Numbly, she realised he had moved his hands away. She glanced up at him and saw he was pointing at the bar. Her first thought was that he was going to demand she pour him a drink, and considering the early hour of the day she wondered if she should add another fault to his seemingly endless list of character flaws. He had already proved himself a bully, a twisted disciplinarian and Hope had indicated that he couldn't be trusted to honestly handle her finances. Now she briefly speculated that he might also be a drunkard.

'Go and bend over there,' he told her.

The suspicion of what he might be planning made her stomach tighten in a sickening knot. She shook her head and started to stammer a refusal, but when he repeated his instruction Charity did as she was told. She couldn't bring herself to be bullied by another of his cruel threats and knew, no matter what protest she made, he would make it clear that she had to do as he said. Walking slowly across the room, she went to the spot he had indicated and bent over.

Her blushes had burnt deep before but now, for some reasons she couldn't fathom, the shame seemed more unbearable. On the comparative safety of his knee she had felt slightly sheltered even while he was spanking her, his nearness affording some level of security. But now, standing alone in a corner of the room, she felt exposed and painfully vulnerable.

She could imagine Todd ogling the pouting lips of her sex, knew they were peeping from between her clenched buttocks, and she dreaded to think of how exciting he found the sight. Her breasts swayed as she bent forward and she closed her eyes rather than study him from the awkward angle of looking back.

'We'll make this part of your discipline brief,' he allowed graciously.

She squeezed her hands into fists until the pressure of her nails hurt her palms. The urge to make some sharp retort was dangerously close but she didn't dare say anything that might make him angrier.

'Because I'm prepared to accept that you were frightened by what happened,' he conceded gallantly, 'and because I understand that the situation is new to you, I won't drag this

117

out unnecessarily. But you need to understand that you must keep me informed of all developments.'

She heard the words, and was ready to respond with an apology and a request for him to explain what he was talking about, when he sliced a switch through the air. It whistled musically, chilling her with its unspoken implication of menace, and she was suddenly overcome with the urge to try and escape. She didn't know where he had produced the crop from, but the importance of that detail was way down on her list of priorities. More pressing was her fear of what he might now be planning to do with the implement.

'You don't seriously frickin' think…' She got no further, for he advanced across the room and sliced the crop across her bottom before she could complete the sentence. Once again the musical whistle of the leather sang through the air, and then her backside was awash with a fresh and glorious pain.

For an instant she wondered if she was going to pass out. The burning weal that blazed through her buttocks was more ferocious than any of the torments he had visited on her already and she writhed in an attempt to lessen the severity of the pain. Blinking back tears, too breathless to release the scream that welled at the back of her throat, she started to turn to him and demand that he stop.

But Todd slashed the crop against her bottom for a second blow. This was harder than the first, biting far more cruelly, and she almost fell over with the force of the impact. The flat of his hand had made her cheeks tender and responsive but this latest torment took those sensations to a new level. Staring at him agape, bewildered by the perfect blend of pain and arousal he had managed to inflict, she tried to stammer something that might interrupt long enough for him to stop.

Todd struck her buttocks with a third shot, and Charity groaned.

'We'll keep this to a strict six,' he decided, and with the

back of his hand he encouraged her to spread her legs slightly apart. His knuckles grazed the wet lips of her sex as he urged her to put a little more space between her thighs. A sparkle of raw pleasure prickled through her pussy but she refused to let herself acknowledge that momentary delight.

'Any more than six stripes would be unfair and cruel,' he stated. 'But any less might not get my point across.'

She didn't understand what he was saying, and the idea of responding was completely beyond her. Her sex lips ached for another frisson of his touch and her clitoris pulsed with an immediate and insistent demand, but rather than dwelling on her body's traitorous responses she was more amazed by her own acquiescence as she dutifully forced her feet apart and assumed the position he wanted.

Todd broke the silence between them with another slice of the switch. Charity bit back a shocked cry and flexed her fingers in an attempt to fight off the soaring agony that blazed through her rear. Her body was swathed in icy sweat and she didn't dare turn and look at him in case he saw the arousal she knew would be sparkling in her eyes. She couldn't equate her longing with the suffering he had administered – and didn't want to believe that her body was so weak it could be driven to such extremes of pleasure through punishment – but she couldn't deny that she was horribly excited.

'You'll keep me fully informed in future, won't you?' he barked, and she gritted her teeth as he landed another blow. His aim was infuriatingly accurate, each slice of the switch falling perfectly on top of the weal left by the last. Her bottom felt as though a rusty razor had flayed it and she had to fight for the necessary air to answer, but before she'd managed to respond Todd had driven the crop down once again.

'You'll keep me fully informed in future, won't you?' he repeated. 'Give me the answer I want, or we can turn these six stripes into an even dozen.'

'Yes,' she gasped quickly, the word coming in a rush she couldn't stop, as did the tears that trickled down her cheeks. 'I'll keep you fully informed in future,' she promised. 'I should have told you straight away. I should have—'

A final slice of the crop silenced her babbling, catching the tops of her thighs and taking her to a bright new world of anguished delight. The promise of pleasure came in a rush, transporting her to a divine plateau of unparalleled joy. Every agony was momentarily forgotten as she choked back a sob and allowed the sensations of agonised relief to throb through her rear.

She heard Todd's footsteps as he returned to his chair, listened to the familiar click of his lighter being opened and lit, and caught the crackle of a cigar being brought to life. Quite how she was able to hear over the pounding of blood in her temples was a mystery she didn't bother exploring. She remained where he left her, allowing the tears to trail meaninglessly down her face, and wondering why her body was responding with such elation after the brutal torment he'd made her suffer.

She didn't consider herself to be naïve – she had written enough songs about the pleasures and pains of sex to consider herself something of an expert – but she had never thought it would be possible to be taken to an extreme of satisfaction from such punishing treatment. Slowly regaining her breath, scared that if she moved too quickly she would reawaken the pain in her buttocks and send herself tumbling to the floor in a climactic heap, she surreptitiously stretched her stiff muscles and tried to stand upright.

'Are you fully au fait with our ground rules?' Todd asked.

She took two deep breaths before trusting herself to respond. 'What's your third reason?' she asked, remaining by the bar, clutching the polished wooden surface for fear of revealing her nerves and showing him the telltale tremors that shook her fingertips.

He raised a single eyebrow and regarded her quizzically until she explained the question. Her nudity was no longer an issue and she considered it unimportant that he was seeing her naked, trembling and confused. Not bothering to conceal herself, concentrating only on trying to stand erect without revealing her excited confusion, she took another steadying breath before she trusted herself to continue. 'You said you had three reasons for disciplining me,' she reminded him. 'You've said you want me to retain my virtue, and you've chastised me for not keeping you informed about what happened with Lilah last night.' It was a struggle to keep the bitterness from her voice and she thought she could see his brow creasing when he heard her disparaging tone. Speaking quickly, not wanting to incur a further bout of his wrath, she asked, 'What's your third reason?'

He snapped his fingers and summoned her to return to his lap. She was loath to obey the instruction but, after all she'd already endured, she could no longer see any reason to defy him. Despising him for being such a bully, and hating herself for submitting without a proper show of defiance, she returned to him and bent over his thighs. The pressure of his erection was more noticeable than before but this time, rather than repulsing her, she found the presence of his excitement perversely reassuring. When he placed a hand between her shoulder blades and idly stroked the nape of her neck, she recoiled from the rush of her own excited responses.

Todd spanked her again, effectively removing every one of her forgiving thoughts. His fingers remained around her aching cheek and he squeezed with characteristic brutality. She squealed as his hands casually re-awoke the pain of every stroke from the crop and didn't stop complaining until he slapped her bottom again.

'My third reason is the most important,' he said solemnly,

and Charity struggled to listen, rather than begging him to stop. She couldn't decide if he had taken her to the brink of orgasm or if she was simply suffering the symptoms that came from enduring too much pain. She guessed the distinction was unimportant because she silently vowed that she would never submit to such treatment ever again. Yet the inability to distinguish between those two extremes troubled her greatly.

'Maybe before midnight tonight,' he continued, 'almost certainly within the next forty-eight hours, you're going to be called on to defeat the dark one. If you're going to be strong enough to meet that challenge, if you're going to be able to face whatever he has lined up for you, you have to be immune and untroubled by this sort of discipline.'

The words made her feel ill with worry; rather than remaining unmoved by the spanking, and far from being untroubled by the discipline, every blow had made her more excited. Instead of seeing herself as a champion against the threat of the vampires she could only believe that she would be another victim easily overwhelmed by their irresistible charm. She wiped the tears from her face and sniffed before speaking. 'What will the dark one do to me?'

Todd shrugged. 'He likes to see his women tormented and struggling. It won't be easy for you, and you won't stand a cat in hell's chance if you aren't prepared.'

His callused palm stroked from one buttock to the other, smoothing over the raised weals his crop had left behind, and sliding almost innocently against her exposed sex. Earlier she would have beaten her fists against the floor as she fought to distance herself from the excitement he was generating, but now she could only surrender to her growing arousal.

'You've already seen how dangerous Lilah can be,' he said, 'but she's nothing compared to her brother. The dark one is a truly formidable opponent. Unless you understand your own

122

responses, and unless you're prepared to use those responses to your best advantage, he's going to triumph.'

She heard everything he said but the ability to respond was beyond her. His hand continued to stroke circles against her rear, rekindling every moment of torture through her punished flesh and slipping against her pussy lips. In amongst the barbs of anguish she was treated to the slippery sensation of her fingers teasing her labia, and when he touched her pulsing clitoris she knew he had pushed her beyond the resistance of fighting her orgasm. The surge of joy held her motionless and she didn't dare move for fear of revealing her response. The discovery that pain and pleasure could be such close neighbours was astounding but she didn't want Todd to know he'd already taught her the first lesson. Silently conceding that she would do as he'd asked, and basking in the blistering release of her joy, she told herself she would retain her virtue until after her confrontation with the vampires.

But when she closed her eyes, rather than thinking about Todd or being struck by images of the beautiful Lilah or the menacing figure of the dark one, Charity found herself remembering Danny. It was her recollection of his handsome face that turned her decision and she realised her course of action had already been decided. Regardless of what Todd said or did, and no matter how the vampires behaved, she couldn't turn her back on the one person who had now become important in her life.

Todd continued to talk, unmindful of the orgasm she had just enjoyed and oblivious to the epiphany she had suffered. 'I don't know what Faith and Hope might have told you, but you can't underestimate the danger these vampires represent. If you don't do as I tell you we could all be doomed to a life as their underlings.'

Charity couldn't bring herself to look at him, not trusting herself to speak and hoping that what he said wasn't true. If there was any chance that Todd might be right she suspected all their futures would be bleak because she was now more determined than ever to have Danny as her lover. And no amount of discipline from Todd Chalmers was going to make her change her mind.

Interlude

Part Three

Wendy was a natural in the battle arena. Stripped naked, every curve of her formidable figure on display, she looked like an Amazonian gladiator as she towered over her vanquished opponents. Her massive breasts glistened with a sheen of sweat and her nipples stood hard and obvious. The Royal Opera House footlights silvered her raven hair and bathed her flesh in brilliant glory. Taking centre stage, commanding her subordinates with arrogant ease, she looked comfortable and content in her role as the victorious dominatrix.

And it was clear that none of her opponents stood any chance against her. Helen grovelled at her feet, her naked body supplicated as she kissed the woman's feet and fawned at her ankles. Savage welts adorned Helen's buttocks and thighs and she trembled with either fear or adoration each time she brushed her lips against the newly made vampire.

Equally defeated, coiling her arms and legs around the woman in a petrified embrace, Marcia pressed against Wendy's side and suckled her swollen breast. The few clothes she still wore had become the ravaged and torn testaments to her valour against a superior foe. A nipple was visible through the shredded remnants of her blouse, and her skirt hung in such tatters that it was possible to see her pouting pussy lips as they pressed hungrily against Wendy's leg.

Drained, and finally looking like she had resigned herself to losing, the mulatto knelt between Wendy's legs, burying her face into the vampire's cleft. Her head bobbed and swayed with violent urgency and, each time she pulled back to adjust her position, it was possible to see that her face was lathered with a sheen of musk. Either embarrassed by her defeat, or hungry to taste more of the woman above her, the mulatto quickly extended her tongue and returned her face to Wendy's sex.

But this time Lilah couldn't bring herself to gloat. It was enough that Wendy was proving herself triumphant, and she could see no advantage in remarking that she had been right to recruit her to their coven. More important matters weighed on Lilah's thoughts and she glanced slyly at her brother on the opposite side of the theatre.

Hidden by shadows, and keeping his emotions concealed behind an unreadable mask, he sank into one of the red-plush seats in his box and glared broodingly at the stage. If she hadn't been trying to distance herself from the idea, if she hadn't been trying to deliberately push the thought from her mind, Lilah would have known they were sharing the same fear.

She had negotiated the use of the theatre for the afternoon, needing an arena for Wendy that wouldn't be hampered by the bane of natural light. The Royal Opera House had seemed like the ideal venue because its West End location was ideal for the Covent Garden tube. And although it had meant cancelling a production of Tosca, Lilah had instructed her contacts within the management to make the theatre available. She was determined that the dark one would see the wisdom of her plan and believed another demonstration of her protégée's infallibility should convince him.

But the preparations for this display now seemed long ago and, rather than enjoy the sight of Wendy's winning prowess, Lilah found herself brooding on that one nagging doubt that had been troubling her since her brother fed from the gypsy.

'Drink from me, you little bitch,' Wendy growled. 'Drink

from me and make me love it.' She grabbed a fistful of the mulatto's hair and pulled her closer to her sex. Parting her broad thighs, making it easier for her to be tongued, she growled with pleasure baring her elongated canines. As she continued to writhe on the stage, her curvaceous body made lithe with pleasure, she tugged Marcia's mouth from her breast and forced her head back.

The blonde gasped, but made no other attempt to defend herself. Biting her throat, drinking freely from her, the flood of crimson daubed Wendy's lips as she greedily swallowed. Briefly she tore her mouth away and looked to be languishing in a state of ecstasy as she basked in the pleasure of feeding.

Ordinarily the sight would have sparked Lilah's arousal and whet her appetite for a taste of the same perverse satisfaction. Watching subordinates feed always inflamed her hunger, and since tormenting the virtuous one she hadn't properly sated her needs. But she was preoccupied with matters more pressing than her libido and a single glance across the theatre, to the facing box where her brother sat, told Lilah that the dark one was in the same distracted state of mind. Watching his lips, seeing him silently shape words that she could have read from the frown lines on his brow, she understood they were pondering the same question:

What if the gypsy was right?

She wasn't troubled by the worry that Charity might be unbeatable; Lilah had faced and defeated the unbeatable before. She had achieved victory against all odds on more occasions than she cared to remember, and felt confident that Wendy would be able to best the virtuous pop singer and any allies that she happened to find along the way. It was easy to dismiss that particular threat to the coven as nothing more than a minor nuisance and she doubted Charity would really prove to be a problem. More worrying, and unsettling her with the endless implications, was the gypsy's revelation that she and her brother shared an aura.

'Deeper, you bitch,' Wendy grunted. 'Tongue me deeper.'

Concentrating on her brother, Lilah didn't bother to glance at the stage. Wendy was in absolute control of her three playmates, kicking Helen aside, dropping to the floor and pulling Marcia with her. She moved with the fluid ease of someone confident with their size and arrogant of their enormous power. Her grace was surprisingly feminine and made Lilah think of ballet dancers she had seen on the same stage in more public performances.

Wendy pushed her crotch over the mulatto's face, almost suffocating her as her pussy lips engulfed the diminutive vampire's mouth. Grinding her pelvis down, squirming greedily against her, she directed Helen to continue grovelling before turning her attention back to Marcia.

The blonde looked pale and drained. Whatever pulse was left within her now beat thin and ragged. She no longer struggled against her formidable opponent, and when Wendy resumed her penetrating kiss Marcia could only sigh and give herself to the pleasure of being taken. Her nipples stood stiff and flushed and the deep magenta of her areolae contrasted against her paper-pale skin. The scarlet hue of her lips looked so out of place against her wan complexion it was as though she'd tasted the same crimson flow that Wendy drank from her throat.

But Lilah didn't see any of the interaction on stage. If what the gypsy said was true, her future was no longer as assured as she had always believed. Whatever fate befell her brother would also doom her and she didn't like the implication that she was no longer the mistress of her own destiny. It didn't help that she was noticing too many similarities between herself and the dark one, and the timing of those observations made her wonder if she had simply missed them before, or if they were symptoms of the condition the gypsy had diagnosed.

'Tongue my anus, you little whore,' Wendy demanded.

Lilah sat upright in her seat, her attention suddenly caught by events on the stage. Catching movement from the corner of her eye, she was disquieted to note that her brother shifted position, as though he too was suddenly interested in the staged exhibition.

Wendy had taken Marcia to a dangerous extreme, drinking too much from her and exciting her past the point of orgasm. Weakly, but with unmistakable pleasure, the blonde sobbed her way through a delirious elation, sniffing and spluttering as she tried to break free from the brunette's inescapable embrace. Seemingly tired of tormenting her, Wendy pushed Marcia aside and began to drink from Helen. She urged the trembling Marcia to go behind her and issued her clipped instruction once again. 'Tongue my anus, you little whore. One of you bitches will make me come, or I'll drain the damned lot of you before we leave this theatre.'

Lilah leant over the edge of the box, enjoying the pressure of her leather basque as it pressed against her rigid nipples. The familiar flush of excitement was almost enough to make her forget her fears and she allowed herself the first genuine smile that had broached her lips all day. The pleasurable tingle of arousal was enough to banish her worries and she was able to believe that she and her brother were not really linked by the same aura.

Across the theatre, alone in his own box, the dark one rubbed himself.

Wendy pushed Helen away. Her mouth was bloody and the scarlet on her lips matched the dark red glimmer that sparkled in her eyes. She reached for the coiled bullwhip at her waist and gripped the pizzle-shaped handle tight in one hand. Snapping the whip sharply against the boards, easily producing a crack that echoed around the auditorium, she

129

barked at the confused trio and told them to bend over. 'I'm having one of you as my prize,' she decided confidently.

Lilah and her brother exchanged a glance. Neither of them had agreed to this condition, and it bordered on insurrection that the newly made member of their coven could dictate terms so freely. But rather than fretting about Wendy's lack of respect for their authority, it was the instantaneous way she and the dark one turned to regard each other that Lilah found most unsettling. Across the space that separated their facing boxes, they each regarded the other with a single eyebrow raised.

'I'm having one of you as my prize,' Wendy repeated. 'And I know that none of you want that. So you'd best listen good and hard if you want to avoid what I've got planned.' She snapped her whip against the stage again and the tip produced a flurry of dust.

Helen, Marcia and the mulatto each had their bottoms to the dominatrix and flinched in response to the vicious crack.

'You can avoid being my plaything by following one simple rule,' Wendy announced. 'Stay silent and I won't pick you. Stay silent and I'll move on to the next worthless bitch. But make one whimper, or word of protest, and I'll spend the next twenty-four hours drinking from your throat and any other part of your body that takes my fancy.'

A warm wetness began to spread through Lilah's loins. She crushed her thighs together, savouring the tingle of excitement that the performance was generating. It crossed her mind that she shouldn't have left Nick guarding the front of house, and that he could have been quite useful to her now if she'd invited him to share one of the empty seats in her box, but she knew there was no point in troubling herself with such recriminations. More important than the ways she could have sated her welling desire was the need to believe that her arousal was unique and not something she shared with her brother.

The dark one pushed himself back in his chair. Lilah could see that one of his arms had disappeared from her view and she guessed it was somewhere near his waist. Glancing down at herself, seeing her own fingers were pressed against her crotch, she snorted with disgust and pulled her hand away. The similarities between her and her brother were too many to be ignored and that dispiriting thought killed her appetite for properly enjoying the show.

'Have I made these rules clear?' Wendy demanded.

The three broken vampires nodded. Helen and Marcia exchanged a frightened glance, but always a loner, always content to take her pains and pleasure with characteristic distance from the others, the mulatto held herself rigid and stared blindly ahead.

Wendy cracked the whip down hard, and it moved so fast that Lilah couldn't tell with any certainty which of the vampires had been struck. She saw all three of them stiffen and the crack rang loud in her ears, but it wasn't until she saw the dark red weal blossom on Marcia's backside that she realised the blonde had been targeted.

'If any one of you whimpers you're mine for the night,' Wendy reminded them.

But not without the dark one's permission, Lilah thought bitterly. Movement from the box on the other side of the auditorium caught her eye and she realised her brother was whispering something under his breath. She didn't need to strain her vision to read his lips, or concentrate to hear his words, because she knew what he was saying as if the thought had come from her own head:

'Not without my permission.'

Wendy thrashed her whip down with punishing force and an accuracy that would have served her well as a circus performer. She caught Marcia's other buttock, pausing until the welt had flourished to the colour of a rose, before branding Helen's cheeks with identical crimson stripes. Saving the mulatto until last, and investing her greatest efforts into each shot, she bit the dark-skinned vampire with two blows that would have left a lesser creature howling in agony, but the mulatto bore her punishment in stoic silence.

Lilah pushed her worries about shared auras aside as she involved herself in Wendy's performance on stage. The mulatto had closed her eyes and, although she was a vampire with no need to breathe, her chest swelled with the obvious exertion of containing her response. Marcia and Helen were both trembling, and Lilah could see that they were on the verge of crying out at the mere sound of the whip descending, but it was the mulatto's endurance that held Lilah's interest.

'Not a bad demonstration,' Wendy conceded grudgingly, and snatched the whip hard against the mulatto's rear for a third time. Helen and Marcia both quivered as the crack echoed through the theatre, but the mulatto merely held herself with quiet, dignified composure. Her glossy lips were pouted in an expressionless kiss as she silently sucked in her need to squeal.

Wendy shook her head with obvious disapproval, and storming over to the mulatto, grabbing her buttock and squeezing hard, she hissed, 'You're not endearing yourself to me. These two worthless bitches shit their pants every time I fart or cough, but you're not showing me any response and I'm beginning to think you're doing it to piss me off.'

'Foul-mouthed bitch,' the dark one muttered, and Lilah didn't need to glance at him to know what he'd said; the same thought tumbled through her mind an instant before he spoke. Unnerved, she studied her brother in sullen silence.

'What's it going to take to get a response out of you?' Wendy growled, continuing to clutch the mulatto's rear with one hand, readjusting her grip on the pizzle with the other.

132

Stroking the dome-like end between the mulatto's pussy lips, parting the labia and sliding the handle up and down, she asked again, 'What's it going to take to get a response out of you?'

Marcia and Helen dared to glance at what was happening and their relief was apparent. Lilah had known Wendy would be a formidable opponent and she could see the two subordinates were thankful that the vampire hadn't decided to target them with her wrath. Struggling to remain indifferent, fighting the responses that were being wrung from her aching backside and forced between the pouting lips of her pussy, the mulatto said nothing.

'Do you really dread spending the night with me?' Wendy asked, pushing the pizzle deep into the mulatto's sex, spreading the lips and burying the shaft inside. Rolling the phallus in a circular motion, ploughing the length back and forth with languid movements of her wrist, she continued to claw at the mulatto's bottom and dug her nails into the blemished flesh of her buttocks. 'I could be quite insulted if I thought you were deliberately trying to avoid spending a night with me.'

'Don't you think she's good?' Lilah asked her brother. The distance would have stopped a mortal from hearing her question but the dark one's supernatural abilities were manifold. Even without the suggestion of their shared auras – and Lilah was still trying to convince herself that she was worrying needlessly on that score – she knew her brother would be able to hear what she asked.

'She's good,' the dark one allowed softly.

On stage, Wendy had made the mulatto sit upright. The pizzle filled her sex, impaling her so deeply that her labia were stretched around the massive girth of its base. Still kneading the mulatto's buttocks, gritting her teeth as she vainly tried to coax some cry of submission from her, Wendy looked to have forgotten Marcia and Helen as she concentrated on her chosen victim. 'I want to have you as my playmate tonight,' Wendy hissed.

Almost imperceptibly the mulatto shook her head. Her features were strained with exertion, her body quietly trembled with the effort of containing her responses and she valiantly fought her need to climax. Lilah could see it was proving to be a furious battle of wills, but because Wendy had the superior position, and because she seemed so determined on this point, she didn't think there was any real doubt about which of them would be victorious. However, because she knew the mulatto could be spectacularly single-minded, she knew the dark-skinned vampire would not allow Wendy an easy triumph.

'I could crack my whip across the three of you, and both of those weak-willed bitches would eventually sob for me to stop,' Wendy growled, her mouth inches from the mulatto's ear. 'But I don't want either of them. I want you.'

Again the mulatto shook her head, and fury apparent in her thunderous frown, Wendy pushed the pizzle deeper then bared her teeth as she prepared to bite. The tips of her canines pressed against the mulatto's throat and slender ribbons of blood spilt from the pinpricks of the vampire's teeth.

For an instant Lilah thought the dark-skinned vampire was going to cry out. She could see the woman was hovering on the extreme of an emotion, although it was impossible to say if it was pleasure, pain or a delightful combination of both. She held herself still, watching intently so as not to miss the mulatto's surrender, and was disappointed when the moment passed.

Wendy tore her bite away, a look of frustration twisting her features. 'Keep fighting me and I'm going to make this worse for you,' she warned, raising a finger, not bothering to disguise her fury, but trembling, the mulatto did not reply.

'Why don't you just surrender and let me have you as my

little bitch for the night?' Wendy demanded. 'You know that's what I want. You know I'd rather have you than either of these two simpering bitches.'

Slowly, the mulatto turned to face her tormentor. The pizzle still filled her pussy, its formidable length and girth stretching her swollen labia, and her body was quietly rocked by minor tremors. 'But what if I don't want that?' she asked, fixing her wide-eyed gaze on Wendy, looking obscenely corruptible.

There was a moment's hesitation, as though Wendy was considering her reply. Familiar with the torturous tricks that the likes of her were fond of playing, Lilah believed the vampire was simply timing her next move for maximum effect, and an instant later she was proved right.

With vicious speed Wendy pulled the pizzle from the mulatto's pussy and thrust it into her anus instead. The penetration was swift, brutal and accomplished in a second, and if either Helen or Marcia had seen what was happening, Lilah knew they would have shrieked in protest at the mere sight. If either of those two vampires had suffered such rough manhandling, Lilah didn't doubt their cries would continue to echo around the theatre for hour after hour.

But the mulatto was made of stronger stuff than her contemporaries from within the coven, and although it was clear that she wasn't relishing her treatment at Wendy's hands, it was also obvious that she would never simply relent and do as her tormentor demanded.

'If you don't want to be my plaything for the evening, I might have to make you want that,' Wendy hissed, twisting the pizzle deeper.

The mulatto scratched her fingernails against the stage boards, scarring the timber. Her features were stretched into a grimace of disgusted pleasure and it was clear that she was going to climax regardless of her resistance. Sweat glistened on her brow, her chest swelled and her nipples grew taut, and she began to arch her back in readiness for the explosion that wanted to surge from her body.

'Don't you think Wendy's the best you've ever seen?' Lilah asked her brother.

Wendy returned her lips to the vampire's throat as she took her to the brink of orgasm. Using every trick at her disposal, biting flesh, kneading the mulatto's arse and thrusting the whip handle deeper into her victim's rear, she was rewarded with a faltering cry of release.

Lilah chuckled softly, pleased that she had been right to place her faith in the victor. 'She is the best, isn't she?' she mused, glancing across the theatre, meeting the dark one's inscrutable gaze.

'She's good,' he allowed.

'She's the best,' Lilah assured him.

He nodded half-hearted agreement. 'Quite possibly, but I don't think she's good enough.'

Lilah had been prepared to watch events on stage as Wendy gloated over the mulatto's sobbing defeat, but her brother's contentious remark snatched her attention. 'What the hell does that mean?' she demanded.

'She won't beat Charity,' he grumbled.

Lilah snorted in disgust. 'Charity won't stand a chance against her. Wendy will pussy whip the little bitch before she can remember the shape of her crucifix.'

'Your star pupil might be all right at tormenting seasoned vampires, but Wendy won't know how to deal with the virtuous one. You're putting too much confidence in her and she's going to let you down.'

Instead of angrily defending her beliefs, Lilah smiled. Perhaps her brother was correct, and maybe there was a risk that Wendy might not be able to triumph in a confrontation against Charity, although she seriously doubted he was right on that. But the matter was made momentarily unimportant when she realised they were on the verge of arguing. They were having a difference of opinion and she took that as a sign that her earlier worries had been horribly misplaced. Different opinions must mean different auras, she told herself, which meant the gypsy must have been wrong. Perhaps they did share many drives, ideas and other qualities, but that was only to be expected after living in the same coven for the past two hundred years. It didn't mean they shared the same aura and it certainly didn't mean they were destined to suffer the same fate.

Convinced that she no longer had anything to worry about, Lilah wasn't even troubled when she noticed the dark one's sly smile was a perfect reflection of her own. She was confident that they would be victorious and that shared thought was enough to keep her smiling.

Charity

Act II, Scene III

The view from Parliament Hill was a magnificent vantage point. They had their backs to Highgate and Hampstead and basked in the distant splendour of St Paul's dome and the faraway bar chart of Canary Wharf. A grey base of urban monotony puddled beneath the familiar landmarks and stretched toward and beyond the horizon. The setting sun silhouetted the distinctive skyline against a backdrop of darkening purple. With the lush greenery of the heath spread out below them, Charity could have believed their shared park bench provided a view from the top of the world.

But she wasn't interested in any of the glorious landscape. She didn't notice that the heath was preternaturally quiet: no children or dog-walkers, or hand-in-hand couples, or suspicious looking guys wearing unseasonably long raincoats. Her concentration was fixed on Danny and she watched and waited to see how he would respond to what she had told him. The importance of the moment was so great she held her breath as she waited for him to speak.

'Vampires exist?' he repeated, earnest doubt in his voice. 'Not fiction, not a joke, and you're not saying this for stupid giggles. Vampires really exist?'

She hung intently on his words, aware of the scepticism underscoring his tone. 'Yeah,' she said, trying to make light of the situation. 'It's a big one to accept, isn't it? It's nearly as incredible as that rumour that Santa Claus might be made up.'

Danny pursed his lips, ignoring her attempt at levity.

'Vampires really exist, and you're a virtuous maiden destined to confront the evil leader of a villainous coven? Is that what you're telling me?'

'I won't write it on my CV like that,' she conceded flippantly, 'but that's what I've been told.' With absolute solemnity she added, 'My sources are trustworthy, Danny. I have no reason to doubt them.'

He considered this for a moment, and then nodded. 'And are these revelations supposed to explain why Todd Chalmers dragged you away from me this morning? Or why I haven't seen or heard from you all day?'

'No,' she said, surprising herself with her own display of patience. 'You haven't seen or heard from me all day because I've been locked in the basement recording studio wrapping up the vocals for the final track of BloodLust's next album.'

'And the reason why Todd dragged you away from me?'

'Todd did that because he's a frickin' dick,' she said stiffly, considering mentioning the switch, the humiliating punishment she had been forced to endure and Todd's insistence that she needed that discipline to help her overcome the threat of the vampires, then decided it might be too much to explain in one attempt. 'Todd thinks he's protecting me,' she said carefully. 'I suppose he thinks he's protecting himself as well. He sees my virtue as the last line of defence against the threat of the vampires. Do I need to explain anything else, Danny, or did we just trek all the way up here to discuss my role in contemporary vampiric lore?'

Danny's frown remained defiant. 'Is there anything else to explain or discuss?'

She thought again about the stripe marks on her rear, and the niggling discomfort they added to sitting on the bench. Shaking her head, placing a hand on his shoulder, Charity drew him closer, ready for a kiss. 'We have unfinished business to conclude, don't we?' she whispered.

'Unfinished business?'

'From the kitchen,' she reminded him. 'Before we were so rudely interrupted. Before Todd dragged me away.'

Understanding washed over his face before being replaced by a shred of doubt. 'Todd's not going to suddenly jump out from behind a tree, is he?' he asked, glancing over his shoulder, scouring the desolate heath.

She giggled at the suggestion and pulled him closer. His body had a scent of warmth that became more tantalising the nearer he got. It was a base note fragrance of masculine sweat and musk that made her pulse race faster. 'No one knows we're up here,' she assured him.

Her departure from the house had been as discreet as the text message she sent to his mobile, urging him to meet her on the heath. 'Todd doesn't know we've left the house and the only person who might have a clue is your sister, Angela.' Danny's sister had been hanging around the recording studio when Charity finally left the basement that afternoon. She had looked to be still suffering from the effects of her hangover and barely seemed to hear when Charity said she was going to slip out of the house and meet Danny.

'We're safe,' she assured him. 'We're safe, we're alone, and we're not going to be interrupted.'

The remainder of his hesitation was fleeting and easily overcome. Untroubled by the fact that they were in a public place, and seeming able to brush aside the embarrassment of the morning and the angst of a long day's separation, Danny placed a hand on her breast as he kissed her.

Charity drew a startled breath, pleased that he had accepted her explanation and happy that they would be able to pick up from where they had left off. The brief time she'd shared with him had already made her anxious to experience more, and now they were finally alone she was determined that nothing was going to interrupt them.

She had lost the schoolgirl uniform before embarking on the day's vocals, and gone for the more comfortable feel of a T-shirt and jeans. Now, as Danny's hands roved over the thin cotton fabric and teased the swell of her barely constrained breasts, she wished she had worn something that would make her body a little more accessible.

'We were getting quite intimate in the kitchen,' he remembered, and glancing warily around the deserted heath his eyes narrowed. 'Are you sure this is the right place to do that sort of catching up? The top of Parliament Hill isn't exactly a discreet location.'

Charity placed her hand over his groin and discovered the thrust of his erection distending the denim. Tracing her fingers lightly over the swell of his hardness she could feel the nuances of his shape and the distinct pulse of his desire. Her need for him accelerated, and together they sighed. 'The kitchen wasn't exactly a discreet location,' she reminded him.

He sniggered and she heard enough genuine amusement in the sound to realise he had put all unpleasant associations of the morning behind them. He worked his hand beneath her T-shirt, his fingers chilly but perversely warming, and stole his touch against the soft flesh of her nipple. An instantaneous rush of excitement thrilled her, and regarding him with fresh arousal as he caught the stiff bud between his finger and thumb and then squeezed gently, she revelled in all the glorious sensations he inspired.

Determined that she would enjoy every moment of this first time, anxious to recall the fresh excitement that had made their morning in the kitchen so scintillating, Charity slowly unfastened his jeans. He wore no pants beneath the denim and his erection pushed eagerly into her hand before the third button was released. His heat, and the pressure of his bulbous glans in her palm, made her tremble with renewed desire.

Danny pushed her T-shirt up, exposing her stomach and breasts. While he continued to tease the taut bud of one nipple he placed his mouth over her other breast and sucked. His lips were warm and moist, but it was the teasing thrust of his tongue, probing and exploring her flesh, that made her want to melt against the bench. Charity threw back her head and groaned, the erection in her hand pulsing as though it shared her eagerness, and when she stroked her thumb languidly over the tip she realised Danny was leaking a viscous seepage of pre-come. The discovery was maddeningly exciting, and almost enough to have her begging him to hurry up and fuck her, her need for him accelerating when she caught the musky fragrance of his arousal, but while she was determined to have him, she was also adamant that their union would not be hasty.

'I wanted to make this moment special,' he told her, and she couldn't help smiling, surprised that they were so in tune with each other. Then Danny moved his hands and mouth away from her breasts, and she was a little disappointed that he'd stopped. He had teased her nipples to a state of hardness that was so strong it hurt, and taking his lips from her breast left her exposed to the chilly dusk air, but his hands slipped to the waistband of her jeans and he began to lower her zip.

A light breeze on the top of the heath made Charity vitally aware of her exposed flesh as he peeled down her jeans. He tugged them off, dragging the denim over her thighs, knees and ankles, until she was sat on the bench wearing only a pair of panties and the rucked up T-shirt. Not wanting to hide herself from him, reluctant to cheapen this moment in any way, she snatched the T-shirt over her head and tossed it aside.

His erection twitched, and unable to stop herself she licked her lips. A part of her wanted to see him undressed, and caress his muscular torso and abdomen, but the need within her sex

142

insisted she was already in control of the most important part of his anatomy.

He was tensed with an anticipation that matched her own, and when she pulled the crotch of her panties to one side his eyes grew even more eager. Her heart was racing as she rubbed his swollen glans against the wetness of her sex and revelled in the thrill of his intimate touch. The lips of her pussy were soaked with arousal and her inner muscles clenched hungrily.

'Let me take these off,' he said, reaching for her panties, but she shook her head, and without relenting her grip on his erection, she brushed his hand away. This was the third time they had found themselves on the brink of making love and Charity was adamant that it wouldn't be spoilt. Vampires interrupted the first time, and the second was vetoed by Todd Chalmers's untimely appearance, so she wasn't going to let Danny's discovery of the switch marks on her bottom give him cause to delay or refrain from consummating their relationship.

'I'll keep them on,' she whispered tactfully. 'They won't get in the way.'

He passed her a questioning glance that she brushed aside with the same casual ease with which she'd moved his hand away. She didn't like keeping secrets from him but she knew her claims about the threat of vampires had already stretched his credulity to the brink of breaking point. She couldn't believe he would simply accept that her rear had been striped in a necessary lesson on the rules of discipline that would help her against that impending threat.

'I'll keep them on and I'll explain why later,' she said.

He nodded acceptance, and as she guided him closer he positioned himself awkwardly between her legs. The abrasive weave of his jeans scoured her inner thighs, and then they were exchanging a sultry, passionate kiss. His tongue plundered her mouth as she brought him closer, stroking his

143

length up and down against her sex. She placed the end of his shaft at her entrance, braced herself for the penetration and started to ease her pussy onto him.

But Danny broke their kiss and pulled his hips back slightly, preventing Charity from taking him into her warm confines. 'If you're really the virtuous one, won't this stop you from being virtuous?'

She considered him coolly, not replying at first, only nestling her pussy lips against the delicious heat of his erection. The distinction between the virtue of her virginity and the virtuous bloodline she came from was more theology and mythology than she cared to explain in her current state of arousal. Quite how Danny was able to worry about something so prosaic at this particular moment was a mystery she didn't want to explore, and it was certainly something she didn't want to get into. Shrugging the argument aside, wishing he would understand that this wasn't a time for thinking about such things, she whispered, 'Fuck me, Danny. Don't worry about my virtue. Don't worry about the consequences. Just fuck me.'

It was all the instruction he needed. He pushed into her with a fluid ease that made Charity want to scream. His thickness was broad, fighting against the inner muscles of her sex and thrilling her with the slippery rush of penetration. Her labia melted open for him and the pulse of her clitoris began to beat at a quicker pace. Charity had expected to close her eyes and languish in the bliss of this new sensation, but instead she found herself staring at Danny, sharing his pleasure and marvelling at the gift of joy he had so effortlessly bestowed.

His shaft continued to push into her, filling her more deeply than she would have dared imagine. The pulse within her beat with demanding urgency and she gasped for air as Danny transported her to unexpected degrees of pleasure. When he

144

was buried at his deepest, their stomachs touching, his pubic hairs pressing against her labia and the tip of his length nudging the neck of her womb, she could have happily screamed.

He held her like that for a moment as they savoured their union. It was difficult to read his eyes as darkness swabbed the sky, but Charity could see his approval. His wholehearted appreciation of the moment was a perfect reflection of her own delight, and when he began to withdraw, making the movement slow so she could feel every nuance of his cock, she finally released her breath in a drawn out sigh.

His hands were on her waist, holding her steady as he eased himself into her, but they moved and Charity thought nothing of the shift until he cupped her buttocks.

She gasped. Her rear was still protected by the sheer fabric of her underwear, but the pressure of his fingers was enough to remind her of the wicked discomfort inflicted earlier. Danny's strong hands agitated the switch marks and flavoured her excitement with a sting of unexpected pain. Fresh tremors bristled through the lips of her sex, surprising her with their bittersweet flavour. A sheen of perspiration beaded her brow and swathed her body, tearing her between extremes of guilt and pure joy. She noticed the questioning frown that wrinkled his brow and could only smile in response.

'I'm not hurting you, am I?' he croaked, and unable to explain what had happened or how she felt, Charity simply shook her head and encouraged him to penetrate her again.

He was a more skilled lover than she had dared to hope and his movements gradually became a slow and satisfying rhythm. Basking in the experience, wanting to scream with triumph as he continued to take her to undiscovered realms of pleasure, she realised his lovemaking was exactly what she needed. Aside from the discomfort of him clutching her buttocks it was the perfect moment she had anticipated and her delight came in escalating waves. Each penetration was deliberate and calculated for their maximum pleasure. Charity bit her lower lip to stop herself from crying out but still she could hear herself sobbing softly as Danny fucked her.

She threw back her head and stared up into an inky sky. The fact that night had fallen so quickly eluded her as she rubbed her clitoris against his erection and languished in fresh thrills of excitement. Her breasts swelled with each inhalation and the rush of arousal grew stronger each time she exhaled. The swell of orgasm rose within her, and sure that delaying her climax would make it better, she fought against the impulse to simply surrender. Her breath had turned to ragged pants and she could hear the same change in tone inflecting Danny's respiration.

His hands squeezed tighter. A part of her knew the pain wasn't caused deliberately, and she guessed he might have been more considerate if he'd known about the stripes on her buttocks, but that didn't stop her from reeling from the sensory overload and the pain sparked her first orgasm. The tumult of anguish was more than she could bear and she clenched her inner muscles, convulsed sharply against the bench, and then gave into the sweltering release of her climax.

Charity was amazed by the soaring delight of her release. She had written countless songs, praising the heights of passion and despairing over the agonies of lost love, but she had never thought she was writing about emotions of this intensity. It occurred to her that none of her songs had ever done justice to the extremes of emotion that were properly involved in a relationship, and then he was pushing into her again and all those tumbling notions were forced effortlessly to one side as she concentrated fully on the bliss of release.

She came back from a fugue of pure delight to discover that Danny was still fucking her slowly. His tempered passion was both exciting and maddening and she wished he would give some indication that this meant as much to him as it did to her. With his face held in shadows, and the light of the brightening moon now shining behind him, his mood was impossible to read.

'Coming,' he hissed stiffly, all the warning he could manage before his explosion spurted in a deep and torrential thrust. Charity thought she had been prepared for his ejaculation but the strength of it still surprised her. His shaft twitched and pulsed, a rush of viscous fluid doused her inner muscles, and she could feel a retaliating climax being torn from her. This time her pleasure had a strength that was untainted by the perverse pleasure of Todd's punishment, or the twisted enjoyment of remembering his discipline. This orgasm had a fullness that she believed could only have come from a wholesome experience and she held onto that thought as her euphoria took her to another disembodied fugue of unconsciousness.

They exchanged a sly smile, which spoke more than any words. He tidied up his clothes and found her jeans and discarded T-shirt, but she was happier to sit nearly naked, warming herself against him rather than bothering to dress. Still reeling from all the pleasures he had shown her, and only just getting her thoughts back to their normal order, Charity decided it was the way lovers should curl together after such immense satisfaction.

Danny shrugged off his jacket and gallantly draped it around her shoulders. There was a hesitant frown on his face and she waited patiently for him to speak first. She wondered if he was going to talk about the experience they had just shared, or mention that her backside seemed inordinately sensitive to the mildest caress.

'If you really are a virtuous maiden,' he began.

She nodded, smiling at the idea that he was now, at least, considering her revelation as a possibility. She felt no disappointment that he didn't want to discuss their lovemaking because she had already decided it was everything she wanted and needed, no analysis. 'Go on.'

'If you're really a virtuous maiden, and if vampires do exist.'

Silently, she encouraged him to continue.

'And if there's really a confrontation brewing between you and this coven.'

'Yes,' she said, beginning to wish he would get to his point.

'If all those things are true, why are we sitting on Hampstead Heath, in the dark, overlooking Highgate Cemetery?'

She opened her mouth, ready to tell him that it wasn't that dark, that Highgate Cemetery wasn't an issue, and that there was no immediate element of danger, but before she could Nick loomed out of the shadows with Lilah by his side.

Danny stiffened against her as she pulled the lapels of his jacket modestly around her exposed frame. She glared at the approaching vampires with genuine unease and clutched defensively at the crucifix that hung around her neck, and realised that they weren't just being visited by Nick and Lilah. Behind the two vampires stood a trio of scantily clad women.

And all five of them wore broad, bloody smiles.

Charity

Act II, Scene IV

'Hello Charity,' Lilah smiled sweetly. 'I thought we'd find you up here.'

'Who the hell is this?' Danny demanded.

Charity placed a hand on his thigh and prevented him from rising from the park bench. Shaking her head, she silently willed him to remain quiet and not draw the attention of the vampires. She felt painfully vulnerable because of her near-nudity but, because she knew it was the best hope of defence that Danny had against the vampires, she was determined not show her reservations in front of Lilah. 'You don't want to know who this is,' she said. 'You don't want to know her, or any of her friends.'

'On the contrary,' Lilah laughed. 'I don't think introductions would be out of place.' Addressing Danny, speaking in a low, pleasant voice, she said, 'My name is Lilah.' Pointing to each of her companions she added, 'This is Nick, Marcia, and Helen. And the commanding one at the back is my new girl, Wendy.'

Charity's stomach folded with trepidation. She couldn't imagine anything good coming out of this situation and wondered if this was the start of the confrontation she had been warned to expect. It crossed her mind that she should have kept her distance from Danny, just in case there was any validity in what Todd had told her, but she tried to put that thought out of her mind, scared that her doubts might get the better of her commonsense.

Lilah was oblivious to Charity's swirling thoughts, still

speaking to Danny, studying him with an appreciative leer. 'The five of us are vampires. And since we all know Charity is the virtuous one, that only leaves us needing to put a name to the man who's just been pounding his cock into her virtuous pussy.' Extending a hand, maintaining the deportment of a polite cocktail party hostess, she asked, 'What's your name, handsome?'

'Duh… Danny,' he stammered.

Lilah winked at him and smiled. 'That was quite an impressive show you just treated us to. Could we see a repeat performance? Maybe you could fuck her anally this time? Or get her virtuous mouth wrapped around that chunky little length of yours?'

Danny recoiled from her crudeness, and looked as though he was ready to say something by way of a reprimand, but Charity spoke over him. 'What do you want, Lilah?' she asked, standing up, putting herself between the vampire and her lover. 'Why have you come looking for me? Has it started already?'

'Looking for you?' Lilah laughed. 'Why would I come looking for you? If I wanted to find myself a cheap tart, I could just as easily have gone cruising around the Kings Cross area.'

Charity glared at her, infuriated by the insult and spluttering to think of a response, but ignoring the outrage inspired, but without lowering her gaze, Lilah snapped her fingers and barked commands to her subordinates.

Charity tried to retaliate, but there were too many of them and she was overpowered before she could bring herself to act. Someone pushed her and she stumbled back and sat heavily on the bench, while Marcia and Helen pulled Danny away. Charity tried to resume her footing and struggled to get off the seat, but Nick was holding one hand, the vampire called Wendy held her other, and Lilah towered over her. The jacket had been pulled away from her shoulders, tossed into the darkness somewhere, and the feeling of vulnerability bit more ferociously than ever before. Bitterly she realised her defeat had happened before she even had a chance to gain victory.

'How can you meet anyone's interpretation of the word virtuous?' Lilah asked scornfully. 'You couldn't keep your legs together if I bound you at the knees.'

Charity fought to snatch her hands from Nick and Wendy but they held her tightly and both possessed formidable strength. When Lilah stepped closer, ingratiating a thigh between Charity's parted legs, she realised she was going to remain at the mercy of the vampires until the woman deigned otherwise.

'Your boyfriend looked quite capable,' Lilah observed. There was a salacious lilt to her tone and her smile was offensively genial. 'He made you come, didn't he?'

Charity tried to close her legs but the vampire was preternaturally fast. She slapped a hand onto one thigh and pressed her knee against the other. Stooping so she could stroke her free hand over Charity's sex, tracing an icy finger against her still-smouldering labia, Lilah chuckled softly before raising the hand to her nose. Her nostrils briefly flared as she inhaled the musky scent of Charity's wet sex.

'He's just defiled you,' the vampire stated.

Charity was thankful that the night concealed her blushes and she tried to remain defiant. 'We made love,' she told Lilah, 'but Danny didn't defile me. There's a difference.'

Lilah nodded, still studying the wetness on her finger as it glistened beneath the moonlight. 'Maybe,' she conceded, dismissing the distinction as though unimportant, 'but this confirms that he had you. This smells like he's had you. I wonder if it tastes like that too?'

Charity shook her head, trying not to be excited by Lilah's

uncouth observations, and ready to tell the vampire she was a disgusting creature with a twisted outlook. But Nick and Wendy tightened their hold on her wrists and the sudden flair of pain stopped her from speaking. Then with a briskness that was daunting, their mistress shoved her glistening finger under Charity's nose.

'Tell me how it tastes,' Lilah suggested, and Charity glared at her, unable to conceal her resentment. But rather than being offended by the hatred she inspired, Lilah seemed to thrive on it. Her smile blossomed and her eyes shone with sadistic glee. 'Lick my finger,' she insisted, pushing it closer. 'Lick my finger and tell me how it tastes.'

Charity tried to turn away, but from her position on the bench it was impossible. The scent of Danny's seed and her own arousal had mingled together to make a rich and intoxicating blend, and while Lilah's suggestion was perversely sickening, Charity conceded that it was also obscenely tempting. Each time she drew breath she could detect the flavour of their lovemaking, and the idea of extending her tongue and licking the vampire's finger held an undeniable, shameful appeal. But she resisted the urge, and summoning her willpower she turned her face away and glanced in Danny's direction.

He stood in shadows with Marcia on one side of him and Helen on the other. There was obvious reluctance on his face, and what she believed was a genuine desire to break free from the vampires and come to her assistance, but Charity could also see other emotions struggling to take control. Marcia had one hand against his chest, stroking and exciting him with her casual caress. Helen, bolder and more eager to sample her victim, rubbed a hand over the crotch of his jeans. Both vampires had their mouths pressed at his throat as though ready to bite. Their lips looked full, bloody and red and their smiles were tipped with razor-sharp canines.

Lilah snapped her fingers, and Charity turned to face her. 'Tell me what it tastes like,' the vampire demanded. 'Tell me what it tastes like, or,' a wicked smile twisted her lips, 'or should I tell you?'

Before Charity could respond the finger was snatched from beneath her nose. She could still catch the lingering scent of their union, as though Lilah had brushed too close and glazed her upper lip with the perfume of their sex, but the aroma was no longer the force it had been. As she watched, Lilah lifted the wet finger to her mouth and licked the tip. Her overly sharp teeth weren't in evidence but Charity could see the scarlet lustre of her lips, and there was no mistaking the crimson shine that lit her eyes as she idly licked. There was also no way she could overlook the glee that illuminated Lilah's smile as she drew her tongue against the finger.

'It tastes like you had a wonderful time,' Lilah purred.

Charity turned away in disgust and frustration. She couldn't find words to explain the cause of her annoyance, but because Lilah had licked the juice from her fingers, she felt as though the woman had stolen something precious that belonged to her and Danny alone. She made another attempt to pull away from the bench but Nick and Wendy seemed determined that she wasn't going to escape.

'It tastes so good,' Lilah enthused, 'I think I want to drink it from the source.'

Aware of what the vampire was planning, outraged that the woman believed she could take such liberties with her, Charity tried to stop Lilah from kneeling between her legs. But as long as her hands were being held, and as long as Lilah forced her legs to remain apart, she knew there was no chance of bettering the vampire. Her efforts only served to help Lilah snatch the panties from her, and she knew she was completely naked and helpless with a vampire kneeling between her spread thighs.

'Look at these marks,' Lilah murmured, and Charity closed her eyes against tears of shame. A chilly finger was stroking against one buttock, the nail scratching the same path made by Todd's cruel switch. She tried to remain unmoved by the rush of warm discomfort, but it was a difficult battle and she felt sure she was going to lose before the inevitable struggle began. When Lilah stroked a second finger against her, scouring the line of a blazing weal, Charity had to bite her tongue to stop herself from gasping out loud.

'Has Toad Chalmers been teaching you a lesson in discipline?'

Charity glared at her with silent fury, then cast her glance in Danny's direction, her fear that he might have overheard Lilah's tactless remark quickly banished when she saw him struggling to keep himself distant from Marcia and Helen. The two vampires had started to undress him, Helen removing his shirt while Marcia unfastened the buttons of his jeans. His length, sticky and spent, was exposed to the night and both vampires were working hard to inspire his arousal. Watching his shaft grow thicker, and slowly begin to stand erect, Charity realised they wouldn't have to work much harder. The idea left her ill with jealousy and she made a renewed effort to pull herself free.

'Stop squirming,' Lilah demanded, but Charity ignored her. 'Stop squirming or I'll have Marcia and Helen take your boyfriend now.'

It was the threat she had been dreading and Charity held herself as still as she could. Nick and Wendy still held her wrists but she no longer struggled to break free, enduring their subtle kisses as they stroked their tongues against the sensitive flesh.

Lilah placed a cool hand on each of her victim's parted thigh and inched her face closer to Charity's sex. 'That's better,' she decided. 'There's no need for you to start going mental on us. We only want a little fun in the same vein that you've just been enjoying.'

Sickened by the persuasive tone of Lilah's voice, and the way her own excitement hatefully rose to that siren call, Charity glared defiantly up at the sky. She was trying to remain unmoved by the kisses to her wrists, and the maddening tickle of Lilah's nose as it nuzzled through the pubic curls over her labia. However, as much as she didn't want to be swayed by excitement, she couldn't stop her body from trembling with a vile anticipation.

'This is where we've been going wrong,' Nick laughed, and aware that he was addressing one of the others, Charity didn't bother to look at him. 'We spend our nights prowling graveyards, and are surprised when we don't find anything except other vampires. We should have thought to come to Hampstead Heath before. This is the place to find naked pop singers sitting on park benches.'

Wendy's laughter sounded forced and uneasy. Lilah's chuckle was more self-indulgent and Charity felt the mirth trembling against her sex lips. More than ever before she wanted to tear herself away from the vampires but arousal, and her fear for Danny's safety, had weakened her will. As much as she was loath to concede the fact, and sure that she would never admit the truth to another living soul, she realised her body craved Lilah's dark kiss.

The vampire's fingers stroked the soft flesh of her inner thighs, smoothing upwards and outwards and making her feel reluctantly receptive. The flesh of her labia tingled with eager need and her inner muscles trembled with a pale shadow of the excitement that Danny had inspired. Miserably, she glared at the vampire between her legs. Lilah's crimson gaze glimmered with menace. Snakelike, her tongue flicked across her lips, her eyes shone with fresh hunger, and then she was lowering her head.

Charity steeled herself against the threat of pleasure, vowing that she wouldn't succumb to the arousal the vampire inspired, but it was a futile argument. Lilah's tongue was cold and unwanted but it touched where Charity needed to be touched. Her labia were parted and teased, the sensitive flesh was tormented by Lilah's inquisitive kiss, and her sex was skilfully penetrated. Listening to the vampire's satisfied sigh, despising the note of approval she could hear and the mocking sound that lay beneath, Charity racked her brains to find some way to escape the humiliation before her will gave out and she surrendered completely, and the task became even more difficult when Lilah flicked the tip of her tongue against Charity's clitoris. A rush of unexpected delight left her shivering. She tightened her hands into fists, considered another attempt to pull away from Nick and Wendy, and then thought better of risking such a bold move. As though reading something of her thoughts, as though pre-empting her response, Nick and Wendy both squeezed her wrists. Nick stroked her arm, reaching for the swell of her breast and kneading it with a rough, uncaring caress. His hateful smile was simultaneously dangerous and appealing and she didn't know whether to cringe from him or melt beneath his seduction.

But the decision became unimportant when she felt the hateful intrusion of Wendy suckling her breast, her teeth poised over the thrust of her nipple, her eyes shining with hunger. Helpless, and no longer sure that she wanted to escape her tormentors, Charity tried valiantly not to lose herself in the pleasure. Her resolve was quickly weakening, and as the pleasures became stronger she realised she couldn't fight the vampires and her own dark needs.

'Sweet,' murmured Lilah, taking obvious pleasure from the flavour of Charity's sex. 'Was it just your pussy he had,' she enquired huskily, 'or did I misjudge your Danny? Did he take you anywhere else?'

Charity closed her eyes over tears of shame, wishing she were able to show her disgust, but that emotion now seemed beyond her range.

'No, I don't think he did,' Lilah ventured, her hands still on Charity's thighs whilst stroking her thumbs against the line of her labia. The chilly touch was an unbearable torment, unwanted but maddening and driving Charity to a frenzy of unsated lust. 'I don't think he would have dared to pop it up your arse,' Lilah mocked, 'but I'd love to know for sure.'

Charity guessed what was coming, but the knowledge came too late for her to respond. She shook her head, made a half-hearted attempt to tug away, and then realised that Lilah had already acted. The vampire lowered her face, pushing her tongue out as she moved, and slipping it into the tight ring of muscle of Charity's anus.

The shock was overwhelming and painfully exciting. The cool muscle slipped deeper into her forbidden hole, stunning her with the perverse pleasure and making her feel ill as the crescendo of an orgasm swelled inside her. Nick continued to fondle her right breast, his kisses chasing lightly over her wrist. Wendy carried on suckling her left breast; the threat of her bite causing a constant discomfort that was both agonising and arousing. But it was Lilah's tongue, wriggling deeper into her rectum, which had Charity teetering on the brink of orgasm. She drew a strangled gasp, chugging air and trying to deny the inexorable pleasure building in her loins. With a determined effort she tried not to think of Lilah's lips, puckered against the ring of her anus as the vampire forced her kiss deeper. But it was impossible to exorcise the image from her mind.

Powerless to resist, carried along by the thrill of so much stimulation, she couldn't help but give herself over to the orgasm when it struck. Her body was battered and buffeted by a headlong rush of pleasure and she heard herself scream into the night.

Lilah chuckled as she pulled herself away. She wiped the back of a hand against her lips without disguising her triumphant smile. 'He didn't take you up the arse, did he?' she goaded, meeting Charity's gaze, silently laughing in the face of her shame, Charity's cheeks flushing as she shook her head. 'He didn't fuck you there,' Lilah repeated, 'but I'll bet you wish he had.'

'Do you want me to rectify that oversight?' Nick suggested, and Charity's stomach folded again as she realised she was being torn between choices she didn't want to make. The vampires were treating her as though she was nothing more than a toy for their twisted entertainment, but she was making the situation worse by responding eagerly to their cruel torment. She was loath to suffer Nick's attention, and horrified by the idea that he might want to use her the way Lilah had suggested... but the idea fuelled her arousal.

Miserably, she decided she had made a mistake. She had been wrong to go with Danny; wrong to believe Faith and Hope when they told her that her virtue had nothing to do with her virginity; and wrong to ignore Todd when he tried to impress her with the seriousness of the threat the vampires posed. She had been wrong, and now she was going to pay for that foolishness.

'I'll get her ready for you,' Lilah told Nick, and without another word her head bobbed back between Charity's legs and the divine splendour of her tongue again touched the ring of her anus. This time she didn't stiffen from the attention or try to pull away; she knew what was coming and, although she knew it was vital that she try not to be swayed by the malicious teasing, she couldn't find the willpower to ignore such exquisite sensations.

Lilah sighed with obvious pleasure, and then moved her mouth back to Charity's sex. 'I think you should use her pussy,

Nick,' she breathed, and Charity felt the tremor of every word against her labia. 'I think you should use her pussy, take her to the brink, and then get her to beg you to fuck her arse.'

Nick sniggered. 'I can live with that suggestion,' he said, but Charity was beyond hearing, squirming beneath the tongue that slipped against her sex, hating and loving the divine experience, tears of self-loathing trailing down her cheeks. She glanced miserably in Danny's direction, appalled to find her excitement increased by what she saw.

Helen had tugged her own clothes free, exposing a breast and revealing the secrets of her sex. Marcia wasn't being as obvious but she had raised her skirt to show a length of glorious pale thigh, and the moonlike orb of one buttock. Trapped between the pair, still struggling but weakened from their superior power and the arousal they inspired, Danny stood no chance of resisting their wiles. His erection now stood hard in Marcia's hand with the glans swollen and dark as it pushed out from the vampire's fist. Although she could see reluctance in the defensive poise of his body language, Charity knew he would have to submit to whatever they demanded, and comparing his dilemma to her own, she realised she couldn't blame him for responding as she had.

With a malicious giggle Marcia stroked the swollen end of Danny's hardness between Helen's breasts, both vampires shivering theatrically as they tormented Charity's lover. Their wicked excitement grew more obvious when Helen turned her back, bent over, and guided Danny's cock to her sex.

'She's almost ready for you,' Lilah told Nick, but instead of answering he made a muffled exclamation and bolted from the bench. Charity glanced up, and was shocked to see him fleeing into the darkness, and then her other hand was free and Wendy was cursing and stumbling away, too.

'How many times do I have to save you?' Todd demanded, pushing Lilah from between Charity's legs and threw her towards Helen and Marcia. Lilah made a half-hearted lunge back in his direction but he was wielding a sturdy wooden cross, and the vampire backed away from him with her teeth bared in a sneer.

Todd sat down on the bench beside Charity, draping a jacket around her bare shoulders without once lowering his gaze from the vampires. 'At the risk of sounding exceptionally dense,' he said, 'would you care to tell me what's going on here?'

Charity glowered at Lilah. 'That bitch has come for me again,' she told him.

Lilah sniffed with obvious disdain. 'Come for you?' she scoffed, nodding for Marcia and Helen to tighten their hold on Danny. 'I haven't come for you. You're my brother's pet project, and before the night is over he's going to have you. No, I've come to take your boyfriend.'

Charity tried to get up from the bench but Todd held her back. 'If you're so certain your brother is going to be triumphant, why do you need Danny?' she challenged, glaring defiantly at the vampire, determined that she was now beyond being intimidated by her.

Lilah glanced at Danny, and then smirked. 'He's what I came here for,' she explained. 'He's my bargaining chip. He's my bargaining chip, and I'm keeping hold of him to make sure you do exactly as I tell you.'

'You aren't going to win, Lilah,' Todd said calmly.

'No,' she agreed, 'I'm not going to win. My brother's going to do that.' She turned to the remainder of her coven, snapping her fingers and effortlessly commanding their attention. 'And speaking of my brother, I believe he wants us at his beck and call this evening. Let's not keep him waiting.' With that said, she led her coven away from the heath.

Interlude

Part Four

It was only when the sun went down that Angela started to feel herself again, but she didn't associate the two facts. It was easier to believe that the rise in her spirits, and the dissipation of her lingering hangover, was caused by the appearance of the mysterious stranger. Tall, handsome and undeniably sinister, he appeared at the mansion's door with his dark-skinned girlfriend hanging on his arm. As Angela welcomed him inside, artfully ignoring the consideration that she didn't know their names, she shrugged off the last vestiges of the day's weariness and found herself remembering the excitement she had enjoyed the previous evening. If there'd been a mirror nearby she would have seen a hungry smile creep across her lips.

Viv was by her side and she smiled easily for the pair as Angela welcomed them. Her hair was the usual disarray of designer-untidy dreadlocks, but because she'd been told they would be meeting a fan, she made an extra effort and wore coal-black eye shadow and charcoal lip-gloss. A grey skirt, off-the-shoulder jumper and laddered stockings completed the image of gothic punk that the drummer always managed so well. 'I hear you're anxious to meet us,' she said, allowing the stranger to gallantly kiss her hand. 'Are you a big fan of BloodLust?'

His sly smile sparkled but it was the closest he came to offering a reply. Stealing an arm around her waist, pulling her into an intimate embrace and pressing his mouth to her bare shoulder, he seemed to think that was sufficient response.

Angela had expected him to make his presence felt with some sort of bold introduction, and made no comment as the pair melded together in the ostentatious entrance hall. She heard Viv's gasp, wondered briefly if she was listening to cries of protest or sighs of surrender, then her fleeting concern was banished when she saw the drummer wrap her arms around the stranger in an eager cinch. One stockinged leg snaked behind his back and Viv's skirt was hitched high enough to reveal a sliver of pale thigh. Her hips gyrated rhythmically when she rubbed her crotch daringly against him and her fingers raked his back as she tried to hold him closer. With obvious delight she sighed and gave herself to his lingering kiss.

'I can smell weed,' the mulatto observed. 'Do I go through there?' She was pointing toward the downstairs rec room – the spacious lounge they'd furnished with a TV, a suite of comfortable settees and a sound system to rival the basement's recording studio – and Angela nodded. Charity's lyrics were screaming from the speakers in the room and, because the door was ajar, Angela thought it looked like the only possible place where they could be having their impromptu get together. But although she sniffed quizzically she couldn't detect the telltale aroma of Lauren's herbal cigarettes, and supposed the mulatto might have simply been making an educated guess and reasoning that, with this being a party hosted by successful musicians, the presence of marijuana was fairly likely. The only other explanation she could think of was that the woman had an incredibly perceptive sense of smell, but didn't give the matter any greater consideration, deciding the stranger's girlfriend wasn't really of any interest. 'Yeah, through there,' she said, shrugging indolently. 'Go ahead if you like. We'll be along in a minute.'

Viv was panting and writhing against the stranger and

162

clearly basking in the intimacy of his introductory kiss. Angela could hear the wet sounds of their exchange, not missing the urgency that rang in Viv's breathless tone or the commanding growls of the man who held her. Wishing she could be a part of what they were sharing, but knowing Viv would never forgive her for intruding, she reluctantly turned her back on the pair and followed the mulatto into the rec room.

Lauren sat cross-legged on one settee, wearing a pair of sweat-suit pants and a low-cut top in the same pastel pink.

Angela knew that, while she was currently being lauded as one of the best backsides in pop music, Lauren was feted for her boobs. Dressing to show off her best assets she sat with faux innocence, as though she didn't know her bounteous breasts looked set to spill from the neckline of her top. The shadows of her areolae darkened the pale jersey fabric and the thrust of her nipples was clearly visible.

She casually rolled a joint before twisting the tip tight then lighting it. Catching her breath, and holding it with an air of practiced skill, she exhaled a stream of sweet-smelling smoke as she glanced up and nodded a mellow greeting to Angela and the mulatto. With a typical lack of tact she fixed her sleepy gaze on the visitor and asked, 'Are you with the superstud?'

The mulatto glanced back over her shoulder in the direction of the stranger and Viv, and then strolling to Lauren's side, plucking the joint from her fingers and sucking on it, she held the smoke for a moment before replying. 'Who says he's a superstud?'

Lauren pointed at Angela. 'She says he's the best lay she's ever experienced. She says if we play along for him, like good little girls, we might get a chance to find out how great he is.'

Angela blushed, but at the same time she could feel her sex clench hungrily. Every thrilling memory that had made the previous evening so memorable came rushing back in a giddy swirl of recollection. Lauren's casual assessment of their

163

expectations added a raw arousal to those thoughts and she clenched her thighs together in a bid to stave off the excitement. Her sex lips felt suddenly damp and, with her interest now focused on Lauren and the mulatto, Angela drew a heavy breath as the pair shared the joint.

'He's not the best lay ever,' the mulatto demurred, nodding in the direction of the door to indicate the subject of her sentence, then tilting her jaw arrogantly she took another draw from the cigarette before whispering, 'I am.'

'...You placed your fingers against my breast; You made me think our love was blessed; Then you tore the heart from outta my chest...'

Charity's lyrics screamed from the CD player, the volume blaring so loud that Angela missed Lauren's response. But although she couldn't hear what they were saying, it would have been impossible to overlook the bass player's sultry smile or the seductive invitation that sparkled in her eyes. And more than that, Angela couldn't miss the sly acquiescence involved when the mulatto nodded.

'You're the best?' Lauren asked.

Angela could just hear her voice over the wail of the music as it subsided from the forceful volume of the chorus.

There was the hint of a challenge in Lauren's tone as she pressed, 'Am I supposed to accept that statement on face value?'

The mulatto shrugged, and with a daring glint in her eye she held Lauren's gaze and asked, 'Would you care to find out how good I am?'

'Why the hell not?' Lauren said, feigning indifference, making it seem as though she didn't care one way or the other. She dropped her joint into an ashtray and nodded an invitation for the dark-skinned girl to join her on the settee.

And that, Angela thought as another tight bolt of arousal spiked her gut, was all it took. Within less than a minute the house had gone from an air of muted expectation to almost orgiastic chaos. The air was thick with the tension of arousal and she knew the dense atmosphere had nothing to do with the cloying smoke from Lauren's cigarette. Glancing back into the hallway she saw that Viv and the stranger were now embroiled on the floor. Her blouse had been torn open, the milky flesh of both breasts was clearly visible, and the stranger was pressing himself urgently between her legs. On the settee in the rec room, indecently oblivious to the danger of being watched, Lauren and the mulatto had become greedily intertwined. Lauren's low-cut top was pulled aside, one glorious breast exposed to the room, and the dark-skinned visitor worked her tongue greedily against the nipple.

A part of Angela wanted to feel peeved that she was being overlooked, but she couldn't bring herself to harbour such an inappropriate emotion. Admittedly she would rather the stranger was with her instead of Viv, and she conceded that she might have missed an opportunity in not being more welcoming to the mulatto, but she knew there would be time for that before the evening was over and she felt confident that both Viv and Lauren would be indebted to her for introducing them to this fiercely capable man and his partner.

Pleased that the party was working out, she went to the kitchen and found herself a bottle of Danny's lager. The respite gave her enough time to wonder where her brother might be, and why both Charity and Todd had disappeared from the house, but because she knew the answers to those questions weren't going to be immediately forthcoming, she didn't bother worrying. Instead, she simply thanked good fortune that she, Viv and Lauren had been left alone in the house this evening and she idly speculated about how much satisfaction she could wring from the night.

The music was loud enough to echo throughout the house but it didn't quite drown out Viv's cries when she reached her first climax.

'Yes! Yes! Yes!' she shrieked, and Angela was stung by a brief pang of envy.

'Yes! Yes! Yes!' Viv proclaimed.

Hurrying back to join them, anxious that she wouldn't be overlooked, Angela wasn't surprised to find that Viv and the stranger were still in the hall. He remained between her spread thighs, sliding forcefully in and out while she trembled beneath him in the throes of ecstasy. A glance into the rec room showed that Lauren and the mulatto were being equally uninhibited and Angela almost dropped her beer with surprise. The dark-skinned woman had assumed a dominant pose over Lauren, pressing her bare sex against the bass player's face. The figure-hugging dress she had worn was now a discarded rag hanging from the arm of one settee. The mulatto moved with a lithe grace that reminded Angela of the dancers they used on stage and video. She arched her back through extremes of pleasure and then curled over so she could dart her tongue between Lauren's legs, the bass player sighing with mounting delight.

'Didn't I promise you this pleasure?' the stranger chuckled, taking Angela in his embrace, his mouth, as cool as iced water, brushing against her neck. He positioned himself behind her and she was tormented by the thrust of his erection pressing against her skirt.

Angela hadn't noticed that he and Viv had finished and she glanced coyly at her spent friend. Viv lay on the marble floor of the hallway, her skirt hitched up to her waist, her breasts exposed and her legs still spread as she squirmed happily through the last throes of an orgasm. Her sex was visible and Angela could see the viscous trail of the stranger's semen seeping from her friend's pussy lips. The sight made her catch a startled breath as another bolt of arousal buried itself in the pit of her stomach, and she observed the other

166

details; the vicious bite marks that marred Viv's breasts, the scratch marks on her inner thighs and the purple love-bite that now blossomed on her throat.

'Aren't I delivering on all those promises I made last night?' he pressed, and she shivered at the sound of his voice. He had a way of speaking that filled her with unbidden lust and she knew, whatever he asked of her, she wouldn't be able to refuse. But determined that she wouldn't be seen to be easy or pliant, Angela forced herself to remain momentarily aloof.

'No,' she said coolly, 'you haven't delivered on any of those promises you made last night.'

She felt his embrace grow stiff with annoyance.

'Last night you showed me pleasures I'd never imagined,' she remembered. 'But before we parted you promised me more. You promised me more pleasure than I would believe possible and you haven't delivered on that promise yet. Are you going to?'

His laughter was appreciative and indulgent. 'You're a mercenary after my own heart,' he told her. 'And, in answer to your question, of course I'm going to deliver on that promise. That's why I have you in my arms right now.'

She held her breath, her heart pounding as he reached for her skirt. Aware of how the evening was going to develop, confident of the pleasures she was going to enjoy, Angela hadn't bothered to wear knickers. The stranger's chilly fingers gracefully caressed her bare buttocks and stole briefly against her labia. She swallowed, infuriated by the way he sparked her arousal and anxious to sate the need he instantly generated. Glancing back over her shoulder, watching the crimson glint that sparkled hungrily in his eyes, she allowed him to press his bite against her throat as he fed his erection between her legs, the implications frighteningly obvious when he moved the tip from her pussy lips to the taut muscle of her anus.

Angela opened her eyes wide with a pang of unease. She glanced doubtfully down at Viv but the drummer simply lay on the floor, still murmuring meaningless words of gratitude as she writhed against the marble. In the rec room Angela could see that Lauren was all but spent beneath the dark-skinned woman.

'You did want more, didn't you?' the stranger asked, one hand cupping her breast, the other holding his erection as he pushed slowly forward. The muscle of her anus was stretched lightly, ready to accept his engorged length and tingling with a thousand deliciously dark associations. 'I don't just want more; I'm demanding it,' she gasped, trying to steel herself in readiness.

The stranger stiffened again, and then nodded, moving his hand from her breast, leaving it to ache with an unsatisfied need for attention. He snapped his fingers and in the rec room the mulatto glanced immediately in his direction.

At some point during their time together the bass player had lost her clothes. Lauren's pale body was sprawled over one settee, looking like a match for the discarded dress that hung over the arm. Like Viv, her throat and breasts were marked with the cherry-red memories of bites and scratches, but judging by the contented smile on the bass player's face none of the abrasions were causing her any discomfort.

Yet it wasn't Lauren the stranger was summoning, and when he snapped his fingers again the mulatto came out into the hall. Angela felt no shame that the woman could see her in such a compromising position, and only a flicker of hesitation when the stranger indicated for his companion to kneel down. She could sense what was coming, and although she knew many would consider it excess and a depravity, it was exactly what she wanted.

The mulatto touched her tongue against Angela's sex. Her lips and mouth were as cool as the strangers but that didn't stop her from inflicting a pleasure that left Angela breathless. She chased the tip of her tongue against febrile labia, plundering between the soft folds of flesh before teasing the nub of her clitoris.

Angela choked back a cry of gratitude, and the stranger began to ease forward, his length pushing hard against the centre of her anus, and she could feel herself opening in readiness for him. Seeming content his shaft was in the right place, and no longer needing to direct his subordinate, the stranger cupped both Angela's breasts and kneaded them as he started to slowly penetrate her rear.

She bit back a scream of elation and trembled between the pair of them. The mulatto had a hand on each thigh, scourging her nose through Angela's pubic mound as she diligently worked with her tongue. She flicked the dewy lips of Angela's labia, occasionally pushing inside and exciting her clitoris, but she was also lubricating the stranger's partly embedded cock. Angela felt the woman's mouth brush against her anus, heard the man behind her sigh when his shaft was teased by the woman's tongue, and thought she had never been involved in anything so wonderfully hedonistic. The escalating euphoria made her want to scream in anticipation of the climax she knew they would squeeze from her.

'You've made this so easy for me,' the stranger murmured. 'I really don't know how to thank you.'

She considered telling him that he was already thanking her, and although she didn't understand what it was she'd made easy for him, she was happy he was pleased with her efforts. But her side of the conversation only existed within her own mind, and even if he had given her the chance to speak she didn't think she would have been able to find the energy for the words. His cock was ploughing deeper into her rear, amazing her with the wealth of sensations he was creating, and transporting her to a climax she hadn't dared to anticipate. The mulatto's tongue was stroking miracles through her pussy, pushing deeper, taunting her, and Angela knew the first of her orgasms was close.

When the stranger pressed his bite against her throat, and she felt the wicked pain of his teeth burrowing into her, the first climax of the evening shuddered through her body. It scared her that she could feel him drinking, the coppery scent of blood flavoured each breath she took and she realised he was having her in a way that no man had ever taken her before, but she couldn't bring herself to ask him to stop. Another climax swelled between her legs, she knew the orgasm was going to be cataclysmic, and all that mattered was wringing that final pulse of pleasure from him.

Angela was alone when consciousness returned, a blissful smile spreading her lips and the ache of satisfaction throbbing from between her thighs. She didn't know if the climax had come from the mulatto's tongue, the stranger's cock, or the penetrating bite against her throat. Whatever the cause, she knew it had induced an orgasm strong enough to leave her unconscious.

'...*You had me day and night without any rest; You said our loving was the world's fucking best; Then you tore the heart from outta my chest...*'

The lyrics of the song were no indicator as to how long she'd been laying on the floor. The CD player was invariably set to play tracks in a random order, sometimes taking a couple of hours before repeating a song, and occasionally playing the same one immediately as soon as it had finished. And a glance at the grandfather clock in the hall was no help because, aside from the fact that it had been after sunset, she didn't know what time her guests had arrived at the house.

'Yes! Yes! Yes!'

She looked into the rec room and saw that Viv and the

mulatto were locked in a passionate embrace, their faces buried between the other's legs. Both looked to be in the throes of absolute joy and their elation was only ended when Viv threw herself back and struggled against the carpet in a fit of delighted elation.

Less frantic, but no less intimate, the stranger and Lauren sat side by side on the settee. She had relit her discarded joint from earlier and, while she drew on the remaining roach, the stranger kissed her throat and fingered her pussy. The enjoyment was clear in Lauren's sparkling smile and her usually sleepy eyes were bright with the thrill of impending pleasure. When the stranger pressed his kiss deeper against her throat, making her stiffen on the settee, Angela realised the bass player had just been taken to another extreme of satisfaction.

Gingerly, Angela struggled to get to her legs and started heading towards the rec room, wondering if her body was sufficiently recovered to endure more of the pair's skilful play. The mulatto glanced up as she entered the room and then her gaze shifted behind Angela and into the hall. A frown pursed her full, glossed lips. 'Sir,' the mulatto breathed, nodding at the grandfather clock, 'it's time for us to go.'

'Already?'

'Your sister wants you to see her champion perform again,' she sneered, 'and I've got an errand to run with the rest of the coven.'

Angela saw obvious reluctance on the stranger's face as he nodded and extricated his fingers from Lauren's sex. Still cresting on the wave of a lingering orgasm, the bass player didn't seem to notice he had stopped teasing her pussy.

'Where are you going?' Angela demanded. 'The party's barely started. I thought you'd be here for the remainder of the night, or longer.'

The stranger shook his head. Moving easily to her side,

cupping her face in his hands, he kissed her lightly on the lips. 'We'll only be away for a short while. I have other things to attend to but I'll be back before the night's over. I might even have some other friends with me who could enjoy playing these games.'

Angela regarded him doubtfully. 'Was that all you wanted from me?' she asked softly. She glanced at Lauren and Viv's spent bodies, catching a tight breath and marvelling at the tawdry carnage the stranger and his girlfriend had left in their wake. 'Was that all you wanted from us?' she amended.

He shook his head. 'It wasn't quite all I wanted,' he admitted. 'But I have to admit it's been very satisfying so far.' Speaking solemnly, addressing her with deadly earnest, he added, 'There's one more small favour you'll do for me before the night's over.'

Angela nodded, sharing his certainty that she would do his bidding. 'Whatever you ask,' she promised. 'Anything.'

He paused at the door only to wait for the mulatto to slip the scanty dress back over her slender frame. 'Your lead singer, Charity, you didn't tell her about this meeting of ours, did you?'

'You told me not to,' Angela reminded him. 'And I always stick to my side of a bargain.'

'Of course you do.' His smile was perfunctory as he glanced at Viv and Lauren, spent and listless. 'I'll be returning this evening, and I might need your assistance. You can do that for me, can't you?'

From the corner of her eye Angela saw that Viv and Lauren had started to rise from their exhausted euphoria and were eagerly nodding. Her own reply was a mere formality but she knew she was speaking for the three of them when she answered. 'Whatever you want,' she assured him. 'We'll be there for you.'

Charity

Act III, Scene I

Todd took her into the house through the building's back door. The heavy thump of music came from the rec room, along with the sounds of what she guessed were Angela, Viv and Lauren holding a comparatively subdued party. As he hauled her through the kitchen and along one of the more discreet corridors, Charity was thankful he had spared her the humiliation of being exhibited past her fellow band members. It would be bad enough having the other girls see her suffering this indignity but the idea of their guests witnessing her predicament left her cold with dread.

'You can't keep punishing me like this,' she complained.

'Damned right I can't,' Todd snorted. 'And I'll stop as soon as we've got the message through your thick hide.'

She made a final attempt to pull away from him, loath to subject herself to his hateful discipline again, but he was far more powerful and he dragged her into his office without any show of effort, then while Charity crouched miserably on the chesterfield he locked the door and walked over to the bar. She didn't bother turning to watch as he poured himself a glass of scotch and lit a cigar.

'Faith, Hope and Charity,' he declared, his voice laden with contempt, and from the night-mirrored surface of the French windows she saw him raise his glass in a mock salute. 'And the greatest of these is Charity. The greatest what, I wonder? The greatest pain in the arse? The greatest one for ignoring instructions and just doing whatever the hell she pleases?

The greatest one for spreading her legs for members of the covens?'

Charity turned to glare at him. She was naked, cold and miserable and his insults brought her to the brink of tears. But determined that he wouldn't see her upset, she asked, 'Is this your way of helping me recover from the trauma of being attacked by vampires?'

'Didn't I rescue you?' His glare was filled with fury and she could hear that he struggled not to add the word 'again' to his response. 'If you'd bloody listened to me there'd be no need to help you deal with that particular trauma. If you'd bloody listened to me I wouldn't have had to bring you back here for a spanking.'

She opened her mouth, ready to explain what had happened and tell him that he had no right to be shouting, but his use of the word 'spanking' made her hesitate and wonder if she should tell him that she wasn't going to endure that sort of treatment, but he didn't allow her the chance to speak. With unquestionable authority he slammed his glass down, stubbed his cigar on the top of the bar, and dropped by Charity's side on the chesterfield.

She considered struggling away from him, then realised it wouldn't do her any good. When Todd grabbed one wrist and forced her across his lap she fell into the position as though it was natural for them. Perversely, she thought, something did feel right about having her breasts pressed against his thighs as she surrendered. And she couldn't deny there was an excitement in having her bare backside raised for him. Each time she'd been forced to endure this mistreatment before she fought an instinctive impulse to enjoy the experience. Now, sure that she didn't deserve this punishment, and still smouldering from the heat that had seared through her loins on Hampstead Heath, she decided it was only fitting that she try and take some pleasure from

Todd's discipline. It was a twisted idea, viciously appealing on a dark, rudimentary level, but she couldn't shake the notion that it was the right thing to do.

'Let's see if we can get the message through to you this time,' he growled, but Charity barely heard him. His hand was on her bottom, stroking one cheek and stimulating the peach-like orb. It was all too easy to submit to the prickle of arousal and she held herself rigid for fear that Todd might notice the effect he inspired, and there was no respite from her excitement when he moved his hand away and raised it in the air. She held her breath and waited for the belittling pleasure of being spanked.

'Tell me you're sorry for putting yourself in jeopardy.'

She despised the condescending way he demanded her apology and was appalled that she found the humiliation thrilling. Controlling her breath, unwilling for him to hear the ragged tone of her respiration, she wished he would hurry up and conclude the indignity so she could put the episode behind her. There was an unsatisfied pulse beating between her legs and she quietly craved the private sanctuary of her bedroom so she could exorcise that insidious heat.

'Tell me you're sorry,' Todd insisted.

Keeping her voice low, trying to hide the mounting arousal she knew would be clear in her voice, Charity whispered, 'I'm sorry, Todd. I'm sorry.'

He smacked her bottom. The first slap was heavier than she expected and she stiffened against him. His palm warmed an entire cheek and she knew it would only take a few more blows before she was brought to a state of lascivious need. The idea left her weak with desire and she quietly cringed from the wicked gluttony of her sexual appetite, but more unnerving was the horror that Todd might notice her response.

He spanked her again, and this time Charity couldn't contain a small cry. Both cheeks were already blushing and that mild heat was slowly encroaching towards her sex. The pulse between her legs beat with a fluid ease and she realised he had already sparked her longing. Quivering against him, secretly enjoying the humiliation of each slap while despising it at the same time, she held her breath as she waited for the next blow.

'Tell me you're still prepared to face the dark one,' he demanded.

A glance in the shiny black surface of the French windows reflected the scene perfectly, and Charity could have sobbed when she realised how low she had sunk. Todd held one hand high, ready to slap again, and she could see her own naked body curled over his legs. The image made her feel simultaneously embarrassed and excited: thrilling her with a sense of audacity while crushing her with the shame of her predicament. Wrenching her gaze away, not sure she could watch the humiliation of having his hand land against her rear, she closed her eyes and braced herself for the impact of his palm.

'Tell me you're still prepared to face the dark one,' he repeated.

'I'm ready,' she croaked.

Todd drew a sharp breath and landed his hand with more force than before. Both cheeks were bristling from the sting of the punishment's aftermath but she was no longer trying to deny the pleasure. Her body felt alive and vibrant, and while this wasn't the wholesome pleasure she had surrendered to with Danny, she knew it was nothing like the sadistic enjoyment the vampires inspired. Her clitoris throbbed dully and, as she held herself still, she was made painfully aware of the greedy cramps that gripped her loins.

'Are you genuinely ready to face the dark one?' Todd asked. 'Or are you just saying that because you think it's what I want to hear?'

Charity struggled to follow the question, and then couldn't decide how best to respond. She hoped she was ready for the impending confrontation, but she couldn't honestly say that she was prepared. Fretting that he might punish her for not responding, secretly hoping the tips of his fingers might brush her sex the next time he struck, she writhed against him as she tried to formulate an answer.

'Are you genuinely ready to face the dark one?'

Not daring to speak, unable to find the breath for words, she nodded.

He brought his hand down again, and Charity lifted her head and exhaled noisily. 'I'm ready,' she gasped. 'I'm genuinely ready.' Her pussy lips felt as though they'd already melted open for him and she couldn't bring herself to imagine how her body might respond if he continued to strike her rear. It was obvious that Todd had noticed her arousal because the pressure of his erection was, once again, pressing up from his lap, nudging her tummy.

Sickened and amazed by the discovery, she told herself it would be wisest to ignore his response. Yet although she didn't want to think that her suffering was giving him pleasure, she felt pleased that she was responsible for his arousal. Trying to make the movement innocent, and quietly savouring her own gall, she shifted position on his lap and gently rubbed her side against him.

Todd's length twitched forcefully, and he drew a sharp breath and landed his hand heavier than before. She squealed with the impact, her sex felt wetter than ever and her inner muscles trembled with hungry anticipation.

Todd stood up quickly, almost throwing her from his lap in the process, and quickly turned his face away from hers. Puddled on the floor, startled by the sudden change from being across his knee to being sprawled on the carpet, Charity didn't try to meet his eyes. There was no doubt in her mind that she would see a reflection of her own libidinous appetite in his expression and that was something she didn't want to witness.

'I do believe you've outgrown our spanking sessions,' he said stiffly, and she shivered, but made no attempt to rise from the floor. He was still angry with her and she knew he would only prolong her discipline if she stood up without his permission.

'Of course I've outgrown the frickin' spanking sessions,' she returned bitterly. 'I've been trying to tell you that much since you dragged me in here yesterday.'

He either wasn't listening, or simply wasn't paying attention. Walking back to the bar, drinking swiftly from his scotch glass, he snatched the riding crop that was kept there and sliced it through the air. She guessed her affect on him had been greater than he was admitting because, when he used the switch to point at her, she noticed the tip wavered a lot more than it had previously. Everything else about his composure seemed calm and in place, but the trembling end of the crop seemed to indicate that he was concealing his excitement.

'Get on all fours,' he demanded. 'We'll have to do this more formally.'

She shook her head but knew he wasn't going to accept any refusal, and being honest with herself she knew she wasn't really going to offer one. A part of her wanted to steal another glance in the mirrored surface of the French windows, and watch as she supplicated herself for him in the centre of the room, but she didn't dare. It had been enough to see what she looked like when she was bent over Todd's lap and she didn't think she needed to see any more. Obeying without thought, not dwelling on the sensations of holding her bottom high, or the ache of her tingling nipples as they hung beneath her, she did as he demanded and got down on all fours.

Todd stepped behind her and drew a deep breath. She was attuned to every detail in the house, from the fragrance of his cigars to the distant music that came from the rec room. She could detect the scent of an expensive cologne, the creak of Todd's leather shoes as he shifted his weight from one foot to the other, and the throaty undercurrent to his respiration. His arousal so clearly matched her own that she couldn't allow herself to think about their similarities. When he tested the switch, slicing it through the air, she was grateful that the whistle of leather cut cleanly through her thoughts. If she had brooded on their matching needs for much longer, she feared she might have come to a conclusion that would be ruinous for both of them.

'As enjoyable as these lessons might be,' he said sternly, 'you really do need to start learning from them.'

Charity said nothing; her only sound a small grunt of protest when he swatted the crop across her buttocks. The flare of pain was enormous, blazing across both cheeks and sending a pernicious heat quivering through her pussy lips. The pulse of her clitoris was now in perfect rhythm to the dramatic pounding that beat through her temples and she marvelled over the fact that her body was held on a tightrope of pleasure and pain. Perspiration glistened on her brow and her breasts, back and buttocks, and between her thighs she could feel the musky warmth of arousal seeping from her sex.

'Are you going to start learning from these lessons?'

He gave her no opportunity to respond, even if she could have thought of an appropriate answer. The switch bit sharply across the top of her thighs, branding a ferocious wire of pain and leaving her breathless. The tears she'd been trying to blink back came with a sudden rush and she frantically wiped them away with the back of her hand. Todd slashed the crop repeatedly, filling the room with the brisk whistles of each blow. Charity stiffened and melted every time the switch struck, and rather than suffering the glowing pleasure of his hand warming her bottom, she could feel herself succumbing to a feverish heat that was like a symptom of her depraved appetite.

'Are you going to start learning?'

Her teeth clenched and she didn't know if she was fighting the pain or the threat of an orgasm. Whichever it was, she knew she was losing the battle and bit her lower lip to stop from sobbing in despair.

'Are you going to learn from this lesson?'

'What do you want me to learn?' she gasped, her voice husky with need and her forearms aching from the exertion of staying on all fours. 'If you tell me what lesson you're trying to teach me I might stand a chance of getting it.'

He paused and she sensed a change in his mood. Stiff with readiness for the next blow she waited through an agony of silence as she braced herself for another punishing welt. Glancing in the reflection of the French windows, mortified by the sight of her naked body kneeling on the floor and waiting for Todd's discipline, she realised he was no longer brandishing the crop to punish her bottom with it.

'This is wrong,' he said quietly.

She started to turn, wondering what had changed his mind, but he acted before she could glance back over her shoulder. His hand snatched her sex and his fingers slipped between her labia. Charity thought she had been close to the brink of an orgasm before but this intimate contact took her to another realm of pleasure. He was touching her more closely than she had hoped, the tips of his fingers squeezing between the lips of her sex and thrilling her with unbidden excitement. The temptation to wriggle, and try to ingratiate his fingertips deeper, was almost unbearable. She bit harder on her lower lip and forced herself to remain motionless as he continued to slide his hand against her sex.

'You're wet and it's the wrong response,' he admonished, and she heard the words but didn't understand what he was saying.

The confusion made her want to sob but she was loath to let Todd Chalmers see he had reduced her to tears. 'What are you talking about?' she asked, wiping a hand across her face, smudging the tears that had already meandered down her cheeks. 'What's wrong with the way I'm responding?'

He squirmed his fingers against her and it was all she could do to choke back a whimper of delight. Her thighs trembled with the effort of holding her position and suppressing an orgasm. She didn't know if it was accidental or deliberate but the tip of his thumb rubbed over her pulsing clitoris, the subtle frisson almost enough to make her collapse on the floor.

'This is wrong,' he insisted with a weary sigh. 'You're being punished, but instead of suffering you're enjoying the damned process. Giving yourself over to the pleasure will let the dark one win, and that's the last thing we want, isn't it?'

Charity could have argued that the last thing she wanted right now was a sanctimonious reminder about how she could best defeat the dark one, but she didn't think that would be a constructive way to continue the discussion. 'The punishment excites me,' she admitted miserably. 'The punishment excites me more than I would have believed and I don't know how else to respond.' Turning to glance back over her shoulder, enjoying the sight of his fingers disappearing between the valley of her buttocks, she gave him a watery smile. 'How else am I expected to respond if it excites me so much?'

He snatched his hand away, leaving her to feel hollow, empty and pathetic. When the crop struck again she fought against the call of its vicious sting and realised she was on the verge of losing her battle against the swelling orgasm. He only needed to deliver one more blow and she was suddenly lost in the sensory overload of her climax.

Her insides convulsed and the ache in her breasts and clitoris became a glorious swelling that erupted in a molten flow. She never knew if she cried out but she didn't doubt that Todd was aware of her release. A glance in the mirrored surface of the French windows told her he was watching intently and she didn't think he could have missed seeing the wetness as it seeped down her thighs or the flushed complexion of her face and neck. However, instead of feeling any of the shame or guilt she had expected, Charity could only acknowledge a sensation of relief and immense satisfaction.

'Well done,' Todd said quietly.

She regarded him through a misty haze of bliss, not sure why he was congratulating her, or what she might have done to earn his approval. She briefly wondered if she had missed a part of the conversation, and if she had said something profound or appropriate as she shuddered through her climax, but the idea didn't seem very likely so she brushed it from her thoughts.

'Very well done,' he repeated.

'What did I do?'

He tossed the crop away and encouraged her to climb from her demeaning position on the floor. 'It's about time you admitted that truth aloud,' he said, guiding her to the chesterfield, tactfully helping her to sit so that she didn't rekindle the discomfort of her freshly striped rear. 'It's been long overdue.' He sounded smugly pleased with himself and Charity was both charmed and repulsed by his hearty smile. 'Now you know that punishment excites you – now you've finally said as much – you're going to have your best chance against the dark one.'

'That's the lesson you've been trying to teach me?' She wondered why he couldn't have simply told her that when he first returned from his trip to Paris. 'That's what all these sessions of discipline have been about?'

'It's the most important lesson you've needed,' he stated defensively. 'Learning that lesson is...'

He broke off as the trill arpeggio of his mobile phone rang. Plucking it out of his pocket, frowning at the display, he returned to the bar as he conducted a whispered conversation. Charity heard some of the words, but not enough to make any sense of what he was saying. She had to wait until he returned the phone to his jacket pocket before she could ask him who the call was from.

'I've just been told there might be a way to avoid tonight's confrontation.' She glanced at him expectantly, waiting for him to elaborate but he seemed annoyingly aloof. 'We might be able to avoid you facing the vampires.'

'How?'

He shook his head. 'I can't tell you.'

'Who was that?'

'I can't tell you.'

He snatched his cigar from the bar and she knew he was about to leave her alone, and suddenly apprehensive she tried to think of a reason to make him stay. The gravity of the situation hadn't escaped her and she understood that it would be wisest to let him try to usurp the need for a confrontation. But now that she had learnt her lesson from his discipline she didn't want to miss the chance to use the newfound skill. 'Do you have to go?'

He tucked the cigar in the corner of his mouth and pushed his key into the lock. 'Can I trust you to do one thing for me while I'm gone?'

There was a subtext to his tone that suggested she couldn't be trusted to sit in the corner like a chastened schoolgirl, but she chose to ignore the inflection. 'What?' she asked churlishly.

'Can I trust you to stay here without fucking another vampire?' he asked sharply. 'Or fucking another boyfriend, should one happen along? Or doing anything else that's likely to jeopardise your alleged virtue? I know it's asking a lot but can I trust you to do that much?'

She bit back a sharp retort and simply nodded. The discipline and her orgasm had left her in no mood to argue and she couldn't be bothered to try and challenge his derogatory opinion of her. Perhaps, she thought glumly, he was right to hold her in such low regard. 'I think I can manage that much,' she sniffed.

He walked to the door and then hesitated. 'I'll be back within the hour.'

'I'm missing you already.' She saw his jaw tighten and knew he wasn't happy with her sarcasm, but she hadn't made the remark for his amusement.

'One hour,' he said stiffly, speaking as he left the room and closed the door. 'Try not to let the dark one suck you dry before I get back…'

Charity was ready to shout after him, and make some comment that the dark one didn't stand a frickin' chance against her, when movement at the French windows caused the words to stall in her throat. Her eyes widened and her heart began to race, and it was unnerving that she recognised all four vampires: and it was unsettling that they each wore bloody, hungry smiles. But the most chilling aspect was the realisation that the French windows were open and the four were bearing down on her.

Charity

Act III, Scene II

There was a crucifix mounted inauspiciously above the study door, a handful of iron and wooden stakes were disguised as paperweights on Todd's desk, and two subtly labelled soda siphons – filled with holy water – stood behind the bar. But Charity didn't notice any of the potential weapons at her disposal. She only saw the advancing quartet of vampires and told herself she had no hope of defending against them.

The mulatto led the way, followed by Nick, Helen and then Marcia. The last two shielded their eyes from the brightness of the office lights but Nick and the mulatto held Charity with unflinching, mesmerising glares. Their lips were full and scarlet, eyes dark crimson, and each wore a smile that glinted with predatory menace.

Charity stiffened and tried not to show her terror. It didn't matter that she was pressing her bare bottom against the ox-blood leather, revisiting the burning memory of every stripe Todd had delivered. Nor did it matter that she was naked and had only her shaking hands with which to cover herself. All that mattered was defiantly facing the vampires and not letting them believe they had caught her off guard.

'We've come to keep you company,' Marcia explained.

'That was me on the phone to Spanky,' Helen added.

'We were getting your oily little protector out of the way,' Nick said.

'So we could spend a little quality time with you,' the mulatto concluded.

Charity's gaze flicked from one intruder to the other, daunted by the way each took a turn to speak and trying to follow what was being said. Understanding came to her in a panicked rush. 'This is a trap?' she exclaimed uncertainly. 'You've deliberately lured Todd away? This is a trap so you can get me alone?'

'You say that as though it's a bad thing…'

'Something you wouldn't enjoy…'

'A thing to be avoided…'

'When it really shouldn't be too unbearable.'

Suddenly wishing she had something with which to protect herself, Charity dared to glance at the crucifix above the study door. It would be difficult to reach but not impossible. Formulating a plan of action she wondered if she could outrun the vampires, make a valiant leap and snatch it down. The sharpened stakes on Todd's desk were closer, but she guessed that might prove a messy and violent way of defeating her tormentors. She also considered the soda siphons filled with holy water to be a non-starter, because she couldn't conceive how to use them as a weapon. Believing the crucifix above the door might be her best chance, she prepared to make a dash across the room.

But Nick sat on her left while Helen dropped casually by her right, and they appeared on the chesterfield so quickly she realised they had usurped her weak plan before she'd even formulated it. She stared bitterly at the crucifix knowing that, for the moment, it was out of her reach.

'Hello, virtuous one,' Nick purred. He placed a hand on her bare thigh. His cool touch excited a delicious tension in the taut muscle. Charity thought he was dangerously near to caressing her sex, the edge of his thumb seemed to drag tantalisingly close to her pussy lips, and she urged herself to find the willpower to pull away from him or make him stop. Helen was pressed closed to her right, the swell of her bicep casually brushing Charity's bare breast, and she realised there was no way to distance herself from either of the two vampires sandwiching her on the settee.

'Hello virtuous one?' Helen snorted, her tone rich with malicious disdain. 'Virtuous slut, you mean. I've seen the stuff her and her sisters get up to. It's enough to make a whore blush.'

'I saw her on Parliament Hill,' Marcia confirmed with prudish authority. 'What she was doing didn't seem very virtuous to me.'

The mulatto stood in front of her, her delicate features solemn, and Charity stared at her expectantly. With mounting apprehension she realised the rest of the coven were watching the dark-skinned vampire, as though awaiting her instruction.

'Virtuous or not,' the mulatto growled, 'she's ours now.'

Charity paled, and glaring at Marcia, the mulatto snapped her fingers and pointed. 'Take her!' Her voice rang with the steel of true authority, then she turned to Helen. 'Make her, if that's all you can do.' She glanced at Nick. 'Fuck her, tease her, and then make her crawl on the floor while she cries and begs for more.' Addressing them all, not seeming to care that Charity could hear everything she was saying, the mulatto pointed an accusing finger. 'This virtuous bitch is a threat to the safety of our coven. She's a danger to the sanctity of our immortality. Do whatever you can to take her now.'

Charity swallowed, expecting the four of them to pounce on her. She didn't dare move, and although her mind was screaming for her to take some pre-emptive action, she knew her body would simply surrender to them as soon as they decided to obey.

'Why do we need to endanger ourselves by taking on this virtuous slut?' Helen snorted. 'Lilah's got everything in place for that butch bitch, Wendy, to eat her alive at midnight. What's the advantage of us putting ourselves at risk?'

The mulatto rounded on her, pointing a menacing finger beneath Helen's throat. 'That butch bitch, Wendy, won't get the chance to eat this one alive,' she hissed. 'She won't get the chance because we're going to finish the job here and now. What's left of the virtuous one won't be fit for an appetiser at the final confrontation.' The tip of the mulatto's fingernail pressed into the delicate flesh over Helen's trachea. 'Do I make myself clear?'

Charity was close enough to see the venomous spite in her blood-red eyes, and Helen returned her glare with cowed truculence.

'Have I made myself clear?' the mulatto demanded, switching her gaze to the others, making sure she stared each one down before she continued. 'We have to take her now. We have to finish this virtuous bloodline here, in this room, tonight. Do you understand me?'

Charity held her breath, hoping fervently that they might continue to refuse the order. If the others followed Helen's lead she knew there was a slim chance she could escape the threat of the coven. She didn't seriously think there was much hope of capitalising on an insurrection but she fearfully conceded it was probably her only chance of salvation.

But that prospect was dashed when Nick shifted against her. The hand on her thigh squeezed and Charity was shocked to realise his knuckles were now grazing her sex. The slippery warmth of her pussy lips nuzzled his fingers as he leant closer and placed his mouth over hers. She considered protesting, and told herself she didn't want to be subjected to his kiss, but arguing was suddenly beyond her. When he inched closer, brushing his chilly lips against hers, she gave in to the kiss he demanded.

Helen snaked an arm behind her, lowering her mouth over the aching bud of Charity's right nipple, while Marcia slipped between her legs and drew her tongue along her thigh. The two women were capable lovers, easily exciting and arousing her, but it was the intimacy of Nick's kiss that held Charity motionless. Not sure why she should be so helpless, she yielded to the promise of passion that came when his lips crushed against hers.

He grunted sardonic laughter. 'You kiss better than your sister.'

Charity couldn't respond. Helen wasn't simply sucking her nipple; the pressure of the vampire's canines bit the hard bead of flesh, thrilling her with a bewildering blend of pain and satisfaction. Marcia's curls tickled the sensitive skin of her inner thighs as her tongue stroked slowly and deliberately upward. The pressure of impending orgasm swelled across her abdomen and Charity suppressed the urge to scream with mounting need.

'I had your sister, Hope, in a Paris crypt,' Nick gloated, the revelation leaving Charity shocked and aroused. She could hear excitement in his voice and instinctively knew he was erect, the temptation to reach for his groin and confirm that thought almost irresistible. But knowing how calamitous such an action would be, she was briefly thankful that her arms were being held. It was all too easy to imagine his erection pulsing beneath her touch, and on an instinctive level she knew that caressing him through his trousers would sound the death knell on any resistance she wanted to make.

'And if your other sister, Faith, hadn't been a lezzer, I'd have probably had her back in Rome,' Nick revelled between kisses, slipping his lips over hers and occasionally teasing his tongue inside her mouth. 'But having Hope was satisfying enough. She was very tight. She was very athletic. It's given me quite a taste for screwing virtuous pussies. I wonder if yours is going to be just as satisfying.'

Marcia chose that moment to stroke her tongue against Charity's labia, the glorious contact enough to take the captive

189

girl to the verge of paroxysms. She held her breath, squirming her sore bottom against the chesterfield, wishing they would take her, make her, or simply get the frick away and leave her alone.

Helen placed a steadying hand on her shoulder, Nick's hand squeezed more tightly against her thigh, and between her legs Marcia pushed her face closer to her sex while holding both her knees. There didn't seem to be a part of her body that wasn't under the control of chilly fingers or crimson lips and the only protest she could effectively manage was a weak, pathetic moan.

'But the greatest of these is Charity,' scoffed the mulatto.

Charity had heard the quote often enough to understand the reference, and she could also appreciate the vampire's disparaging tone. Aware of the picture she was presenting, her naked body being so easily manipulated by the coven, she was able to sympathise with the mulatto's disgust. However, although she didn't like being a plaything for the undead, she couldn't find the will to fight them off or drag herself away.

'She's a lot more receptive than her boyfriend,' Marcia observed.

Nick nodded. 'She's not as irascible.'

'She's tastier, too,' Helen agreed.

Their words brought Charity from a haze of distraction. She didn't know how she'd been able to put the worry of Danny out of her mind for so long, but now she remembered the vampires had taken him away she had to know what had become of him. If they'd hurt him, if he'd been taken or made, she felt sure she would have to retaliate. Sitting upright, brushing aside those hands that tried to hold her, she glared at the mulatto. 'Where is Danny?' she demanded. 'What have you done with him?'

The vampire's sly smile was hateful and Charity knew she

wouldn't tell her anything of value. She glanced from one pallid face to the other. 'Where's Danny?' she demanded again. 'What have you done with him? You have to tell me.'

'Danny's safe,' Nick promised.

'He's tied to a four-poster bed in a hotel room,' Helen told her.

'Not that he seemed to take much pleasure from the bondage game,' Marcia giggled.

The scene was all too easy to imagine. Charity could picture Danny naked, his lean body spread-eagled on a bed, his wrists and ankles bound and the vampire women fawning over him. If she closed her eyes she would see their tongues lapping at his flesh, licking the salty sweat from his body, teasing his erection to hardness and savouring the flavour of his…

'If you've hurt him…' she started, a threat she couldn't complete because she didn't have words to express the extent of her wrath. 'If you've hurt him…' she tried again. 'You'd better not have hurt him,' she finished lamely.

'Hurt him?' Marcia sounded shocked. 'Why would we hurt him? How could we hurt him?'

'He was groaning when we left,' Nick remembered.

'And parts of him did look quite inflamed and swollen,' Helen giggled. 'I think we might have been riding him a little too vigorously.'

Charity fought to keep the image out of her mind but it refused to go. It was all too easy to see her beloved Danny's naked body trapped beneath Helen and Marcia. She could almost hear the wet squelch of one pussy accepting Danny's glorious shaft while the other woman squirmed on his face. The idea left her thrilled by a combination of black excitement and bleak despair. When she tried to pull herself from the settee Nick and Helen held her effortlessly in place, and powerless to properly struggle, she allowed them to continue with their control.

'I've been told it wasn't all bad for him,' the mulatto breathed softly. She stroked her fingers through Charity's hair and tilted her head back. Nick and Helen grudgingly moved aside as the dark-skinned vampire pressed closer. 'I wasn't there but I've been told all about it, and do you want to know which part he was enjoying the most? Should I show you?'

Charity guessed it was a rhetorical question when the vampire elegantly raised one leg and placed it on the back of the chesterfield. The hem of her dress slipped back, exposing a sly glimpse of her shadowed sex, the bare lips glistening in the darkness, and Charity caught the scent of arousal and sex.

She wanted to recoil from what was happening; shake her head; refuse to acknowledge the fragrance; deny what she knew would be demanded from her. But the mulatto was quick and Charity's will was at a weak ebb, and when the vampire eased her other leg onto the back of the settee, gracefully and miraculously balancing herself before sliding forward, Charity could only submit as the woman's sex smothered her mouth.

The remainder of her desire to rebel was vanquished as the rest of the vampires resumed their hateful teasing. Nick's teeth locked onto her left breast, his chilly lips adding contrast to the heat his bite inspired. Helen tongued her right nipple, exciting electric shards of joy from the sore tip. Marcia buried her face against Charity's pussy lips and lapped with greedy abandon. The sensory overload was too intense and it became impossible to believe that she didn't want to give in to them and let them win. Inhaling deeply, valiantly fighting to find the will to resist, she was overwhelmed by the intoxicating aroma of the mulatto's sex.

'Drink from me, you virtuous little bitch.'

It was an insulting instruction, more insidious than any of the wicked commands Todd had given, and Charity told herself she didn't want to obey. She tried to pull her face away, adamant that she wouldn't submit to the torment, but the mulatto was now in control. A fist grabbed the hair at the back of her head and she had to suppress a scream of anguish as her head was forced into position.

'Drink from me, virtuous one,' the mulatto insisted. 'Drink from me, and make it good.'

With no other option available, and urged on by the twisted appetite of her own black desire, Charity plundered the woman's sex with her tongue. She could taste the salt of freshly spent semen and the musk of the woman's arousal, but it was the divine sensation of slippery labia squirming against her face that won her over. The pussy lips melted against her mouth, nose and chin, sliding wetly against her and almost reciprocating the kiss she was giving. The forbidden tang was a barb to her excitement and, hardly aware of her own eagerness, she pushed her tongue deeper.

The mulatto released a throaty chortle. Wetness from her sex flowed more freely in a fluid surge. The pulse of a clitoris beat against Charity's upper lip, and without thinking about what she was doing, merely responding to the hedonism of the moment, she swallowed and suckled on the bead of flesh.

The mulatto groaned and pressed herself more urgently forward. Empathising with the woman's eagerness, Charity devoured the succulent flesh at her mouth. The swell of an orgasm grew stronger with each passing second and she realised her body would soon be carried to an extreme of bliss and well beyond. The fight to resist was forgotten as she revelled in the pleasure. Even when she felt the first tentative nip against her inner thigh, as Marcia tested a wary bite, Charity couldn't find the impetus to flinch from the discomfort. Nick and Helen, acting with a unison that was eerie, pressed their teeth more punishingly into her breasts. The twin stings at her nipples were sharp and uncomfortable. But that hurt pushed her past the brink of orgasm and her climax came in a steamy, delicious burst, and she groaned as the joyous release was dragged from her sex.

'You dirty little bitch,' the mulatto breathed, and Charity glanced up from a haze of bliss. She didn't know when the vampire had slipped away from her, or how long she had languished through the divine torpor of her orgasm. Nick, Helen and Marcia continued to nibble at her breasts and pussy lips and the mulatto's musk – coating her mouth and cheeks – remained wet and fragrant. But none of those factors told her anything about how long she had been unconsciously at the mercy of the unholy quartet.

'You dirty little bitch,' the mulatto repeated. She held Charity's head from behind; razor-sharp nails scratching the delicate flesh of her throat. 'I can't believe such a filthy little tramp is being feted as the virtuous one. You weren't meant to be getting off on that,' she hissed. 'You were supposed to be pleasuring me.'

Petrified, and still trembling from the excess of her release, Charity said nothing. Her sex was sodden and she didn't know whether to be repulsed by the viscous wetness there, or revel in the aftermath of her release. The consideration wasn't made easier by the mulatto's talon-like fingernails perpetually grazing the sensitive skin beneath her jaw.

'I think this one needs teaching a lesson.'

While it sounded like she was addressing the others, Charity knew her tormentor's words were spoken for her benefit. It was hard to concentrate on what was being said but she willed herself to remain as coherent as the vampires would allow.

'I think she needs teaching a lesson for being such a slut,' the mulatto continued. 'And I think the best way we can teach her a lesson is to make her.'

Charity's eyes opened wide. There was no time for her to brace herself because the remaining three vampires acted as though they'd been waiting for this exact instruction. Marcia buried her face deeper between Charity's thighs, lapping and teasing the labia between her teeth. The borderline sensations of pleasure and pain became indistinguishable as the blonde thrust her tongue deep, then gnawed on her pussy lips.

Stiffening, pressing her freshly punished bottom into the uncompromising leather, Charity writhed and struggled to contain her sobs. Fresh wetness daubed her face but she couldn't decide if the tears came from anguish, joy or frustration.

Helen's icy fingers cupped the breast she suckled and she squeezed without regard or sensitivity. Her lips added a subtle pressure to the intimate kiss but it was the anguish of her bite that Charity couldn't escape. She sucked a deep breath and clawed her hands against the settee as she tried to acclimatise herself to the wicked delight.

Nick chuckled softly. He already had her nipple held between his canines, and with a hateful slowness he wrought fresh agony as she hurtled towards the thrill of another climax.

'Make her,' the mulatto demanded. 'Make her now.' Her voice was close to Charity's ear but the words meant nothing. Raw bliss surged through her body and she knew the vampires were biting harder than before. Marcia's greedy slurping was almost as loud as the pounding pulse within Charity's temples. The heady scent of her arousal had become an intoxicating perfume that coloured every breath. But although Charity could feel each gratuitous kiss delivered to her sex, she knew it wasn't the most intense sensation she was being forced to suffer.

Nick and Helen were in perfect co-ordination with each other, biting, sucking, teasing and tormenting. Yet although they sent escalating daggers of bliss searing through her nipples, Charity conceded that they were not responsible for her most satisfying pleasure either.

'Do you want me to bite you?' the mulatto growled, her pursed lips pressed against Charity's throat, resting the promise of a kiss against her jugular. 'Do you want me to bite you?'

The question was laden with muted hunger. Charity held her breath, willing herself not to answer while longing to beg for the vampire to do what she could. At the back of her mind she knew she should be fighting to defeat her tormentors and remain free from danger. But that knowledge didn't stop her from wanting to have the dark-skinned vampire drink from her throat.

The mulatto stroked her lips against Charity's throat, scratching with the tips of her teeth as she excited the sensitive flesh. 'If you want me to make you, all you have to do is ask and you know I'll do it.'

Charity opened her eyes and told herself she should act, but the idea seemed too fanciful to comprehend. They were all relaxed, enjoying her torment and disarmed by their own confidence. Commonsense told her this would be the ideal time to strike and she knew she would have the advantage of surprise. Pushing the four aside she would be able to lurch across the room and snatch the cross from above the office door. It wouldn't be easy to fend off the mulatto, who would most likely regain her senses first, but Charity believed the crucifix would buy her sufficient time and give her a chance to get to the bar. From there she could douse the group with holy water from one of the soda siphons. And while they were panicked, disoriented and struggling to work out what had happened, she could make use of the stakes from Todd's desk and defeat all four of them.

But doing something so bold would have torn her away from the bliss of Nick's kiss and Helen's wicked teasing, and it would have meant Marcia could no longer chase delicate kisses against her pussy lips. But more importantly it would have meant she couldn't surrender to the mulatto's kiss, and the concept of denying herself that pleasure was almost more than she could bear.

It was only when she thought of Danny that she realised she had to do something. The tiny voice of her commonsense told her that if she didn't act soon and stop the coven, her battle against evil would be over forever.

Interlude

Part Five

'You stupid fucking bitch!' the dark one roared.

Lilah had never seen her brother in such a fury but his outrage reinforced her belief that they shared the same aura. Even though his anger was directed at her, and even though she could sense he was close to venting the full force of his wrath, she felt certain it was proof that they were now inextricably linked. It was a comforting thought and left her confident that she would be safe from the storm of his temper.

'Tonight, of all nights,' he ranted, 'you let my entire coven go off on their own personal errands?'

'It's not like they come and ask me for permission before they go anywhere,' Lilah complained. 'I'm only your sister and you've made it quite clear to them that I've got no authority over what they do. I'm not their nanny and you're...'

His crimson glare was deadly. His expression was a challenge that said she should only continue if she wanted to brave the direst of consequences. But because she knew they shared an aura, because her own anger in the face of his outrage proved that much to her, she dared to carry on. 'And you're wrong when you say that your entire coven has gone. We've still got one that's better than the rest of the damned coven put together. She's our best hope against the virtuous one. Time and again she's beaten the greatest of your champions. I thought I'd already proved that to you. I thought we'd already agreed that Wendy was the only one we needed.'

Wendy glanced up upon hearing her name, and an

unpleasant smile broke her plain features as she nodded approval in Lilah's direction.

They were waiting in the cellar of the manor house, biding their time as midnight crept closer. Wendy had been playing a game of solitaire with a discarded tarot deck she found. Lilah and the dark one had been successfully managing to avoid the topic of the impending confrontation until he asked her what she'd done with the remainder of the coven. Thinking back over events, Lilah realised that was when the argument first began.

The inefficient bulb that had exploded during Lilah's last visit had since been replaced by another weak light, and she was thankful that they had brought candles for the makeshift altar to make the cellar brighter and less claustrophobic. Although they shared an aura, and she was convinced they were almost of a like mind, she conceded that better light made it easier for her to read her brother's unpredictable moods and gauge his responses with more accuracy.

Candlelight flickered in the blood-red shine of his eyes and she could see that his fury hadn't abated and remained at a volatile level. 'Do you seriously think this butch bitch stands a chance against the virtuous one?' he snarled, pointing at Wendy, twisting his upper lip into a disparaging sneer.

'She's beaten every vampire she's gone up against.'

He shook his head. 'I'm not talking about putting her up against vampires. I'm talking about this bull dyke coming face to face with the virtuous one. Do you really think she stands a chance?'

Lilah thought Wendy stood more than a chance, and believed the vampire's victory was a foregone conclusion, but while she was still trying to understand the point her brother was trying to make she realised he had already decided on a change of plan. Before Lilah could intervene, before she had any chance to stay him, the dark one grabbed Wendy. He snaked his fingers into the hair at the back of her head, dragged her into his embrace and then pressed her against a wall.

If Wendy made any attempt to pull away it was rendered unnoticeable by the dark one's commanding authority. She could have struggled or tried to resist, but all Lilah saw was the vampire being lifted from the floor and melting into her attacker's arms. When he forced his leg between her thighs, then cupped one breast with a forceful hand, Wendy merely quivered as though anxious for him to continue. The smile on her lips looked hungry but not with the avaricious leer Lilah was used to seeing on her face. Now Wendy seemed hungry for something else.

'Fight me, you bitch,' the dark one demanded. 'Show me how you're better than the best of my champions. Prove my sister right. Show me how you'll defend me against the virtuous one. Fight me.'

Lilah watched, her eyes widening with excitement. Wendy was quietly struggling to retaliate but her attempts were stilted and ineffectual. The muscles of her arms were taut with exertion, her thighs tensed with the effort of trying to pull free, but none of her heroic endeavours came close to helping her escape or overpower the dark one. She seemed powerless to prevent him from tearing the basque from her body and only able to surrender when he placed his mouth over her throat. His fingers lingered at her freshly exposed breast, teasing the stiffness of one nipple and rolling the hard bud of flesh between finger and thumb.

'She won't stand a chance,' he snarled derisively, snatching his lips from Wendy's throat, glowering at Lilah with a bloody frown.

'She's beaten everything we've thrown at her so far,' Lilah protested. 'She's invincible.'

He shook his head. 'You've brought me a Goliath to go up against a David.'

The biblical reference surprised Lilah, and made her wonder if he had plucked that thought from amongst her own. Her brother didn't trouble himself too greatly with religion and she could think of no other reason to find him using analogies that referred to the Old Testament. 'She'll defeat the virtuous one,' she insisted, shaking her head to dispel the incongruity, trying to make him see sense so he would release his hold on Wendy.

'I don't think she will.' As if to prove his point, the dark one pressed his bite against the vampire's throat. Lilah watched his teeth sink through her flesh and noticed Wendy stiffen. A look of absolute pleasure was torn across her features and she briefly turned rigid before melting against him. Rather than struggling to get free the vampire moulded herself against him as though she needed the comforting contact of another body. Riding her pussy lips against his leg, urging him to squeeze and knead her bare breasts, she had been instantaneously transformed from an intimidating dominatrix to a submissive, yielding whelp. As she threw back her head in ecstasy, sighing with the obvious delight of surrender, Lilah saw the expression of acquiescence lighting the vampire's eyes.

'Fucking great!' Lilah snapped. 'Absolutely fucking marvellous!' She knew it wasn't wise to challenge her brother's decisions, but this time her own fury was impossible to contain. 'Your coven choose tonight to go walkabout. You have an impending confrontation with the virtuous one, I give you a last line of defence against the virtuous one, and you go and fucking break her!'

The dark one wasn't listening. His mouth was pressed over Wendy's throat and he drank greedily. The wet slurp of his thirst reverberated from the walls and was underscored by the gratuitous pant of his victim's arousal. With burgeoning need Wendy rubbed against him and melted into the torment of his penetrating kiss. When the dark one moved his hand, shifting his hold from her breast so his fingers could plunder the wet folds of her pussy lips, Wendy's growl of contentment turned into a satisfied sigh. She writhed onto him with an urgent greed that was shameless and embarrassing to watch. Her sex engulfed his hand as she thrust her hips him with pure, wanton need.

'No!' Lilah roared, but neither of them paid any heed to her outrage. Her brother pressed more lewdly against Wendy, pushing his pelvis to and fro as though riding in and out of her. Lilah could see they weren't that close, and knew the dark one was still dressed, but Wendy responded as though she could feel every inch of his penetration. The vampire's eyes blazed with ferocious passion and she grunted with wild abandon as she gave herself to him. The wetness around her sex lips grew more copious and her guttural growls became more demanding.

'No!' Lilah insisted again, and knowing she had no other choice, determined that her brother wouldn't spoil all the hard work she'd invested in preparing Wendy, she forced herself between the pair, hauling the female vampire to the floor. 'You can't do this,' she protested. 'I won't let you.'

Wendy landed on her backside, legs spread to expose the shining flush of pink flesh that blossomed at her sex. There was a bewildered look in her eyes, as though she was puzzled by how she had ended on the floor, but it was difficult for Lilah to read that expression. Too much of Wendy's smile was made up with avaricious desire and raw, sexual need and it was clear she was now devoted to doing whatever the dark one demanded from her. Given the opportunity, Lilah knew Wendy would have pushed her aside so she could resume her place in the dark one's arms.

Shifting her glare to her brother, trying not to think that his treatment of Wendy now cast a shadow of doubt over her idea that they shared a like mind, she willed herself to contain her anger. 'Wendy is your best defence against the virtuous one,' she hissed. 'Your coven is missing, you're set to face a final confrontation, and you're drinking from this butch bitch as though she's the party entertainment at one of those nasty little vampire conventions.'

'Are you telling me how to run my affairs?' he asked with deceptive mildness.

'I'm telling you that you're acting like a fool.'

He chuckled and looked set to say something in response, but movement at the bottom of the cellar steps made them both glance in that direction and, as they watched, a tall, masculine figure moved out from the shadows at the bottom of the wooden stairwell. 'Don't stop on my account,' Todd Chalmers said. He reached into his jacket pocket and pulled out a long, fat cigar. Without breaking into the ineffectual circle of light that surrounded Wendy, Lilah and the dark one, he lit it and smiled with impish arrogance. 'Carry on. Act like I'm not here. I don't mind waiting until you've finished.'

'Toad?' Lilah whispered.

'Chalmers?' the dark one muttered. He shielded his eyes to peer further into the darkness. 'Is that you, Chalmers?'

'Like I said,' Todd mused, tipping a mock salute in the direction of Lilah's brother, 'don't stop on my account. I always enjoy watching a good show and you guys never fail to put on a fantastic performance.'

Lilah started towards him but the dark one placed a warning hand on her shoulder. She turned to glare at her brother. 'Don't you want me to take him?' She was poised and ready to hurl herself at the intruder. Aside from the rudeness of the interruption, she had old scores to settle with Chalmers that she had vowed to finish at the earliest opportunity. 'Don't you want me to take him, sire?' she asked again, glaring at her brother, stiff with tension and the need to feast.

'No one's feeding from Chalmers,' the dark one mumbled. 'That's never been on my agenda.'

It was impossible to contain her disappointment. 'You can't mean that.'

'I can.'

'But…'

The dark one held up a finger, stopping her interruptions before she could say anything further. 'Chalmers ably controlled my affairs before your little display of dominance,' he reminded her. 'And if we're nice to him he might consent to do that again.'

Todd shook his head. He toyed with his cigar, as though the action helped him find the right words before finally speaking. 'It's generous of you to consider letting me back into your clique,' he said quietly. 'But things moved on in your absence and I don't think we can go back to the happy arrangement we shared before. Your sister wasn't as appreciative of my services as you always were. And she made it clear that my position within your organisation was only temporary.' Flexing his disarming grin, exuding a charm that Lilah found repulsive, he told her brother, 'You'll probably consider me a turncoat but I've changed my allegiances from the dark side to a nobler purpose. Nowadays I'm genuinely trying to assist the virtuous sisters.'

The dark one shrugged. He plucked Wendy from the floor and took her back into his embrace. Licking a sliver of spilt blood from her throat, returning his kiss to her neck, he resumed his hold on her as he had before with one hand on her breast and the other pushed into her sex. Lilah could hear the vampire's soft, needy sobs, and although they sounded like they were coming from someone powerful, it was possible to detect a weakness that hadn't been there before. Lilah quietly cursed her brother's inopportune appetite and struggled to think of a way to rectify the situation.

The dark one paused from feeding from Wendy long enough to glance in Todd's direction. A ribbon of spilt blood trickled from the corner of his mouth. 'I'm currently too preoccupied to contemplate retaliatory action,' he explained patiently. 'But I expect I'll have to wreak bloody vengeance on you and your kin.'

'Fair enough,' Todd agreed. Drawing thoughtfully on his cigar, he looked to be considering the threat before asking, 'I take it that bloody vengeance will only happen if you're the victor in tonight's confrontation?'

The dark one nodded. He started to turn his face back to Wendy's throat, and then paused. 'It might help your case, possibly make my disposition a little more lenient, if you were kind enough to transfer the coven's finances back to my control,' he said, testing an affable grin.

Todd considered this before nodding his agreement. 'If we both make it through the night, I'll start preparing the paperwork first thing in the morning,' he said easily. 'I'll pencil you in for a twilight appointment in my office should we both still be alive.'

Lilah glowered at him. Watching her brother feed from Wendy had been both maddening and exciting. She didn't want to see her champion drained but she couldn't deny that the sight filled her with a lecherous need. The arousal that had come from seeing her surrender to him sparked a pulsing need between her legs, and in turn her sexual hunger made her want to feed. Glaring at Todd, seeing the pulse at his throat beat implacably, she resisted the impulse to pounce on him and drink from him, but it was a hard-fought battle. 'If you haven't come to beg for your old job back,' she sneered, 'what are you doing here, Toad?'

His sly smile was galling, reminding her of all the reasons she had wanted to discharge him from her brother's employ. 'I thought one of you might know what I'm doing here,' Todd replied. 'I got summoned by a phone call. I was told that if I came here, now, I might be able to negotiate a way for the night to end without anyone having to fulfil the demands of the final confrontation.'

The dark one didn't glance up from suckling Wendy's neck. His fingers still pushed in and out of her sex but she was clearly weakening as she gave in to climax after climax. The breathless cry of her excitement whispered from the walls of the cellar as he repeatedly pushed her up to and beyond the brink of orgasm. Speaking with his mouth against the vampire's throat, sounding gruff and disinterested, he said flatly, 'You were told wrong.'

Lilah saw her brother's exclamation as more proof that they shared an aura. The dark one had used exactly the same words that she'd been about to growl. A smile of bitter triumph spread her lips and she twisted the expression into a sneer for Todd's benefit.

'You were told wrong,' the dark one repeated. 'The final confrontation happens at midnight and your presence here only means that you'll get to see your virtuous protégée being drained and taken.'

Todd shrugged as though the matter was inconsequential. 'At least it wasn't a wasted journey,' he conceded. 'It gave us all a chance to catch up on old times.'

Her brother wasn't listening. He had his mouth around Wendy's throat and drank with frenetic hunger. The woman in his arms no longer looked like the ferocious warrior who had bested each of the coven. The dark one had already drained most of the fight from her and she merely remained in his embrace. Instead of looking like she might be trying to pull away, Wendy's only drive seemed to be the urge to give herself to him.

'Sire,' Lilah warned anxiously.

'Let him enjoy her,' Todd said calmly.

Lilah flashed a warning glare in his direction then turned her attention back to her brother. He had changed position, pushing Wendy face first against the cellar wall while his hands stole over her buttocks. Most of their interaction was concealed from her view but Lilah could see her brother parting the woman's buttock cheeks and teasing the ring of her anus with his fingertip. He tormented her until her gasps for more were chilling, and then returned his hold to the swell of her breasts. Once his grip on her was secured his pelvis banged against her in a vigorous parody of intercourse. Chuckling above her cries for him to have her, the dark one lowered his mouth to the open wound on her throat and began to drink again.

'Sire.' Lilah voiced her reservations more loudly this time, and with a greater degree of authority, but still he didn't bother to acknowledge her. From the corner of her eye she saw Chalmers raise his cigar, as though about to make another observation, and she silenced him by merely snapping her fingers and flashing a warning glare in his direction.

Wendy was sobbing, the sound borne from a seamless meld of pleasure and pain. She cried out repeatedly and her shrieks were carried on sighs that mingled gratitude with pleas for mercy. Tremors shook her, from the tips of her fingers to the thrust of her nipples, and when the dark one pulled her away from the wall, turned her to face him and blithely considered her nudity as though trying to decide where he should attack next, Wendy merely pushed herself into his arms.

Lilah vaguely considered that it was a fitting torment for the woman. She was aware that Wendy had taken much satisfaction from dominating the rest of the coven, and her brutality had been cruel and untouched by any display of mercy. But she knew that rationale wouldn't help to keep her champion prepared for the impending confrontation. 'Sire!'

she shouted, clutching her brother's shoulder and wrenching him away from the vampire.

The dark one turned to glare at her, and no longer supported by his powerful arms, Wendy slipped to the floor, a smile of dreamy ecstasy remaining on her drained lips as she collapsed in a lifeless heap. Lilah glanced down at the fallen form and realised there was no longer any point in trying to argue with her brother. 'You've just drained your last hope of defeating Charity,' she said solemnly. 'It's almost midnight, the rest of your coven are nowhere to be seen, and you've got no first line of defence against the virtuous one. What's your next great plan, sire?' she sneered sarcastically. 'Are you going to get us all to wear crucifixes? Or should we start gargling with holy water?'

He was on her in a second. Even when he had been threatening to end her life, Lilah always secretly believed she was safe from her brother's wrath. That notion had been stronger since she learnt they shared an aura, and although she knew he resented their close link, it reinforced her belief that he would never hurt her. But she could see he was now intent on proving his authority.

A hand went to her breast, icy fingers exciting her nipple through the leather of her waistcoat, and Lilah fought not to be aroused by the maddening touch. The pressure of his thigh rubbed against the crotch of her trousers and she was darkly excited by the frisson of his leg against her thinly clothed labia. Holding herself rigid, not daring to move in case she showed the arousal he had managed to generate, Lilah held his gaze with the most commanding stare she could muster. 'Do with me what you will,' she challenged.

'I intend to.' He licked his lips and she could see the remainder of Wendy's blood staining his smile. His breath had the coppery aroma of a recent feed and she quietly wished she had helped him finish the vampire rather than berating him for his lack of foresight. But the idea was gone in an instant, and she told herself it was as repulsive as the touch of her own brother's hand against her barely restrained breast, but those thoughts didn't stop her arousal from swelling in a hot, urgent need.

'Do with me what you will,' she said again. 'But it won't change your predicament. It's nearly midnight, the confrontation is almost upon you, the rest of your coven are nowhere to be seen, and you've no first line of defence against the virtuous one.'

Her brother's eyes shone with wicked glee and the fist around her breast squeezed tight, thrilling her with a shock of unbridled pleasure. 'You're wrong,' he smiled. 'I do still have a first line of defence against the virtuous one.' Pressing his thigh more forcefully against her sex, sparking blisters of twisted need through her pussy, he said, 'I still have you.'

She balked from the idea, ready to raise a thousand objections as to why she couldn't go up against Charity. The concept of becoming one of her brother's champions was more galling than having to submit to his animal arousal. But as she considered each objection, she realised that none would be sufficient to sway his opinion.

'I still have you,' the dark one repeated. 'And given the fact that we share an aura, I know you'll protect me as though your life depends on it.'

'You've finally decided to believe what the gypsy told us?' she said. 'You're finally accepting that you and I share the same destiny?'

His look of triumph disappeared in a scowl of frustration and he pushed her away. 'It doesn't matter what I believe,' he growled. 'Since you've let the rest of my coven go out on their own private errands, you're the only one I've got left.'

Lilah picked herself from the floor and laughed at his obvious unease. 'You're worrying needlessly,' she assured him. 'It's not as though they haven't been out prowling by themselves before. And if they've survived all these years, I don't see why you should be concerned about them on this particular evening.' Shaking her head in the face of his consternation, she added, 'Those four reprobates will be fine. They'll probably come hurtling down those stairs in the next few seconds.'

'No they won't,' Charity said.

Lilah turned to glare at her, wondering how the naked girl had appeared so effortlessly from the shadows. Charity stood by Chalmers's side and looked eerily confident. Her bare body was lean, athletic and annoyingly arousing to behold.

'The rest of your coven won't be fine, because I've just vanquished all four of them. I've staked all four to the walls of Todd's study and doused them with holy water.' Licking her lips, passing her smile from the dark one to Lilah, exuding confidence, she added, 'I only have you two to deal with now.'

Lilah shook her head. 'No,' she said firmly, placing her hands on her hips, cocking her head defiantly. 'The only vampire you'll be dealing with tonight is me.'

Charity

Act III, Scene III

'Charity?' Todd glanced at her with an expression of mild surprise, his brow wrinkled with tight lines. 'I thought I told you to remain in my office. What are you doing here?'

Charity didn't let her gaze waver from Lilah. 'Your office filled up with a hoard of vampires,' she explained. 'They weren't very nice to me so I…' she grinned to herself and concluded, 'so I got a little cross.'

He grimaced as though the remark had pained him. 'Jesus, Charity!' he exclaimed. 'Crack one more nasty pun like that and I'll help the dark one and Lilah defeat you myself.'

Ignoring the mild reproof, trying to ready herself for what had to be done, Charity motioned for Todd to stand back as she concentrated on her adversary. This, she realised, was the confrontation that had been building for the last two days and the enormity wasn't lost on her. She knew it had been building since before her sister, Faith, first encountered vampires in an Italian cemetery and that thought turned the air in her lungs to lead. She refused to acknowledge the fluttering butterflies that flailed in her stomach and kept her hands balled into fists, held rigid at her sides, so that no one could see whether or not she was trembling. Her legs were taut, as though the muscles had locked and she knew, from behind her, Todd would have an unfettered view of her tight buttocks.

'You're early,' Lilah observed.

'Do you want me to go away and come back when you're

ready to face me?'

The vampire's smile was a mask over her hatred. Her teeth were bared and her bloody leer shone bright and hungry. 'You're an arrogant little bitch,' she snarled. 'It's going to give me a lot of pleasure wiping that sanctimonious smile off your face.'

Charity took a breath to try and steady her nerves. 'Try it,' she said simply.

Lilah was tall and commanding but she looked especially daunting this evening. The glistening leather of her waistcoat and trousers caught the reflection of a dozen guttering candles and made her appear as though she'd been cast from bronze. The muscles on her arms looked like they'd been moulded from steel and Charity didn't think it would be possible to face a more intimidating opponent. The vampire wore a bullwhip on one well-defined hip, and when her hands fell to her waist, Charity expected the woman to be reaching for the weapon. It was only when Lilah began to unfasten the buttons on her waistcoat, revealing a small triangle of her stomach, then exposing the shadows where her breasts were concealed, that Charity realised the vampire was making herself comfortable for the confrontation.

'I'm going to enjoy having you,' Lilah growled.

Not daring to show her nerves now that they were so close to beginning, Charity said nothing. It didn't trouble her that the dark one lurked in the shadows behind his sister, or that she could see the fallen prey of one of their victims sprawled on the floor at his feet. Charity wasn't concerned about being naked, or anxious about the humiliation she might suffer in front of Todd. All that mattered was holding Lilah's mesmerising gaze and not losing her resolve to win. If she could manage that much, she felt quietly confident that she would see the other side of this confrontation as the victor.

Lilah uncoiled the bullwhip from her hip, and when she

drew back her arm the swell of one toned breast was revealed from inside her waistcoat. Her nipple was hard, the areola flushed, and Charity wondered if the woman had been aroused before she entered the cellar or if the prospect of what was coming fired her excitement. Warning herself not to be lured by the sight, determined to see beyond the distraction, she switched her gaze back to Lilah's crimson eyes.

'I'm surprised you didn't bring a weapon,' the vampire remarked. 'Toad keeps his hideaways stocked with stakes, garlic, holy water and crucifixes. I'm disappointed you didn't try to catch me off guard with one of those devious little trinkets.'

She shifted her weight from one foot to the other as she spoke. Her eyes twinkled with malicious cunning and she had never looked more like a predatory animal. At the crotch of her leather trousers the gusset moulded the shape of her pussy lips. Drawn to the sight, excited by a dark hunger that the image evoked, Charity quickly pulled her gaze back to the vampire's eyes.

Lilah's smile sparkled, as though she knew where Charity's thoughts had been, and unsettled by that prospect Charity blushed.

'Seeing you standing there,' the vampire continued, 'seeing you all naked and defenceless, I can't help thinking about lambs and slaughterhouses. Is that what you are?'

A quiver of gooseflesh freckled Charity's arms but she maintained a show of defiance. 'I'm not a lamb being led to the slaughterhouse,' she said quietly. 'I'm the virtuous one. Corinthians: thirteen, thirteen. Faith, Hope and Charity. But the greatest of these is Charity. You must be familiar with the passage. And you must know that's me. I guess you also know I don't need crosses, holy water or stakes to deal with you. Todd's told me I have the ability to tear the heart out of your chest, and that's what I'm going to do.'

Lilah's cruel smile tightened as she flexed the whip to its full, intimidating length. It skittered across the cellar's dirt floor like a snake in search of prey. The movement made Lilah's waistcoat fall open again to reveal another tantalising glimpse of bare breast. Charity thought the cerise hue of the woman's areola was probably the most inviting colour she had ever seen and this time the struggle to wrench her gaze away was a lot more difficult.

'Perhaps you could tear the heart from my chest,' Lilah allowed, 'but there are two things that might stop you.'

Charity tilted her jaw, encouraging the vampire to explain.

'First, you have to still be virtuous,' Lilah informed her.

This time Charity didn't blush, despite the salacious note to the woman's voice. 'What's the second thing that might stop me?'

Lilah scowled. 'The second thing that might stop you is the fact that, to tear my heart out you have to get close to me.' Without further warning she snapped the whip, the crack resounding like gunfire in the cellar and Charity was stung by a pernicious strike against her thigh. She tried not to show her response to the flare of pain but it was severe enough to make her wince.

The second blow caught her breast, the tip shrieking against her nipple. It had been a struggle to contain her reaction before but this time it was impossible. She gasped, instantly hating the hurt sound of her own exclamation, but unable to contain the cry. Clutching herself tight, cupping one breast and trying to back away as Lilah advanced upon her, Charity wondered if she might have made a terrible mistake by venturing down into the cellar.

'I can't believe we were all so scared at the thought of facing you,' Lilah scoffed. She snapped the whip a third time, striking dangerously close to Charity's pussy. The tip scoured the inside of her thigh and left a weal that throbbed deep and furiously. Anguished tears filled her eyes and she blinked them back for fear the vampire might mistake them as a sign of weakness.

'I even went to the trouble of kidnapping your little boyfriend,' Lilah complained. 'I had my brother's minions tie him to the bed of some poxy Kensington hotel, and I only did that so I'd have an edge over you.' Sneering with contempt, pulling her arm back to wield the whip again, she added, 'But you clearly weren't worth the effort.'

The fourth whip-crack scored Charity's other breast, her nipple bitten by the sharp tip of leather and a howl of anguish torn through her chest. The sensation was exquisite and breathtaking and she stared at her tormentor with wary respect. It crossed her mind that she should take the opportunity to turn and flee, but she couldn't bring herself to move. Her commonsense was shrieking that she needed to retreat to the study, retrieve what was left of the holy water and maybe grab the crucifix, but she couldn't immediately find the impetus to escape, and by the time she urged movement into her legs there was no time to act. Still clutching the whip, smiling with a fury that bordered on the maniacal, Lilah was on her in a second.

From the corner of her eye Charity saw Todd take a tentative step in her direction, and she knew he was going to come to her defence. She didn't know whether to warn him back or embrace his assistance but she wasn't allowed the opportunity to do either.

But Todd stopped moving when the dark one held up a hand. 'You know better than to interfere in confrontations,' he intervened. 'We have rules, you know.' Todd nodded but didn't immediately retreat. 'Get in their way and I can't promise that Lilah won't take you,' the vampire said solemnly, glancing at his sister, frowning dourly. 'I won't be happy if she takes you; I'd be severely displeased. But while the rules of a confrontation are in process my abilities to intercede are limited.'

Reluctantly, Todd stepped back to his place at the edge of the shadows. The lines striped deeper across his brow and the way he now held his cigar looked fretful, as though he was suddenly anxious. It was an emotion that had Charity's wholehearted sympathy.

She only saw the interaction from the corner of her eye but it seemed to make more sense than her own predicament because Lilah had been faster than she anticipated. Before Charity could gain a proper perspective as to what was happening, the vampire had assumed a superior position. There was a brief moment when Lilah was embracing her, the vampire's cool body gliding easily against hers, and Charity was shocked by the sudden pang of arousal the woman inspired. The leather trousers were like a second skin over Lilah's legs and it was almost as though she was feeling a naked woman pressing against her. Bare breasts pushed against her, a rigid nipple grazed her mouth and Charity realised she had no chance against an opponent who could move so swiftly. Her hands were forced behind her back and the thin end of the whip tied her wrists. Lilah pushed her to her knees, and fearfully Charity realised she was bound, helpless and at the woman's mercy.

'I expected so much more from you,' Lilah mocked, and Charity tried not to listen. There was no sense in struggling because she knew it would do her no good. Lilah had looped the tapered end of the bullwhip around her wrists but she continued to hold the pizzle-shaped handle, and as she circled the kneeling girl she chuckled with merciless glee. Each time she stepped behind her, Charity stiffened as the whip's handle was slapped viciously against her bottom, every crisp smack quivering through her frame.

'We were daunted by your reputation,' Lilah mused, another

stroke of the pizzle landing heavily across Charity's buttocks. Both cheeks were quickly warmed from the punishment and she blushed at the idea that her sex might now be showing the symptoms of arousal. Before the confrontation she told herself there was no shame in what she was doing and no embarrassment in what she might have to endure, but that thought hadn't come whilst kneeling on the floor and displaying her wet pussy lips to her tormentors. Her face burnt scarlet as her blushes deepened.

'We felt threatened by you,' Lilah laughed. 'And now that idea seems so ludicrous.' She swept the handle down hard and it struck like a paddle, crushing the cheek where it landed and making Charity perniciously aware of a tingling heat in the pit of her stomach. She drew a deep breath, not sure if she was trying to steady her nerves or steel herself against the prospect of perverse pleasure.

'We felt threatened by you,' Lilah repeated, 'and all you've turned out to be is a weak… ineffectual… little… girl.' Her last four words were punctuated by further spanks to Charity's rear, each blow reverberating through her and the final one bringing her to the brink of tears.

When Lilah appeared in front of her she seemed to take additional pleasure from seeing the glassy expression in Charity's eyes, and it was almost possible to hear the promise of laughter in the vampire's voice. 'Is this all familiar to you? Has Toad been giving you your spanking lessons in readiness for this event?'

Charity remained silent and tried to bear the shame, while wishing Lilah would turn her humiliation to a different topic. It was only when the vampire repeated her question, sweeping the pizzle down with an insistent flourish, that she understood she would have to give an honest answer. Hesitantly, she swallowed.

Lilah remained behind her, stroking the whip handle from

one buttock to the other before slapping her again with harsh force. 'Has the Toad been reddening this plump little arse of yours?' she insisted. 'Tell me, you little bitch, I want to know.'

Charity stifled a sob, refusing to let the vampire hear her cry. 'Todd's prepared me to face you, if that's what you're asking,' she whispered, drawing a slow breath, hating the electric taste of excitement flavouring the air.

'Did he spank you?'

'Yes.'

'Did you like it?'

Charity closed her eyes and wondered if it might be possible to die from shame. She could feel her face burning as bright as her reddened bottom and she wished the vampire would stop tormenting her and do whatever she thought she needed to do to win the fight. No matter how bad the punishment, Charity didn't think it could hurt worse than the shame of the probing questions.

'Did you like it?' Lilah asked again. 'Did you get off on it?'

'Yes,' Charity admitted.

Lilah sniggered with delight. 'And tell me again, what was it all for?'

Charity glared up at the woman. 'I've already told you. Todd's been preparing me to face you.'

'Well, I don't think he's prepared you very well,' Lilah goaded, leaning close; so close her lips almost brushed Charity's ear.

'Take her or make her,' the dark one demanded ominously, 'but do it quickly, Lilah. I'm growing weary of this sport.'

Ignoring him, Lilah once again circled Charity before disappearing behind her. Chilly fingers stroked the burning skin of her buttocks and the lips of her sex were subtly caressed by the vampire's cool hand. Charity braced herself for another blow from the hated whip handle, but rather than use the pizzle to strike Lilah slipped the bulbous tip against her sex. The dome-like end squirmed against her pussy lips and the promise of penetration was never more than a whisper away. She could feel the threat of its length perpetually poised and ready to impale her, but Lilah was an expert at taunting and continued to ride the length against Charity's labia. Reluctant excitement inveigled its way through her loins and she almost cried out with desperate need, and when Lilah rubbed the end over Charity's clitoris that internal fight became infinitely more difficult to quell.

'Why did you come down here, Charity?'

Trembling with greedy need, the girl didn't trust herself to respond.

'Can't you tell me?' Lilah pressed. 'Did you think you had a chance against us? Or did you come because you knew you'd enjoy the greatest pleasure you're ever likely to suffer?'

The sob fell from her mouth as she tried to distance herself from the joy. Lilah held the tip of the handle so it hovered on the brink of entering her and Charity had to struggle not to push back onto its hateful, wonderful length.

'Take her or make her, Lilah,' the dark one repeated. 'I won't tell you again.'

Lilah didn't bother to acknowledge her brother. 'I doubt there's a virtuous bone left in your body,' she whispered confidently, her mouth so close to Charity's ear the others couldn't hear what was being said. 'I think, after all you've been through, there couldn't be any virtue left inside,' Lilah taunted, her voice low and insidiously exciting. 'But just so I'm sure of that, shall we get you begging for something really unwholesome? Do you think I could get you begging for a taste of this?' Lilah hissed, rubbing the pizzle back and forth against Charity's sex lips, its dome lubricated by the wetness that seeped from the kneeling girl and gliding against her with infuriating ease. The friction was unbearably intoxicating, making her sex yearn to melt open and suffer the penetration, but Charity resisted the urge to beg for that indignity.

'How about I give you a taste of it?' Lilah suggested. 'How about I let you enjoy a little of what I'm offering, then you can beg for some more.'

The pizzle pressed harder against her sex, the rounded end probing. She was torn between the need to push onto it and the desire to pull away. Her body remained immobile through a combination of fear and indecision, but as Lilah eased the length inside her, Charity realised she had made her choice by simply doing nothing.

The stout shaft filled her sex, spreading her inner muscles and promising to satisfy the greedy need growing within her. The pain Lilah administered had whet her appetite for satisfaction but it was the delight of having the whip's handle in her pussy that promised to sate her lust. Startled by her own response, instantly cresting the waves of a cataclysmic orgasm, she squeezed tightly around the length and wished for the pleasure to take her.

But Lilah tore the pizzle quickly from her vagina, its sudden departure leaving Charity breathless with shock and disappointment.

'Do you want to feel that again?' the vampire asked, brushing the shaft back and forth. 'Would you like that, you virtuous slut?'

No longer hiding her frustration, allowing tears of torment to stream down her cheeks, Charity nodded. The final confrontation was forgotten and the enormity of her responsibility was too much to consider. All she cared about was having Lilah slide the gloriously thick shaft back inside her sex and she wouldn't allow herself to think about anything else until she had.

Obligingly the vampire urged the pizzle back into her victim's pussy, making no allowance for sensitivity and thrusting it in aggressively… and Charity sobbed with gratitude, writhing on the splendid length, the prospect of an explosive orgasm never closer. Blood pounded in her temples, her head hung low, and she clawed at the dirt floor as an animal need overwhelmed her.

Lilah held the pizzle steady for a moment before slowly withdrawing it. Charity clenched her teeth; fearful she might plead for its return if she didn't make a concerted effort to remain silent. The pulse in her clitoris beat relentlessly, the ache in her sex growing more obvious than any of the whiplashes Lilah had scored against her body, and the demanding need in her sex shrieked for more.

'Do you want to feel it again?' Lilah whispered. 'Do you want to have this buried deep inside you one more time?'

'Yes,' Charity gasped.

Lilah chuckled. 'Why don't you wet it first?'

The pizzle was pushed under Charity's nose, its length coated with the fresh aroma of her musk. She wanted to recoil from the scent of her own sex but she was sorely tempted to do as Lilah suggested, the idea of extending her tongue, lapping at the fragrant length of leather and savouring her own intimate flavour so darkly appealing it was almost irresistible.

'Wet it first,' Lilah said quietly, 'then I'll put it wherever you want it. I'll slide it inside your pussy, or I might even slip it into your tight little arse.'

'Stop teasing her, Lilah,' the dark one commanded. 'If you're going to make her, hurry up and make her. If you're going to take her, then go ahead and do that. You get too much pleasure from your nasty little games. Mark my words: it'll prove to be your downfall.'

Lilah glared at him and looked ready to snap a tart response, but Charity spoke before the vampire had a chance to retaliate. She was teetering on the brink of an orgasm, desperate for satisfaction and bewildered that everything had turned out so badly. Trying to make a last show of defiance she raised her voice, glared at the dark one, and said, 'I've beaten your entire coven.' Both vampires turned to glower at her tear-streaked face, but she didn't back down. 'I've beaten your entire coven and I can beat the pair of you. All I have to do is defeat you two and I'll have destroyed all your evil forever.'

The dark one's laughter rumbled around the cellar. 'Is that what you think you're doing here?' he asked, the humour in his voice hateful. 'Do you really think you're going to rid the world of vampires if you defeat Lilah and I? Is that what you're telling me?'

Charity had thought that was what she was telling him but his mirth undermined her assurance, and the dark one didn't give her the chance to answer his question. 'I don't know about other vampires in the world, but I've already been bolstering the numbers of my coven. Do you want to meet my latest hoard of recruits?'

She paled as he snapped his fingers and glanced in the direction of the cellar steps, and when he nodded encouragement for someone to join them Charity struggled to turn and see who he'd called, her spirits plummeting as out of the shadows and calmly pushing past Todd came Angela, Viv and Lauren. Each of her fellow band members had a rich, bloody smile, and when they bared their teeth Charity was appalled to see the flash of overly long canines.

'Here they are,' the dark one beamed cheerfully. 'Here are the latest additions to my coven.'

Charity

Act III, Scene IV

It was the curse, Charity thought bitterly. It was the Harker family curse, and once again it had chosen her as its victim.

Until this evening her life had been successful. There had been fame, fortune and the promise of a blossoming relationship with a young man whom she believed she loved. She had even been coping with the enormity of fighting vampires while maintaining her career in the cutthroat world of the music industry. But, as was always the way with the Harker family curse, everything looked set to change… for the worse.

'Ladies,' the dark one smiled as the rest of BloodLust entered the cellar, 'I'm so glad you've come down here. Your timing is impeccable.'

Angela's complexion was deathly pale, set against her sunken eyes and scarlet smile. Viv's curly hair looked lank and lifeless: polished jet against her porcelain complexion. Lauren licked her scarlet lips, tracing her tongue carefully over her wicked smile. The corners of each girl's smile had the vampiric lilt of elongated canines.

Lilah was distracted by the new arrivals. 'Who are these bitches?' she demanded. 'What are they doing here?'

Not letting herself dwell on the demanding ache that throbbed inside her sex, Charity tried to reason if there was a way to use this interruption to her advantage. Lilah was distracted, and if she hadn't had her wrists bound this might have been the ideal time to act. She tried in vain to pull her hands free, succumbing to a wave of despair; considering what appeared to have happened to the rest of the band it looked like she was already too late to help.

The dark one's victorious smile was nauseating as he beckoned the three band members to step closer. 'You timed your arrival perfectly,' he enthused. 'You can show your lead singer that her quest to rid the world of vampires hasn't been much of a success story.'

Todd stopped Angela from leading the others to the dark one's side. Surprising them all, he released a sharp laugh and shook his head with what looked like genuine amusement.

The dark one regarded him uncertainly and then scowled. Lilah flashed her frown at him but he continued to chuckle despite the obvious warning being signalled by both vampires.

'You may have decimated my coven,' the dark one said, ignoring him and talking to Charity, 'you may have destroyed them all. But as you can see I've been recruiting new members. Even if there had been a chance of you defeating me or my sister, you'd have had to go on to kill your former friends and colleagues if you genuinely wanted to rid the world of all vampires.'

Lilah chose that moment to wipe the tip of the pizzle against Charity's upper lip, the scent of sexual musk made fresh beneath her nose and its glorious taste kept her teetering on the brink of a climax. She didn't know how it was possible to suffer so many emotions in one instant but she felt sure her body was currently suffering from terror, dread, defeat and arousal. And despising her own weakness, she realised it was the latter response that continued to hold the greatest sway over her reactions.

'Did you hear what my brother said, virtuous one?' Lilah sneered, one hand cupping Charity's breast, the nipple caught between the vampire's knuckles. As Lilah squeezed Charity could see the woman's cruel smile tighten. It took an effort not to cry out as her flesh was clamped between chilly fingers but she struggled to retain the little dignity left to her. Glancing into the shadows of Lilah's open waistcoat, she was disquieted to note that both nipples stood hard with excitement.

'Did you hear what my brother said?' Lilah demanded. 'If you destroy us you'll have to go on to destroy your friends. Is that what you want?'

Todd puffed triumphantly on his cigar and shook his head. 'That's not quite true,' he said coolly, not flinching from the dark one's scowl or Lilah's threatening glare. 'You picked the wrong three girls.'

The dark one's frown was ominous. 'What are you telling me, Chalmers?'

'I'm telling you that for a vampire who's been around for so many centuries you're not terribly au fait with the rules. I thought you knew you weren't supposed to feed from nuns or gypsies.'

'What the hell has that got to do with anything?' Lilah snapped.

Todd shook his head with unconcealed disgust. 'You don't feed from nuns because they usually have a crucifix close to hand. And you don't feed from gypsies because Romany blood can only be taken: it can never be made. They're protected by birthright, so you can't make gypsies into vampires.'

Lilah continued to regard him as though he was insane. 'No one's tried to make gypsies into vampires,' she snapped impatiently. 'My brother was just showing you that he's…'

The dark one waved her silent and regarded Todd with grudging respect, his smile combining a sinister blend of approval and loathing. 'You recruited the rest of the band from gypsy camps, didn't you? Aside from Charity, all of

BloodLust are from Romany stock.'

'I thought it might be a prudent move,' Todd said smugly. 'I had an inkling of what was coming, and like any good boy scout I got myself prepared.'

He snapped his fingers and Angela, Viv and Lauren turned to face him, and for the first time Charity noticed that their bloody smiles and overlong teeth were nothing more than the theatrical prosthetics they used for live performances and video sets. Comparing them against the reality of Lilah and the dark one, she marvelled that she hadn't noticed such an obvious detail straight away.

'You'd best get yourselves out of here, girls,' Todd said stiffly. 'This isn't a place where you want to be right now.'

Angela shook her head and Charity was dismayed to see a flicker of the lead guitar player's fiery defiance. 'He promised me a party we'd never forget,' Angela said, pointing at the dark one. 'I've already had a taste of what he's offering and I'm not missing out on that for you or for anyone.' She glanced at Viv and Lauren. 'None of us are missing out on that.' Viv and Lauren nodded surly agreement, the three of them folding their arms and looking resolute.

Todd shrugged with typical indifference. 'Stay if you want,' he said generously, 'but I'll warn you now, remain here and I'll see to it that I lose your invitations for next month's music awards.' A sly glimmer touched his lips. There was a moment's hesitation but Charity could see he had, once again, triumphed with his effortless powers of manipulation. It came as no surprise to her when Angela slumped her shoulders, unfolded her arms, and nodded for the other girls to follow her out of the cellar.

The dark one watched their departure with obvious dismay, and halfway up the steps Angela paused and glanced back at the circle of light in the centre of the cellar. 'Charity's not normally into kinky games,' she said to Todd, lowering her voice to a confidential whisper. 'Is she going to be all right with this?'

Todd chewed on his cigar. 'There's no need for you to worry about it; I'm here to make sure Charity's all right.'

While the rest of the band seemed satisfied with that reply, Charity found no comfort in Todd's words. Listening to their footfalls recede she heard Lauren humming a tune from their first album, and remembered the lyrics.

'...*You placed your fingers against my breast; You made me think our love was blessed; Then you tore the heart from outta my chest...*'

Her memory of the lyrics mocked her. Perhaps, she reasoned, the dark one and his sister were the last pair of vampires in existence, but that didn't change the fact that she was still on her knees and being kept alive by nothing more than their failing mercy.

Lilah suddenly slapped the pizzle hard against her bottom, and unable to contain the sound Charity groaned as she realised the torment was being resumed. An air of dark foreboding told her that this might be the last time she had to suffer at the hands of the undead, and she cringed from the mortifying shame she knew would now be coming.

'Aren't you lucky?' Lilah sneered sarcastically. 'The noble Toad is here to make sure you're all right.' She swept the pizzle down again, stinging both buttocks and making Charity grimace. 'Doesn't that make you feel so much better?' Not giving her an opportunity to respond, pulling on the whip and dragging her by her wrists to the centre of the dingy room, Lilah knelt down in front of her. Her cheeks were lightly rouged with anger and the blush of colour suited the twisted fury of her leer. 'Aren't you lucky having the wonderful Toad to watch over you? Or do you think it's just going to be another pair of eyes in the room to see you being drained?'

'Just take her, Lilah,' the dark one snapped, sounding weary and bored. 'I swear, you really do get too much pleasure from these nasty little games. It will prove to be your downfall.'

Lilah turned to glare at him. She snatched hold of Charity's hair and twisted her head so that her throat was exposed. The tips of her canines glistened like daggers in the candlelight and they looked so sharp Charity could almost feel the pain they would inflict. Her heartbeat hastened to a frantic pace.

'Do you really want me to take her?' Lilah asked her brother. 'Are you telling me you don't want a piece of the little bitch before I'm finished?'

The dark one raised an eyebrow and Charity could see his interest had been easily captured.

'Are you saying you don't want a piece of her virtuous pussy while it's still warm and wet? Are you saying you don't want your dick in her virtuous mouth?' She began to lower her face as she added, 'Because if you don't want to sample her, I can take her right now.'

Charity blushed, sickened by the vampire's words and appalled by her own libidinous response. She didn't know if the dark one did want to have her but she couldn't argue that her body suddenly craved him. Her sex trembled hungrily and her labia melted as though yielding in anticipation. It was a small consolation that Lilah was promising to take her instead, but she realised even that prospect held an infuriating appeal.

'You're offering me the chance to share your spoils?' the dark one asked.

Lilah smiled for him. 'You're my brother and we share an aura,' she explained. 'I think it only fitting that we both enjoy the little bitch before we end this confrontation once and for all.'

He needed no further encouragement. Charity heard his footsteps approach and then he was standing in front of her. She hadn't seen Lilah discreetly step behind her but she wasn't surprised when the end of the pizzle thrust against her sex. It was stout and wet and ready to penetrate and she realised she wanted it desperately. Holding her breath, not wanting to give in to the torment being teased against her pussy lips, she raised her gaze to meet the dark one's menacing glower.

He had removed the erection from his trousers and it hovered in front of her nose. A part of her insisted that she didn't want this depravity and that she needed to distance herself from the vampires and their carnal appetites, but there was a stronger voice inside her suddenly anxious to take his length in her mouth. Staring up at the swollen glans, hungrily anticipating the taste of him, Charity licked her lips.

'Enjoy her, sire,' Lilah encouraged, and as she did she fed the pizzle deep inside Charity. The thick shaft spread the walls of her sex as the length burrowed into her wetness. Her clitoris throbbed with urgent fury and Charity could feel herself being carried along by a rush of pure joy. 'Enjoy the virtuous little slut,' Lilah insisted.

Charity choked back the urge to scream but it was as much resistance as she could manage. Knowing a huge climax was almost upon her she thrust her face forward and took the dark one's cock between her stretched lips. He gasped and there was no mistaking the pleasure in his cry, but Charity barely noticed the exclamation. The taste of him was despicable, cold and exactly what her hunger needed. A trickle of pre-come seeped from the tip of his dome and its flavour was a sickly combination of salt and cream. She fought an instinctive urge to gag and quickly swallowed the syrupy flavour. As she sucked on him, cheeks hollowed and eyes wide with the effort, she could feel the steady pulse of delight preparing to sweep through her. If she closed her eyes she knew she could succumb to the rush of pleasure and bask in the glory of a powerful release.

Behind her, Lilah slowly withdrew the whip handle before

plunging it back inside. Her wrist action was slow and steady and she effortlessly ignited bolts of bliss deep within Charity. 'Does she still feel virtuous?' Lilah sniggered, and as though sharing a private joke, the dark one chuckled and Charity could feel the tremors of his mirth travelling through his shaft. Eagerly she sucked harder, and when he stiffened and a small squirt of semen jetted against the back of her throat she knew she had gone beyond the brink and was now hurtling towards a second orgasm. Without thinking about her actions she swallowed the saline taste of his ejaculate.

'She has the best mouth I've ever enjoyed,' the dark one reflected.

'Then maybe I should try it?' Lilah mused. 'I could do that while you explore her other holes.'

Charity felt ill with fresh lust as she listened to their exchange. She didn't want to be had by the pair, and was sickened by her own vile acceptance of their treatment, but she couldn't refute that she was enjoying the experience. And worse – infinitely worse, she thought miserably – was the way her arousal soared each time they voiced their despicable plans. As soon as Lilah made her suggestion Charity's inner muscles convulsed hungrily, her breath grew stilted with anticipation and she knew she wanted to be had by the two vampires while the dark one was behind and she was able to devour Lilah's pussy.

'Haven't you tried her mouth?' the dark one asked conversationally.

'I don't mind trying it again,' Lilah replied, discussing her as though she was totally inconsequential, their cool disregard taking her responses to new heights. She closed her eyes to fight back tears of shame and then gave in to them as a fresh surge of pleasure rippled through her body.

The dark one eased his cock from her mouth and the pizzle was pushed deeper into her sex. He then disappeared from her sight in the same instant that Lilah stood before her, and while she knew the vampires were blessed with supernatural speed, it still unnerved her that they could change places with such disconcerting ease.

'Eat my pussy, virtuous one,' Lilah demanded.

Charity didn't know when the vampire had removed her clothes but she was now without her waistcoat and jeans, and the sight of her shaved pussy, so neat, pink and inviting, tied a knot of fresh excitement in her stomach. The desire to obey the woman was almost unbearable and she struggled to get closer and do as she'd been told. The whip around her wrists felt slightly looser but there wasn't sufficient freedom to release them, and she would have tumbled awkwardly to the floor if the dark one hadn't grabbed her from behind, his erection probing between the cleft of her buttocks. The pizzle remained buried inside her pussy, and even before he guided the bulbous tip of his length to her anus she knew how he planned to take her and sighed a pitiful, ragged moan.

Lilah lay on the floor and parted her thighs. 'Eat me, you little bitch,' she insisted. 'Don't make me tell you again.' Her sex looked pink and juicy, wet with arousal and obscenely tempting, and governed by an insatiable impulse Charity pushed her face down to it.

The musky taste of feminine juices was unbearably satisfying. As she chased her tongue against the folds of flesh, lapping and licking hungrily, she realised the pleasure was going to carry her through her second climax, the prospect warming and almost enough to distract her from the observation that the binding around her wrists had loosened a little more.

The dark one slapped his ice-cold hands to her hips. Charity stiffened, never hesitating from licking Lilah's sex, but bracing herself for the inevitable penetration she knew he was planning. His rigid cock pressed against the puckered ring of her anus and she was aware that he steeled himself to sink into her forbidden passage. The idea left her cold with terror and wet with arousal and she decided it was better not to dwell on her responses and merely give in to the moment.

Broken echoes of that thought tumbled through her mind as he pushed inside. The pressure of the pizzle within her pussy was made more forceful as he speared her rectum, and she was thrilled by it, the penetration leaving her bathed in a chilly sheen of sweat. Charity's body felt so cold she wondered briefly if they had already turned her into one of their coven, and that thought made her drink more greedily from the copious dew at Lilah's cunt.

'You were right,' Lilah groaned, Charity hearing the colour of arousal in the vampire's voice and taking a small thrill of pride that she had been responsible for that excitement. She despised Lilah, hated everything the vampire had ever done against her sisters and the torment she'd made her endure, but it still pleased her to know she was satisfying the woman's depraved appetites. 'You were right when you said she's good with her mouth,' Lilah qualified to her brother.

Behind Charity the dark one made no reply. He pushed deeper and filled her rear with his long, broad cock. The scrub of his pubic hair irritated her sensitive buttocks and she gasped as another torrent of euphoria threatened to take her. The pleasure was too much and promised to overwhelm her. Straining her hands against the restraints, subconsciously forcing the bindings to relent a little more, she didn't know if she was in the middle of an orgasm, or if her world had simply become one long climactic experience. The joy was relentless, and as the dark one rode in and out of her rear she knew she was cresting on a huge tide of delight.

'Go on,' Lilah insisted, the satisfaction Charity had heard before now layered beneath a growl of impatience. 'Make me come! Eat my cunt and make me come!'

Snuffling against the vampire's labia, forcing her tongue as deep as she could, Charity struggled to obey. She swallowed the cloying musk of Lilah's arousal, drinking a greedy swallow before pushing her mouth over the woman's clitoris. The muscles in Lilah's neck tautened and she grimaced with relief. The dark one's length stiffened inside Charity's rear and she held her breath, sure he was about to erupt, and it was a terrible anticlimax when he paused, pulled himself slowly from her and said, 'No, not yet.'

Charity tried to glance back over her shoulder and see what was wrong. Her sphincter contracted, pulsing softly as it returned to its former size, and the sensation inspired her with a series of dull shivers. But it was the dark one she wanted to see and she strained to find out why he had pulled out of her bottom.

'No…' Lilah growled, grabbing a fistful of Charity's hair and forcing her face back between her spread thighs. The humiliation for Charity was almost complete, and too enjoyable to be denied. She lapped obediently at Lilah's pussy and had to rely on her other senses to work out what the dark one was doing. The hardness of his erection brushed against her buttocks, and she could sense the need for a climax trembling through him, but it was when he pulled the pizzle from her sex that she realised how he planned to conclude her torment.

Unhappily she closed her eyes as the length of leather exited her inner muscles, urged on by the involuntary clench of another climax, and trying to snatch it from her more quickly, clearly anxious to enjoy his orgasm whilst buried inside her pussy, the dark one loosened the bindings at her wrists.

'Now, Charity!' Todd roared. 'Now!'

All three turned to glare at him, but only Charity reacted to the shouted prompt. She snatched her hands away and the binding at her wrists fell away. The distraction of the pleasure the vampire siblings had induced was gone instantly, and with clarity of thought that shocked her, she knew what she had to do. 'Your brother was right,' she said with menace, leaning over Lilah, thrusting a hand into the vampire's chest and tearing her heart out, 'you did get too much pleasure from your nasty little games; and it has proved to be your downfall.'

The dark one watched his sister struggle pathetically to clamber to her feet, her face frozen by shock and surprise, then slump back to the grimy floor. A look of horror gripped his features too, and with bulging eyes of disbelief he clutched his chest. His shoulders hunched, as though he was either suffering from a blow or bracing himself for one.

Charity scurried to her feet and tried to work out what was happening. From the corner of her eye she saw Todd raise a surprised eyebrow as he watched the vampire. She couldn't understand what was wrong with her nemesis but she didn't think now was the time to run the risk of being tricked.

Then slowly, hesitant at first but with increasing relief, the dark one began to smile. 'The gypsy lied,' he laughed.

Charity glanced at Todd and watched him shrug.

The dark one stood erect and clenched his hands into fists. 'The unscrupulous little gypsy bitch lied!' he bellowed, proudly beating his chest, passing his glare defiantly between Charity and Todd. His eyes shone a crimson made increasingly malevolent by the candlelight. His smile was more avaricious than ever, and in the gleam of the brilliant white enamel of his overlong teeth, Charity saw that he intended to carry on making and taking victims for another four hundred years.

'There never was any shared aura, the gypsy bitch lied,' he announced again. It was impossible to tell if he was furious or overjoyed. His sonorous tone echoed from the walls of the cellar in a deafening roar. 'Our destinies weren't intertwined. Lilah's death didn't mean that mine would immediately follow.'

'No,' Charity agreed, again gathering her courage, 'Lilah's

death didn't mean that yours would immediately follow…'
she punched her hand into his chest and tore out his heart,
'but I never planned to make you wait too long,' she told him,
speaking to his lifeless corpse as it sagged to the floor.

Epilogue

Todd stepped to her side and placed his jacket over her bare shoulders. Glancing down at the dark one's body he shook his head with obvious reproof. 'You understand what this means, don't you?'

'No,' Charity said quietly. 'What does it mean?'

'It means he won't be keeping his twilight appointment for tomorrow evening.'

Rolling her eyes, Charity started up the cellar steps.

Todd remained standing between the fallen vampires. 'It also means I get to keep the coven's money,' he grinned. 'All in all, this hasn't been a bad night's work for my finances. Percentage-wise it goes off the scale.'

'I don't know what my sister sees in you,' Charity grumbled. 'I just hope she doesn't decide to marry you, because the idea of having you as a relative makes me think I should tear one more heart out tonight.'

He chuckled. 'If I didn't think you'd blush, I'd tell you exactly what your sister sees in me. I can give you the measurements in feet and inches if it gives you a clue.'

She wrapped the jacket tight around her shoulders and paused at the top of the steps. Stooping so she could see what he was doing, not bothering to disguise her impatience, she called, 'Can you come away from those corpses and give me a lift?'

'A lift where?'

'A lift to Kensington and whichever hotel the vampires were staying at. I need to find Danny.'

Todd frowned with sudden concern. The expression didn't

make her like him, but it lessened her antipathy. 'Do you think he'll be...? Do you think he'll be okay?'

Charity nodded. 'He'll be fine,' she said. She couldn't find the words to qualify that instinct, but she knew it was right. Something deep inside told her that, once and for all, the Harker family curse had finally ended.

The full range of our titles are now available as downloadable ebooks at **www.chimerabooks.co.uk**. For a copy of our free book catalogue please write to

Chimera Publishing Ltd
Readers' Services
PO Box 152
Waterlooville
Hants
PO8 9FS

or email us at
sales@chimerabooks.co.uk

or purchase from our extensive range of titles at
www.chimerabooks.co.uk

We now also offer hundreds of the best and most innovative adult products from around the world, all intended to help you enjoy your sexuality.

Are you shopping for sexy lingerie, sex toys, lotions and potions, fun and games or bondage play? Whatever your desire, you'll find it at **www.chimerabooks.co.uk**. Or write to our Readers' Services for a copy of our **Emporium Catalogue**.

We just know you'll love our selection of products to set your pulse racing!

You can now contact people from around the world and make new friends, find companionship, and perhaps even meet your perfect partner at our new website

www.chimeradating.com

Chimera Publishing Ltd

PO Box 152
Waterlooville
Hants
PO8 9FS

www.chimerabooks.co.uk
info@chimerabooks.co.uk
www.chimeradating.com

***

Sales and Distribution in the USA and Canada

Client Distribution Services, Inc
193 Edwards Drive
Jackson
TN 38301
USA

***

Sales and Distribution in Australia

Dennis Jones & Associates Pty Ltd
19a Michellan Ct
Bayswater
Victoria
Australia 3153